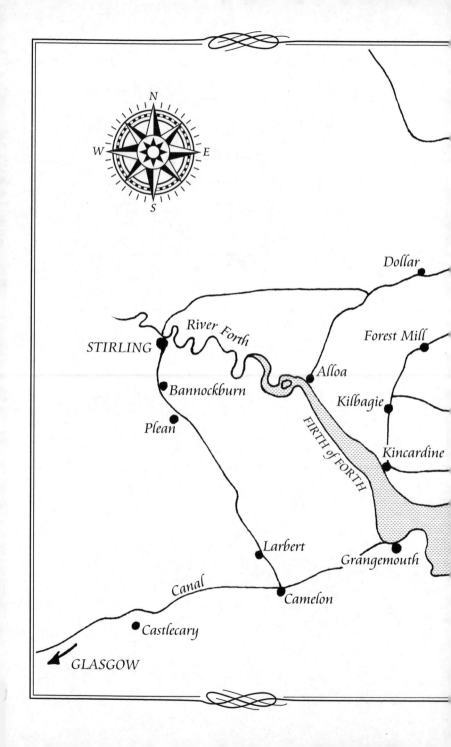

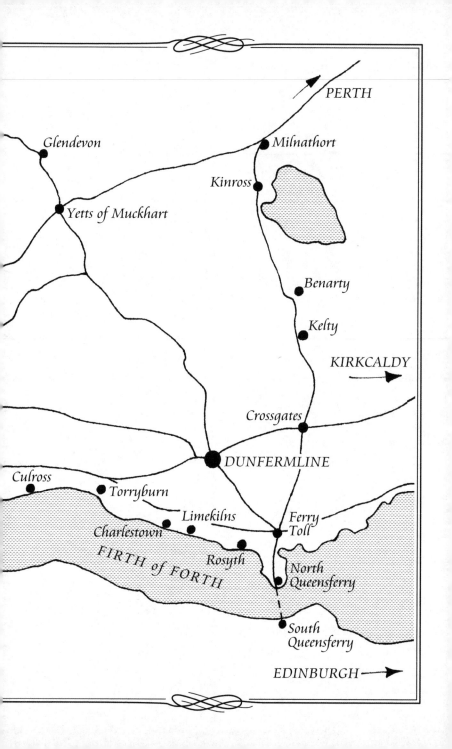

JOHN ORRASON

JOHN ORRASON
Or The Adventures of a Social Castaway

A West Of Fife Story

Daniel Thomson

Edited by Dr Jean Barclay
Illustrations by Iain Wilkinson

DoubleBridge Press
Dunfermline Heritage Community Projects

This edition published 2010.

© Copyright Dunfermline Heritage Community Projects.

ISBN 978-0-9557244-1-1

Illustrations by Iain Wilkinson
Jacket illustration and maps by Clive Willcocks
Design and typesetting by Kevin Hicks, CFA Archaeology Ltd, Scotland
Production management by Lawrie Law
Manufactured in Great Britain by Bell & Bain Ltd, Glasgow

The sign of the DoubleBridge Press is derived from the celebrated double bridge in Pittencrieff Glen, Dunfermline, Fife, Scotland.

LIST OF CONTENTS

List of Contents

List of Contents

ACKNOWLEDGMENTS

On behalf of Dunfermline Heritage Community Projects (DHCP), I should like to thank everyone who has helped with this publication of Daniel Thomson's story *John Orrason: or the Adventures of a Social Castaway.*

First of all our thanks are due to Fife Council for two grants, one a Culture Grant and the other from Celebrating Fife 2010. For authority to reproduce this tale we are grateful to the late Mrs. Deirdre Romanes, Bill Livingstone and other representatives of the *Dunfermline Press* (copyright holder) where the story first appeared in 1897. Library staff in Edinburgh, Kinross, Kirkcaldy and Stirling helped with local and historical details, while the Mitchell Library in Glasgow supplied information about Wilson's Charity School. The ever-helpful staff at the Local History Library of the Carnegie Library, Dunfermline, patiently photocopied the many pages of the original and assisted with information as the work progressed.

Jenny Laurie, author of *St. Andrew's in the Square* showed me round this old parish church in Glasgow, which appears in the tale, and the landlord of the White Hart in the Grassmarket, Edinburgh, allowed me to photograph an old print of the inn, which forms the backdrop to one of the illustrations.

My DHCP colleagues, especially those on the Publications Committee and at the Dunfermline City Archives have added their support, and I am particularly grateful to Bert McEwan and Sue Mowat for their comments on the original draft and Robin Sharp for his role in preparing the final draft for publication.

Above all I should like to thank Clive Willcocks, Chairman of the Publications Committee of the DHCP, for his unfailing support, enthusiasm and hard work, and Iain Wilkinson for the many hours he spent on the meticulous and attractive drawings.

EDITOR'S INTRODUCTION

This Scottish tale of intrigue, adventure and romance is presented as a tribute to its author, Daniel Thomson of Dunfermline. In the late nineteenth century local newspapers frequently carried a serial to interest readers and promote sales, and the tale of *John Orrason: or the Adventures of a Social Castaway – a West of Fife Story* appeared weekly in the *Dunfermline Press* from January 9th to July 3rd 1897.

Daniel Thomson, 1833-1908, was a remarkable man. Born into a Dunfermline weaving family which fell into dire poverty, he became a hand-loom weaver as a boy but took advantage of slack times in the trade to study mechanics, mathematics, literature, music and art. Apart from a spell in a warehouse in Jamaica Street, Glasgow, he gradually took better and better positions in the new power mills in Kirkcaldy, Kinross and Montrose until in 1878 he could return to Dunfermline, his beloved 'auld grey toun', for the rest of his life. Here, he became a respected linen factory manager, a representative of working men, a musician, a journalist, a local historian and the author of articles, verse and industrial history. For the last twenty years of his life Daniel Thomson was a director of the Scottish Wholesale Co-operative Society, travelling to Europe, Asia, and North America on the Society's behalf and publishing detailed accounts of his journeys. In Dunfermline, Thomson is best known for his books *The Weavers' Craft* of 1903 and *The Dunfermline Hammermen,* which was published posthumously in 1909. He also intended publishing 'Anent Dunfermline', his nine volumes of manuscript and printed items about his home town, but died before the work was completed. Daniel Thomson was married twice and had four children. Older residents of Dunfermline may remember his son Daniel, watchmaker and jeweller, who established a family business at 131 High Street.

Although it is fiction, *John Orrason* is founded on fact and many of the incidents in the story can be traced to events that happened from the 1790s to the 1820s in Dunfermline, Kirkcaldy, Stirling, Glasgow, and in the British colonies. The 'cast-off child', the pressgang in

Kirkcaldy, the body-snatching riots in Stirling and many other incidents that turn up in our tale can be traced back in history. Some items, indeed, are recorded in `Anent Dunfermline` in the 1890s and were thus fresh in Thomson's mind. The authenticity of the seafaring part of the story probably owes much to Daniel Thomson's younger brother, James, of Kirkcaldy, who went to sea as a youth and spent many years `before the mast`, writing of his experiences in `Yarns of an Old Tar`.

In editing this story, I have changed little of Thomson's original work, apart from correcting errors in dates and places and making occasional adjustments to grammar and spelling. I have used dialect as Thomson did, but have added a glossary of Scottish words and unusual terms. A few notes and references have been added for interest and clarity. My friend Iain Wilkinson has skilfully redrawn Thomson's small illustrations (which were something of a novelty in the newspapers of the time) and added others of his own.

I hope you enjoy the story of *John Orrason: or the Adventures of a Social Castaway.*

Note: John Orrason's life, which features weaving, the press-gang and a rise through Naval ranks, resembles that of Fife-born Lieutenant James Clepham, a hero of Trafalgar, of whom Thomson was probably aware. A short biography of Clepham appeared in *The Scotsman* on October 22nd 2009 and I am grateful to Iain Wilkinson for this reference.

JOHN ORRASON
Or The Adventures Of A Social Castaway

A West Of Fife Story

By D. Thomson, Dunfermline

AUTHOR'S INTRODUCTORY NOTE

The following narrative begins with the recital of actual occurrences and may be said, with some slight license, to finish with the same elements of personal history. Old people in the City of the Crooked Stream may still be able to recall the echoes of a strange story, told to them in their youth, of a severe wrestle in the Court of Session by certain great folks in the district, of the sudden disappearance of a gay and richly-dowered young lady, and of the sudden and strange collapse of the case before the Law Lords of Session [1]. Fragments of personal history – telling how a certain foundling was disposed of – may also come to their recollections as they read the story of 'John Orrason.' They may not be able to call up corroborative remembrance of the castaway's return, for the incidents connected therewith hardly, in any way, stirred the social life of the district. But these incidents may be accepted substantially in the form in which they appear in the closing chapters of the tale. With these whets and suggestions to the enquiring genius of West Fife, the story of John Orrason may be allowed to speak for itself.

Daniel Thomson

JOHN ORRASON

The Old Toll House, North Queensferry

CHAPTER I

The hero is introduced – The 'Ferry Toll' – A North Queensferry Jehu –
A midnight adventure near Kinross.

'Orrason! Orrason'! I think I hear the reader say. ``Tis surely a strange name for an actual Scotchman`. I have always thought it strange myself though, having a knowledge of how it came into the list of family patronymics, it must be less strange to me than to the reader who comes across it for the first time.

There is something pleasing in the commodity of a fair and well-rounded name, and in days of yore the name was always a valued appendage of the man and descriptive of him. Nowadays, we are much more anxious to obtain and maintain names that are indicative of rank and social standing than such as are suggestive of our origin and the circumstances of our birth. Our hero was always proud of his name, not because it indicated a long line of ancestors – for it did not do that – nor because it carried the name of a family of adventitious wealth, or perpetuated the designation of acres broad and wide domains – for it did not do that either. He loved the name, because it told how he came to be named at all, and he cherished it

1

because it kept alive the memory of the period of his life which, long, dark and mysterious to himself, came at last to be the most deeply interesting part of his existence.

In several of the weekly newspapers for May 25th 1894, there appeared the cut of a small, one-storied house which the Sheriff-Substitute of West Fife had kindly rented and fitted up as a holiday retreat for our guardians of the peace [2]. The appearance of that little engraving became an active suggestion to me, reminding me of a life that had almost fallen out of our local remembrance. The house was interesting – very interesting – to me, and possibly may prove of interest to even the hurried everyday reader, ere the story of John Orrason is told.

The house possessed a much wider degree of interest at one time than it does now, and was regarded with intense consideration by past generations of Highland drovers who, in the old times of Hallow Fair, brought here their herds of hairy, horned Highland cattle preparatory to their passing across the firth at Queensferry – for the house here was the house at the Ferry Toll.

The days have long since become but memories of the past; and the nasal-voice, gaelic-shouting men in trews and plaids, that brought from the far north these cattle supplies for Auld Reekie and the south, are now wholly unknown in the social life of the lowlands. But this little house – dedicated to a social and friendly purpose, and blessed by the sweet words of a noble lady – has an interest for me beyond anything experienced by the now shadowy drover, or even by the keen-eyed toll-man, counting his pence, and drawing distinctions among his cattle. Yet I never lived there, and have only at distant intervals looked upon its somewhat prosaic and hard-lined roof and walls. In its humble interior were spent the first years of a human being's life, which, though neither noticed or praised, was yet a true, noble and happy existence.

Somewhere among the last few years of the last century – just about a hundred years ago – was born one more member of the human family. It was of the hardier sex, and he doubtless made his advent known by the usual outcry – the usual disclaimer of responsibility – when he came amongst us.

His birthplace was long an unsolved mystery to everyone- the beginnings of his life were shrouded in darkness. His parents, his relatives, where and how he came to be a dweller on earth, were all to himself – till he reached the ripeness of manhood – unknown quantities. To his friends and acquaintances these items of his life were equally unknown and equally mysterious.

'Ah'! I think I hear the reader say, 'You are about to tell the old, old story of the foundling- the child placed o'ernight on somebody's doorstep, and picked up, nursed, cherished, and brought up to manhood without anyone knowing who he was, and who suddenly disappeared, no one knew how, and never again was seen by those who had saved his life and made him a man. That indeed is the old story, though generally full of flavour and fascination, and we shall hear and judge of its merits as you go on'.

Well, gentle reader, that is hardly the line of John Orrason's life; and though the foundling has been the theme of endless myths, tales and dramas, and has even inspired the poets to some of their highest flights, I can hardly claim the name, or attach the character to my hero.

He was not left under any tree to await the approach of the inevitable milk-maid, as he waked the echoes of the early morn with his wailing cry. Neither was he found nicely wrapped in a cosy basket-parcel, and left at a roadside inn in the old coaching days, as foundlings so often were. But he did come first into notice in close connection with these same coaching times, and introduces himself to you and me from the recess of a coach and pair.

Frankie Murray had been known for years as one of the best and safest drivers among the select coterie of hackney coachmen who, during the latter half of the last century, waited for pay and passengers at North Queensferry. Frank had the best hung machine and the finest pair of horses on the stand. Local people and the regular travellers were always anxious to secure the engagement of Frankie, since they knew he would drive safely and in comfort, and keep to time. They were a gay, rude, boisterous, and thoughtless company these hackney coachmen of the old time; and managed, with admitted success, to keep the little, bustling ferry village from day to day supplied with constant cause of excitement.

When, however, they came early one November to know that their fellow-Jehu, Frankie, had been out on a night excursion, and that he could give no good account either of himself or his mission except that he had been well paid for time and trouble, their wise heads were laid together, and the whole place was filled with conjecture and stories, true and false, over the matter. They drank Falstaffian quantities of heather ale and peat-reek whisky, in the Ship Inn ³, and broke into wild and lurid language over the difficulties of the case. Even though Frankie kept to a plain, unvarnished tale of his adventure, that tale wanted as many links to give it the due and proper form of a story – with a natural beginning, middle, and end – that they voted it almost unanimously to be 'a guid deal made up'.

Frankie's story will, however, bear repetition, even in his own form of speech:

'Weel, chaps', he repeated for the twentieth time, as he and some half-dozen others sat the evening after the occurrence round the kitchen fire of the Ship, 'you micht notice, some twa days syne, a little, dark, wirakow o' a man-body cam' in aboot sperrin' for me – hoo he got my name I canna tell, and what his was I'm no likely to learn – but he cam' doon frae the Well Head ⁴ speerin' for Frankie Murray. I gaed doon as far's the pier wi' him, an' heard a' he had got to say. He trysted me up to the Ba'hill ⁵ road – a mile or twa to the wast o' Milnathort – and to be there just after nightfa', to drive canny to the wast and to hing on till anither coach wad meet me, an' then I was to be tell't what I was to do, an' to keep dark till a' was o'er'.

Frankie took a long draught from the jug of heather ale, reached over to him from the table, and then resumed.

'That was to be as last nicht fell, an' ye wad a' noticed that yesterday I gaed awa' in guid time i' the afternoon. Darkness is noo weel on by aboot six o'clock, an' I ettled to be at the spot raither before than efter the oor. The beasts being in guid fettle, an ha'in little to draw, speel'd ower the grund in graund style, an' I got up to the grass-grown stretches o' the Ba'hill Road juist i' the nick o' time. It was a'maist completely dark when I heard the crunchin' o' carriage wheels, an' I drew up a' at ance, an' weel to the roadside. In the crack o' a whup, the carriage was up to whar I was waitin'. It moved amaist without soond alang the saft roadside, an' I could hardly believe my ain een when the coach stood still close beyont me.

Oot jumpit the same little dark-vised man, an' comin' hard up to me, he whispered in a hurry, 'Turn your horses an' be as quick as you can'. I had them roond in a jiffy – for the beasts seemed noo to ken there was something ado. The strange coachman, sittin' up on his dicky, never opened his mouth, but pulled up his carriage close alongside o' mine.

He was a quick-set deil o' man – the little dark ane. He ordered me up to my seat, then he opened the door o' the hackney – though I could hardly see him for the darkness – lifted something like a basket an' a bundle or twa out o' the carriage, and, packing them gently within the hackney, jamp inside an' ordered me to drive on – an' we were soon aff an' alang the Ba'hill Road to Milnathort an' Kinross, leaving the strange coach with its dumby driver standin' alane i' the darkness'. At this point, a sudden commotion shook off the listening attitude among Frankie's audience. The kitchen window giving a view of the landing stage, the Queen Margaret passenger boat was seen nearing the pier, and cries from the outside of 'the boat's in, the boat's in' drove in a second every hackneyman from the fireside of the Ship. Then, as now, every man was anxious to secure a fare, and get himself and his vehicle hired for the day. Frankie's story was an inviting one but it could be taken up again, and impatient passengers must be attended to at once. So the Jehus o' the 'Ferry hurried out to their posts, and, forgetting for the time the narrative of their neighbour Frankie, were only anxious to buttonhole the shivering ferry loupers from the boat.

CHAPTER II

Our hero starts life in a carriage – A colley-shangie in Kinross – A run by Crossgates and Inverkeithing to the 'Ferry Toll' – The 'greeting bairn' – The black-a-vised man.

The interruption to Frankie Murray's story of his drive through the darkness was, like our other afflictions, only for a season. The listeners to the earlier part were, indeed, oftener in the kitchen of the inn than Frankie was and, though tale-telling and gossip mongering was then the only constant industry of the place, Frankie could not always be got to company his audience and complete his narrative.

When, however, the inevitable opportunity came, and the heather ale and clear Kilbagie [6] were again inspiring alike the story-teller and his hearers, Frankie was not unwilling to take up his parable, and fill in the latter half of his weird and misty story.

'When we got to the Ba'hill Kirk, a gentle tappin' on the side o' the hackney made me look roond, an' there I saw the curly, craw-fit features of the little man lookin' up at me, an' makin' signs to stop. I pulled up as gently as I could an' pat doon my ear to hear him.

'Gang straicht doon by Kinross', said he, 'then tak' the road by Kelty an' Cantsdam, an' on by Mucklebeath an' Crossgates to Inverkeithin'. When ye get fairly through the toon there, tak' the road roond the hill, an' stop whaur a' the roads meet near the Toll-house. Wull ye mind a' that'? An' the little man lookit at me like a whitrick watchin' a rabbit.

'Nae fear o' me forgettin', I said, 'I ken the road ower weel to lose myself there', an' awa we gaed ance mair.

I saw the weavers' cann'le lichts blinkin' through the shop windows as we drove through Milnathort, an' the Salutation, opposite the Parliament Close in Kinross, was blazin' bricht as we got doon the brae to the Juck Inn [7]. Here we had to draw up for naething mair than a colleyshangle – two chiels fechtin` and a crood roond them – on the Quiech Brig [8]. By we couldna get – though the little man was ay lookin` oot an telling` me to hurry on – till I cam` doon frae the box, an`, crackin` the whup weal roond me, took the horses by the head and forced a passage through the feckless shawl weavers stannin` on the brig, waitin` to see wha among the fechters got the first doonfa`.

I was just mounting the dicky again`, Frankie resumed, ` when, as sure as I`m here, I heard the weak, greetin` cry of an infant bairn comin` oot for an instant frae the inside o` the carriage. I drave awa but wondered mair an` mair what the little cry cood mean, an` hoo it cam` that a man an` an infant bairn should be sittin` thegither in a close carriage on a dark nicht, an` a hale cloud o` mystery roond them. I was sae muckle ta`en up wi` thae thochts, that I near-hand let the machine i` the ditch when we were passing below the hill o` Benarty. But the same thochts gar`d me tak` a` the mair tent, as we cam` doon the steep brae at Cantsdam, whaur mair nor ain o` ye`, he said, turning to his listeners, `has come mair than aince to grief`. All laughed at the too truthful reference of Frankie.

A passing resort to the sparkling Kilbagie occasioned but a short interruption, and when all present had followed Frankie`s example, he proceeded to finish his two-in-hand story. `To mak` a long story short`, he said, `I may just say that the rest o` the road was naething but an even-on-drive. The colliers were a` sleepin` an` their hooses dark as we cam` doon through the Beaths an` past the Crossgates an` we saw no a cratur in Inverkeithin` as we ran through the High Street, but daft Sandy Semple stannin` at the Cross coontin` the horns o` the moon, that juist then gied a bit glower frae the back o` a dark-bankit cloud. Sandy was left i` the darkness when she disappeared, an` we got doon by the wast loan an` on to the Ferry Toll without disturbin` a single bailie i` the auld burgh`.

A general laugh followed this last sally of Mr. Murray. The Knights of the Ribbons [9] were not seldom in the adjudicating hands of the bailies referred to, and their approach to magistrates in general, and these bailies in particular, was ever on the principle of `letting sleeping dogs lie`.

'But hoo did ye get on wi' the little man an' the greetin' bairn', queried a chorus of voices as Frankie gave indications of moving off. 'I never saw them again', he answered. 'I had just gotten past the sooty wark an' was in deep darkness at the wast end o' the hill, when the curious cratur stoppit me an' got oot. He lifted doon a kind o' saft-lookin' parcel an' set it for a moment on the brae side, then he drew oot anither tichtly faulded up bundle, paid me a fair round sum for hire an' horses, an' then tell't me to drive awa' whaur I liked. I cam' roond the hill to the Ferry, leaving him, as I left the coach an' driver on the Ba'hill Road, staunin' alane in the darkness'.

'An' what aboot the greetin' bairn'? for his listeners would have the last fragment of Frankie's experiences in this strange affair. 'My suspicions', he replied, ' were fully confirmed before I pirted wi' my black-a-vised friend. The cauld air o' the nicht had wakened the sleepin' wee thing- for such it was – an' a low wailin' cry o' discontent broke frae the parcel juist as I was leaving'.

'Good nicht', quoth I, 'an' tak' care o' the bairn'. 'Good nicht', answered the little man, 'an' tak' care o' yoursel''. An sae we pairted. I cam' on to the Ferry, an' he was left alane by the roadside'.

Such was the story told at first by the chief hackneyman at the Ferry, and reported by him for years afterwards without essential variation. Even after he had come to know the further movements of his black-a-vised friend on that eventful night, he refused to mar the symmetry of his first narrative by adding any lop-siding items that came to him by after knowledge. Frankie's story, however, proved useful as the only public record we have of that part of our hero's life, during which he was wholly unconscious of the treatment meted out to him, or even of his own existence. Frankie had no tale to tell apart from that which connected itself with his own hackney and, though it did grow somewhat hackneyed in the recital, it was always fresh and gustful to the teller.

And now the reader may wish to know the identity of the dark, thin, diminutive man, who thus was made the vicarious executioner of a hidden decree – a decree directed by a party, evidently rich, possibly powerful, in the land – a decree fixing the fate and deciding the life of an innocent child. He revealed himself in feature, form and limb to Frankie Murray. He will yet be bound to reveal himself to others and the reader, in courtesy, should equally become an acquaintance of such a worthy gentleman.

Charley Graham, though he might rightly be described as a many-sided man, could scarcely be said to be other than single-faced. His features could hardly bend to any but the one expression of cunning inquisitiveness and greed co-mingled, and if the leer of a satyr shot at times from the corner of his grey eye, its effect was soon obliterated by the thin flickering simper that played with persistent constancy over his countenance. He was at once, however, tailor and pedlar; and was fairly well-known on the road which led, and still leads, over the Cullaloe Hills, and in some degree was he also known in the two towns between which the hilly highway leads. He was not infrequently seen in Dunfermline and on rarer occasions in the Lang Toon [10]. He was appraised for his trustfulness, and employed for his powers of insinuation. He was a born detective and would have made his fortune in this business had he not been doomed to see the light before private detectives were known in the land. These qualities made him useful and valuable to those who were in straits, or anxious to learn what concerned them not, or to find out private weaknesses, or to hush up unwelcome events, and also to assist in concealing the evidence of personal or family errors.

Such was the man Charley Graham – mean, contemptible, if not indeed despicable in his conduct; yet possessed of faculties capable, under due direction, of being turned to uses of excellence and good effect in this murmuring, grumbling, ever-active beehive of men. In this expedition of the carriage and the child, Charley had evidently hired himself to accomplish purposes which the light of day dared not shine upon, and which the public ear must not learn. What these purposes were, what the intent and what was to be concealed, or what destroyed, was unknown to all but himself and his employers for well-nigh a generation after.

Let us now, however, follow his movements, and thereafter, if we can, the life movements of the unconscious infant now resting on the cold hillside, with the midnight winds of autumn sighing over him. When Charley found himself alone, he carefully lifted his precious basket-parcel and tried to still the weak wailings that came from within. He lifted also certain other parcels and, thus laden, he carefully picked his way to the southward, bending his steps as softly as he could over the rough road, and making for the houses built on the edge of the sea cliffs at St. Margaret's Bay, known then as the Ferry Toll. While he wends his way across the few hundred paces that intervene, we may explain further as to Charley, his mission and his burden.

CHAPTER III

Three years by the sea shore – The `nurse-mother` – How the hero got his name – Branded by a Christian world – A sad parting.

Graham had been seen at the Ferry Toll before the evening and events we have just described. By means known only to such inquisitive minds as his, he had come to learn the circumstances of the people, or at least of a family, living there, and presumably found that these circumstances would suit the carrying out of a scheme, with the execution of which he was entrusted by parties unseen and unknown.

Mrs. Macintyre was the wife of a tacksman at one of the quarries close by, and occupied, when our story opens, the same house which the kindly-disposed sheriff has now set aside for a laudable purpose [11]. She was a young, comely and finely-formed woman, and animated with those gentle and loving qualities which form the highest dower of beauty a woman can possess. She was the happy mother of several children, but her last-born, after growing in its mother`s affections for a few short weeks, had been suddenly taken from her by the great child-devourer – death – and left her for the time bereaved and desolate.

It was at this juncture that she had one day towards the end of October 1796 – only a few weeks before our story opens – received a visit from Charley Graham. He had called in the evening, and chosen a time when only the wife and husband were present, and his purpose was to offer the family- and especially Mrs. Macintyre – the custody and upbringing of another person`s child. He stated his terms which were ample and generous. He laid down his conditions which were stringent, narrow and unsympathetic. The child would be given to Mrs. Macintyre, and guerdon abundantly sufficient would be paid to her, but the child was to have no name, other than such as she chose to give it. She was to nurse it carefully and well, and give it back whenever its relations desired its possession. She was to ask no questions, nor endeavour to find its parentage *or connections.*

To all this she could agree, but the one point of giving the child back to its discarding parents. She knew well the pain such parting would cause, and she would fain have escaped the stipulation; but this could not be, and she ultimately agreed to be mother to the unknown babe, and to love it and cherish it as a mother should.

Graham had called even after this last interview, and fixed as near as might be the hour when he and his charge might arrive.

When, therefore, Charley Graham, after the departure of the hackney, approached the cottage in the manner we have described, he was not surprised to find, though it was close on midnight, a light burning in one of the windows, and spreading a fan-shaped line of illumination across the deeply-rutted roadway. A gentle tap brought the future nurse-mother to the door. Without a moment's delay the closely wrapped up baby was handed over to Mrs. Macintyre's loving embrace. She hurried with it to the warm atmosphere of the kitchen, undid with swift fingers the bountiful swathings round it, and pressed it to her life-giving breast.

She was delighted with the look of the child. `Thank ye for the bonnie boy-bairn`, she exclaimed, as she saw it warming into movement, `but I ha'e to speir at least ane question, though it be against the bargain. What am I to ca' the laddie? The bairn maun ha'e a name o' some kind`.

`Nae doot, nae doot`, answered Charley, `but ye may ca' him onything ye like; there's no a living cratur likely to be the least particular on the subject`.

`Ah! But I wadna like to be namin' the bairn myself. It's no for a woman to be stickin' names on nameless bairns; that belongs mair to your ain kind. What will I ca' the winsome laddie`?

`Weel, weel`, retorted Charley, somewhat curtly, `I've gi'en ye my answer already. Ca' the unlucky cratur onything ye like. He's but a pickle early corn at onyrate – a kind o' hauvre-meal bannock ower soon frae the fire. If he live, an' things gang richt, he'll be the orra son among the lot, an' ye may as weal ca' him that at aince`.

'An' his first name', persisted the good woman. 'His first name', said Charley in surprise, 'Ye want a marrow to the ither ane? Weel, weel, since the puir thing's never likely to come to muckle, either in luck or possessions, just ca' him Johnnie. Scotch folk langsyne thocht the name unlucky, but it canna be unlucky to a brat that's ne'er to have hae luck o' any kind'. As Charley spoke he rose, drew the stiff six-inch neck of his coat up over his ears, and muffling his thin limbs against the night air, made for the door.

Mrs. Macintyre was incensed by this last remark, and could not help launching after him, as he opened the door and went out: 'A name o' ill-luck, did ye say? It's the brawest name ye can gie the bairn. A' the great folk o' the world hae been ca'd John, an' nae doot, my bonnie bairn' – now speaking to her little charge – 'ye'll thrive as weel's my ain man, an' his name's John, too'. And the good Mrs. Macintyre said 'guid nicht' to the darkness, and closed the door on herself and the future man, John Orrason.

Such was the form of introduction between her unconscious charge and Mrs. Macintyre. Such the beginning of that faithful nursing and tending of hers, which, extending over the first three years of Orrason's life, was to lay the foundation of a splendid physical manhood. Here, in her keeping, he grew to strength and beauty, and often stirred the prideful gaze of his foster mother, as she watched him crawling over the stretches of smooth turf, or tossing the shelly-pebbles on the sandy beach that then bounded the pretty little bay at the Toll-house.

At this time, the existence of the toll made the little hill-and-rock-girded bay the centre of attraction for all whom, from the north, east and west, sought their passage-way by the ferry. The rounded hill, on which the sheriff's residence now stands, was then open, from base to summit, to every roving foot. The yellow bloom of whins and broom spread over the wood-covered slopes, and wandered down over broken rocky ground to the margin of the Forth. St Margaret's to the south-east was equally free to the invading rambler. Great clumps of blackthorn, with whins and heather and hazel, spread over the braes. Linties flitted from bush to bush, while the chaffinch and yellow hammer twitted to each other their morning hymn. Mavis and

13

Merle vied with each other as the evening fell and made music round the house where the child of dread forgetfulness was being reared into the semblance of a man.

That Charley was informed of the child's parentage and connection, and was fully aware of the circumstance of his birth, we may at once conclude, alike from the incidents of the enterprise in which he had been engaged, and the hints he let fall while conversing with Mrs. Macintyre. From the latter there can be no doubt as to one particular connected with the birth of John Orrason. The Scotch phrases – ancient and colloquial as they were – by which Graham characterized the child, left no room for evading the conclusion that its birth had not been sanctioned by the ceremony of marriage.

The child – as with many millions more – had not been welcomed to the world, even by its parents, and must be looked on by 'respectability' with averted eyes and conventional dislike. It is indeed a saddening thing to contemplate the fate too often meted out to the illegitimate. Branded from his birth with a name of evil omen – often of cruel, disqualifying effect – he goes through this Christian world of ours, branded with a stain and cause of rejection he has neither incurred nor deserved. He is spoken of with bated breath, and pointed to as a tainted being, lettered and marked off from his fellows. He may be cast aside and eager relatives, and sometimes eager parents, too, may be solely concerned to find some place and means of concealment, where the living, suffering, innocent evidence of their frailty or folly shall be for ever hidden from view. Such was the destined fate of our as yet unconscious hero – our social castaway, John Orrason.

The first three years of his life were spent by our hero at the Ferry Toll. Carried or guided daily by the rippling beach, or along the hillsides that bloomed and glowed in beauty all around the dwelling of his nurse-mother, he learned to know and love, and to have the impress of each strong feature in the little region indelibly engraved on the tablets of his infant mind.

The period was marked with no incident, and would have been entirely without interest, did we not feel that, even at this early period of our existence, the future of our life is being founded. Had our castaway been treated to the too common fate of the farmed out child, his whole future life, mental and physical, must have been reduced in tone, his conceptions of existence cast on a lower level, and his capacity for happiness and length of life narrowed and shortened.

But the three years were drawing to a close. The child had wrapped himself round the affectionate heart of his faithful nurse. She had fulfilled her duty, and elevated that duty to the level of devotion, by the love that dominated every action. The child was as one of her own, and though she had often, and fearfully, thought over the possibility of separation, the idea of its near approach had never dawned upon her trustful, faithful soul. Yet the hour of parting with the loved and darling child had now come.

Whatever the plans and schemes as to the final disposal of the unwelcome child, maturing in the breast of those responsible for his existence, and who, even yet – from their dark and hidden position – directed his life and fate, no one was permitted to learn. Even Graham – much as we may suppose to his own chagrin – could only execute his orders without knowing their purpose – and Graham was once more in this strange matter of watching and warding a child, set to change our little hero's place of being.

Mrs. Macintyre had never, in all the past three years, seen the gleaming eyes or wrinkled features of the little man, and when he once more in the darkness of an autumn evening, made a visit to the Toll-house, she knew that one more of the trial hours of life had come upon her.

Charley was cool, firm, and indifferent, yet – as far as his nature would allow – tactful and cajoling, and all his heart went with him when he lied and deceived. He deceived the good woman as to the place whither the child was to be carried. He lied when he said the child's real mother wished only to assure herself by sight that it was well, and he cruelly misled her belief when he assured the noble nurse-mother that the child would soon be returned. The truth was as Charley afterwards explained – that his employers had been seized by some sudden fear that the identity of the child was being traced or that the nurse-mother had learned something of the parentage and connections of the child. The danger of full disclosure must be removed by the child's removal. Haunted by the demon of ultra-respectability, they dreaded nothing so much as the discovery of their shame and cruelty, and to prevent this, the innocent must be sacrificed.

With slow-reached consent, with many dread forebodings of evil, with tears she could not conceal, and fears she could not express, she gave up the loved and dear one to Charley's cold, unfeeling care. How she spent the days and nights, and long years of hapless waiting and bootless longing for the return of the lost one, we need not enquire – our quest is with the child. Graham had everything ready. No sooner was the child, wrapped in many protecting folds, given to his arms, than he hurried with it outside. A close carriage was in waiting, and this, on receiving Charley and his sleeping charge, was driven off into the darkness. The heart-grieved nurse-mother listened to the sound of the wheels and horses' feet as these died away in the distance, and then retired to sit down in silent, overpowering grief.

CHAPTER IV

The castaway is carried to Glasgow – A midnight adventure in the `Auld Grey Toon` – From Torryburn to Glasgow by coach and boat – Child life in the `Refuge` – The felt want of a `loving hand`.

The motives actuating the conduct of those who now directed the removal of the child will be laid bare by the parties best able to tell ere our little history comes to a close. The varying age, with its varying tests and measures of what is called respectability, furnishes to each mean and truckling or ambitious and unprincipled soul various excuses for cruelties and immoralities.

The modern reader, living in an atmosphere of comparative freedom, is hardly in a position to measure the anxieties of his fathers of a century ago, nor proportion the risks, expense and trouble taken by the relatives of our castaway to cover up and bury the proof of his connection and identity. To appreciate or in some degree to explain their movements, a fair knowledge of the deep-set, social prejudices of a by-gone age is necessary alike to fairness and accuracy.

At the time referred to – though the age was even less moral than the present – any falling away from the prevailing code of accepted rectitude was at once made the subject of church investigation, of ecclesiastical exposure, and even social degradation and humiliating confession. These possibilities directed the conduct of the common people and guided the hypocrisies of the rich. They also marked those paths of escape – submission in the one case and concealment in the other – which each pursued.

The bare chance of a child of unwarranted birth being traced to a family of position and respectability was at that time regarded with feelings of repulsion which we, in these latter days, can hardly estimate. To such a state of social and ecclesiastical apprehension must we assign the unfeeling and unnatural conduct of those who dominated the fate of little Orrason.

When Graham, as narrated in the last chapter, left the house at the toll, the carriage was driven at a steady speed by the Dunfermline road to the precincts of that ancient city. The warmly wrapped-up child slept contentedly, not even responding by cry or movement to the occasional jolting of the carriage. Sweetly unconscious of his fate, he dreamed not of the change – the saddening bitter change – awaiting him.

The driver was apparently as unfamiliar with the by-paths of the Grey Toon as he was unacquainted with his fare. He received constant instructions from Graham at every dubious turn in the roadways, and threaded the streets as one entirely strange to their twists and turns. He found himself passing strangely shaped ruins and ancient buildings, and looked with curious interest at the flickering lamps of the watch-men who stood around the Townhouse. Further north, by wondrous windings and narrow streets, creeping down into steep gullies and climbing up steep braes, Charley and his man found themselves at last on that height where now the North Kirk nods its twopenny spire o'er the slopes of Mount Allan [12].

Here Charley, alighting, was met in the darkness by a woman more muffled up than himself, and who maintained an absolute economy of speech. She at once relieved that worthy – her husband – of his delicate and precious burden, hurried out of sight, and left Charley to settle with the coachman, who waited orders with all the simulated patience of his class.

Graham, knowing that service prompt and faithful, would be required on the coming morrow, was careful to see both man and horse lodged in comfort, and leaving his orders for the remainder of the journey, soon found himself at his own fireside at the top of 'the Path' [13] helping his guidwife to still the now constantly uttered discontent of their new charge. The task proved an irksome and exhausting one, and drew forth many a peevish and even profane expression of irritation and wrath from Charley and his wife ere the night was done.

In the small hours of the following morning, the same hackney carriage might be seen driving westward by Castle Blair, Milesmark, the 'check' road [14] and by successive well-known ways to Torryburn. Here one of the passage boats was soon procured, and a man and woman stepped on board carrying a loudly complaining child. The boatmen pushed off, the wonder-struck coachman drove away, and Johnnie Orrason was afloat on the quiet upper waters of the Firth.

Grangemouth was soon reached, and a passage secured to Glasgow in one of the 'swift boats' of the Forth-Clyde Canal [15]. Here, in the great mercantile metropolis – small by comparison with its vast modern bulk – the now sleeping bairn was carried to a house in the higher reaches of the city, near the Rotten Row, and left in the hands of practiced officials. With a stretch of decorum – for such things were often loosely managed in the early years of the century – the child's name, marks and possessions were all carefully entered in the books of the 'Refuge', as the house into which our little hero was now ushered, was called [16]. When finished the entry stood:

'John Orrason, nearly three years old, full grown, healthy. Mole or dark spot under the right breast. Left by C.G. and his wife, C. – 25th October 1799.'

Here the imprisoned castaway of social respectability passed more than ten years of his young life. He was well cared for, fed, educated and trained to habits of regular application. At first he missed and sorely mourned the loss of his nurse-mother – the only mother he had ever known. Gradually, as might be expected in the case of a formalised child, the agony of separation calmed down, faded into dim, shadowy memories, and in the later years of his life in the Rotten Row, only came now and then like views of a far-off landscape, where everything seems fair and bright, yet where nothing can be detailed.

The one great element of endurable and happy existence – the element of love – was wholly left out of his child life in Glasgow, and this proved to him a bereavement which nothing in afterlife could make up or relieve. This gap in his young and affectionate heart increased with his growth, and deepened in intensity as the years passed on.

At the Wilson Charity School in Montrose Street [17], where he and the other children hailing from the Refuge were sent at five, he found that his companions each had his or her list of friends and relatives – their loved ones. But he had none. He could not, as they did, talk of his father and mother, of his sisters and brothers. Cousins, uncles, aunts and other relations had no counterpart in his experience, and the meaning of the names and phrases in which the loved ones were enshrined had to be explained and made clear to his wondering apprehension.

These explanations, while they opened up a world that was all new to him, also tended to sadden the time of growing reflection, and to deepen the mystery of his own strange fate.

Why had he no brothers or sisters to love him and play with him and where were the other endearing relations, which gladdened the lives of his playmates? Whence had *he* come that no one lived for him or loved him, or cared to whisper in his longing ear – `This is my boy – my son` or, in equally sweet sounds, `This is my brother`?

These thoughts did not, it is true, fully shape themselves in his young mind, but the feelings from which such thoughts arise were ever with him; and as the thought grew up behind the emotion, the two gradually combined to form in John Orrason the conception of a tangible and intelligent sorrow.

The touch of a loving hand and the tone of an affectionate voice were seldom heard in the prim parlours and orderly apartments of the Refuge at Rotten Row. He was kindly and fairly treated, his child needs were all duly ministered to, but the great desire of the human heart, and the very life blood of that of a child, was not found there.

As his intellect expanded, and his emotions swelled within him, life in the `home` became evermore filled with a deeper mystery, and the sadness of his young life was fast settling into a fixed habit of half-dead thought and feeling, when the needed change came to his thirsting heart.

He had already spent ten years within the home. He was now thirteen and the unseen power which had already, and more than once, changed the current of his life seemed again to have decided on one more change.

White Hart Inn, Grassmarket, Edinburgh

CHAPTER V

The castaway finds himself in Kirkcaldy – A glimpse of Dunfermline and Kirkcaldy weavers a century ago – From Glasgow to Edinburgh and the `Lang Toon` – An eccentric weaver and his wife.

The merchants and manufacturers of Fife – of Dunfermline and Kirkcaldy specially so – had in former times a much closer, more friendly and couthie connection than is either existent or possible in more modern times. The manufacturers of the one town had workmen in the other, and the merchants of the one place sometimes had their most constant customers in the other.

A manufacturing concern of ninety or a hundred years ago in the County of Fife was conducted on lines as different from the system of 1896, as could well be imagined. Not a single parallel is now left, and

21

no fragment of resemblance now exists between the method of the old time and the new.

The manufacturer then might frequently be seen mounted on his grey mare, his packs of goods swinging ponderously on each side of his faithful beast; or he might possibly be observed traversing the rough country roads with an unequal lop-sided pace as he carried his own parcels of stocks or samples [18]. The road over the Cullaloe Hills between Dunfermline and Kirkcaldy, the Lang Toon, was often thus traversed by the flax-spinners and weavers of both towns in these old times and an intimacy existed between the Grey City and the sea-shore Burgh to which the existing generation of traders are wholly strangers. The industrial trade of the country was then held in smaller portions and by more numerous hands than now; and it may be said with equal truth that the feeling of friendly helpfulness and free, open-handed intercourse was also far more prevalent than in these latter days.

It is necessary to keep these differences and distinctions in mind, since our hero will shortly find himself in Kirkcaldy, and be introduced to a state of industrial and social well-being as new and strange to him as it will be to the reader who knows only the great capitalist mill-owners and the wide-spreading mill or factory, in which possibly thousands of human beings toil and struggle amid the roar of machinery, and in an atmosphere of stifling dust and evil odours, for a pittance barely sufficient to yield the necessaries of life.

It is also right to mark these differences, since they help to explain the presence in Kirkcaldy of one of the men in our story. Charley Graham had found himself in the Links of the Lang Toon and, while he was able to explain that he came there on purely 'wab and weavin' business', it was well-known to himself that he had other and ulterior purposes to serve, purposes which were connected with the fortunes of the lad, John Orrason.

It would be impossible to say whether the feelings of dislike which the hidden arbiters of his fate had hitherto exhibited in action towards our hero were beginning to soften, and the sense of justice to the innocent was about to get the upper hand of pride and prejudice, but in March 1810 the ostracized and banished laddie of the Refuge in Glasgow was now suddenly informed he was about to leave the institution. He was now thirteen years of age, pale-faced and bathochtit, and with the appearance of being stagnant alike in his physical and mental growth, yet with the fire and spirit of youth still capable of being roused into flame.

He was lifted with official care into the coach plying between Glasgow and Edinburgh, consigned to the driver's keeping, and waved off in formal adieus from the city of his imprisonment.

The day was one of the spring's reviving and inspiring days. The sun shone clear, clouds swept away before gusty, hopeful winds and soft lights played in grey and blue across the sky. Buds were forming in the hedges, coltsfoot blinked in bright yellow stars on the sloping banks, windflowers were appearing among the trees, and blackbirds led the choristers of the year with their blithe, unmeasured carol. Orrason and the coach left Glasgow before light was in the sky, and reached the Grassmarket of Edinburgh with the fall of the evening. Among those waiting was an honest-looking man, half town and half country bred, who, approaching the passengers as they alighted, enquired of the driver 'Hae ye ane o' the name o' John – John – guidsake! I'll forget the name yet. Whaur's the paper Betty pat i' my pouch afore I cam' awa'? Here it is', and the newcomer spread out a crushed and crumpled bit of foolscap. 'Here it is, an' the name is John – John – Orrason. Has ye sic a passenger in a' your lot'?

'Yes', replied the driver, 'here he is. Are you to take charge of the boy? If so, take this and that and these other things with you. They all belong to Orrason'; and he loaded his interrogator to his full carrying capacity with parcels, bundles and other nameless impediments.

The newcomer was a man of middle height and age, homely, intelligent, kindly and pawky in all his ways. He was a weaver in the Links of the Lang Toon by the name of Peter Saunders and had come to Edinburgh fully commissioned, though he hardly knew by whom, to take charge of and convey to his house in Kirkcaldy the boy named John Orrason. This task he had readily undertaken and was now, in the execution of his mission, standing with a hold of the boy's hand, and surrounded with parcels, on the pavement in front of the White Hart, one of several inns to be found under the shadow of the Castle in the Grassmarket.

The journey home could not be undertaken that night, and so Peter Saunders, swirling every economic consideration through his mind as he stood questioning the half-bewildered lad, at last resolved to 'bide the hail nicht through' in the White Hart, and 'tak' the road i' the morning'. Ensconced in a corner in the common room, the weaver and his charge discussed the chief items of a simple and wholesome supper, while the elder plied the younger with an endless stream of queries as to his previous life, his family, his forebears and all those *et ceteras* of existence which only the thorough-bred male gossip can discover.

'An' whaur did ye say ye were livin'? In a house i' the Rottenraw o' Gleska? Some folk ca'd it a Refuge, did ye say? A city o' refuge nae doot in a desert o' brick houses. A kin' o' sanctuary an' place o' hidin' frae a cruel an' wicked an' perverse generation. Nae doot it was something' o' that kind whaur ye pat up. An' hoo did ye mak' a livin', my mannie, when ye were there? What do ye say? Ye didna work at onything? Had ye nae looms for working dowlas or dook or sackin' aboot the place? It was sheer temptin' o' Providence to hae a stoot laddie like you gaun aboot daein' naething. Your folk surely had forgotten that the Deevil finds mischief enough, an' naethin' but

Forth Ferry, Leith Harbour 1822
(from a Daniell print)

mischief, for idle hands to do. Ye was at the school, was ye? A` weel, ye micht hae been at a waur place, but ye micht hae been twistin` webs, or fillin` pirns i` the forenichts, an` gaen to the school too`. Thus did Peter Saunders run on till the weary laddie`s eyelids were gumming themselves together and he was falling asleep. Peter then rose from his seat, shook up his young charge and, guided by `the gilpie lassie` as he named the chamber-maid of the White Hart, both retired to rest.

In the morning the weaver and his charge crossed from Leith to Pettycur, near Kinghorn, and thence found their way by `Shank`s naigie`, as Peter Saunders phrased it, to the Links of Kirkcaldy. Here the gudewife Betty – a steer-about, cracky, clashing kind of a woman – soon set our wondering wanderer quite at his ease. Putting, and answering her own questions, pressing him to `pree the parritch, and sup them oot`, telling him about the Links, its history, the folk that lived in the place, the weavers, cobblers, bakers, and tailors, and nearly all their queer and questionable attributes, she occupied the first two or three hours of our hero`s sojourn in the Links of the Lang Toon.

`Ye`ll find the folk o` the Links are no ill-set to strangers like yersel`, but ye mustna` cross them, nor misca` them, for their a` kind o` tied thegither, an` fell clannish among themsels. They hae some queer half-dottal sort o` habits among them, but ye`ll soon learn their ways, an` learn to like them too. Hae ye plenty milk to your parritch? See an` fill your wame, an` make a gude breakfast o` what`s on the table. There`s mony a graun` man been fed on parritch – parritch an` kail, an` maybe a whang o` bannocks noo an` then, or ait cakes to sherpin your teeth on. That, wi` a sma` bit o` kitchen at an orra time, should mak` ye grow like a mushroom an` swal out like a bailie – an` that`s weel mindit tae, an` I maun tell ye this. We`ve a bailie o` oor ane i` the Link; an` if ye want to get alang on easy terms, dinna lie across the path o` the baron bailie [19]. He lives o`er i` the jailhouse there, wi` the black hole below his kitchen floor, an` the baron bell cockit up on a belfray on the tap o` the hoose. Aye, they`re a fell folk, the Links folk. A bien an` couthy, an` furthie an` sonsie folk An` noo ye`re fairly dune, are ye? Weel, gang awa` oot an` look aboot ye, an` let the folk see ye, an` hear what they have to say but – gudesake! – dinna tell them ye cam` frae a house o` refuge, or they`ll never let it doon on ye`.

In this way did good Betty Saunders maunder on, giving a history that had no connection in the listener`s mind, and in a language which he could only faintly comprehend.

The door, however, stood invitingly open, and the city-bred urchin – soothed with the comparative stillness of the street and the rhythmical hush of the waves as they broke on the sands at the bottom of the Bell Wynd – soon found himself in the rough, half-paved roadway and, for a time, the observed of all observers as he was subjected to careful scrutiny by old and young in the narrow street.

Whatever might be the ultimate trade-destiny of this the youngest citizen of the Links he was first indoctrinated by Peter Saunders into the mysteries of the weaving craft. And possibly no better fate could have befallen him. The occupation was light and cheerful and, while it offered abundant opportunities for those pensive musings to which he had become accustomed, it also presented every possible means of varied thought, lively conversation, and all that give-and-take between one and another which gently, yet surely and quietly, opened to his surprised and happy eyes the wondrous *arcana* of life.

The Old Jail House at the Links, Kirkcaldy

CHAPTER VI

Life in the Links eighty years ago – A change of occupation – 'Who was his mother'? – 'A sma' crater o' a man' – First love.

At this time the Links of Kirkcaldy was made up of a purely industrial population. Nearly every one of the trades or callings common to Scotland was carried on here. The weavers were the most numerous though, and, unlike the custom in most parts of the country where flax weaving is the ruling industry, a large part of the work was done by women and girls. Every weaving shop counted its contingent of the fair sex, and the long summer evenings which succeeded Orrason's advent in the Links showed how thoroughly men and women found a joy and pleasure in each other's company in both occupation and leisure.

If the tide was out, the sands were literally alive with a rejoicing crowd of human beings. If the tide flowed, innumerable boats plied on the waters of the bay, and one great ambition of the younger men was to become expert in the management of sail and oar. Excursions were made by pleasure-seekers to Inchkeith, or by partan-hunters to the Vous Rocks. The high braes above the glen at the mill-dam would often echo to the music of solo and chorus, rung through all the woods by choirs of part-singers, and the fruit gardens of Dawtle Mill[20], further up the wooded dell, were oft the haunt of those who, deeply smitten with life's great master-passion, would ponder in its shades each other's fate.

This life to Orrason – or, as he was here universally named, Orson – was a revelation so complete, so wonderful and so happy as to surpass to him anything ever conceived in a fairy romance. It spread a light in his heart, warmed up his intellect and touched the dull elements of his emotional nature, as with the fire of a heavenly inspiration. Human beings were now no longer to him mere masses of animated clay, but creatures of joy and beauty; living and breathing with himself, extending to him on every hand gladness and sympathy.

Labour was no longer a task, and active exertion of mind and body became but the exponents of the happiness within. At first dull and insipid, Orrason soon threw off the incubus of his former life, and expanded into the glowing health of thought, and limb and passion.

While exploring in his evening leisure, and making himself familiar with every spot of beauty landward round his new home, the sea proved to him the great field of attraction. The shore, the sands, the glittering and ever-restless surface of the waters were objects of enduring interest. Life at the fireside and in the weaving shop of Peter Saunders, relieved and crowned as it was with a rich and glowing friendship with external nature, passed away to the poor soul like a dream of quiet and unutterable bliss. Weeks and months sped onwards in his life with a speed he could not comprehend. Time had lost its tortoise pace, and now spieled the braes of eternity with the winged feet of Mercury.

He had been some two years at the loom when, with the same silent celerity that had marked his former changes, some occult power informed Peter Saunders that the lad Orrason must be turned to other work.

Damask Handloom

He had evidently, in the estimation of this hidden arbiter, outgrown the seat-tree, and heddles and treddles were to be laid aside for manlier pursuits. Orrason was forthwith – as the lawyers have it – sent to a carpenter's workshop, and there taught the use of planes, gauges and chisels.

The new employment was even more to his taste now that he had out-grown his sad frame of mind than was the occupation of the immortal Bottom, cheerful, lively and song-full though it was. Yet now he thought more than ever about the conditions of his life and it was clear to him that his existence was not like that of any other he had yet met – barring his companions at the Refuge – and he began to feel renewal of an insatiable desire to know something of his parentage.

Who was his mother, and why was it she thus hid her identity behind an impenetrable veil? Could it be this same mother who prompted and compelled the changes in his life, and had arranged, unseen and at a distance, the sordid concerns of his past existence? Had he a father living; and if so, what and where was he? Was it more likely *he* would be the mover and impeller of the dramatic scene shiftings he had been compelled to obey?

It seemed to him only too plain that his birth had not been warranted by all the social sanctions of the time, but, while his reason was conclusive in this direction, it left a vast number of irritating questions still floating in his mind.

It is very true that even this point did not shape itself to his young intelligence in definite and logical form – he felt and acknowledged the emotional conclusion, rather than the mental conviction, as to its truth. Yet, in the same way, and by the same distressing path, did his mind flit about and ponder over innumerable other *might-bes* and possibilities in his enigmatic existence.

It was Saunders, his weaving master, who brought the news of his coming change. But even he could tell little more than that the injunction had gone forth, and must be obeyed. The same power – the same man – who, some two or three years before, had commissioned and instructed him to wait John Orrason's arrival in Edinburgh, had again laid the burden of this duty upon him.

'He was a sma' cratur o' a man', said Peter, 'an' spak but little; nae doot he thocht a great deal. His een were sharp as needles, an' blinkit like a bawbee caun'le when a flou o' saut has fa'en o'er it. He had a richt braid hat on, an' ye could a'maist think ye saw a wee bit will o' the wisp dancin' aneath the brim. The rest o' his claes were in keepin' wi' the black tint o' his beaver, an' he had plenty o' siller to mak' his commands effective'.

In the utter poverty of power to satisfy his curiosity, it need be no surprise that he abandoned all further search for the fact and felt about with a restless instinct for a mind that moved in warm sympathy with his perennial grief. This faculty of sympathy has no particular residence with rank, sex or age, and if prayer can be indicated by the heaving of a sigh, so may sympathy by voice or tone or look.

In the weaving shop where Orrason spent the two first years of his Langtonian life, he had as a constant companion a girl of about his own age – one who was quiet and reserved rather than otherwise, yet who, when jibes and jeers confused at first the young and heartsore lad, contrived to show that her sympathies were with him. The perception of this trait was like soothing balm upon a smarting wound. He never forgot the few, sometimes decisive, words she uttered and, even after he had forsaken the loom for the joiner's bench, he found, not seldom, his way to his old haunts, and rejoiced his heart in a crack with Mary Seaton.

Gradually and surely, this oft-repeated act of friendship ripened into love. He did not, however, perceive its growth, and Mary seemed unconscious of its presence. Time flowed on with an unswerving stream in the experience of both – now quiet and deep, now shimmering down the rapids of enjoyment, now shading itself in the retirement of unconscious modesty.

How pleasant for each if such life as this could flow on for ever! So we all think, yet how poorly were the purposes of life served did the floodgates of adversity never come upon us. Such a period comes to us all, and the bright day in Orrason's journey was now about to be clouded over and drenched in a hurricane of disaster.

By the autumn of 1814 Orrason had grown into a strong, lithe and stalwart lad of seventeen years. His two years at the hardening occupation of the country wright and general house and jobbing joiner had given compactness to his frame and firmness to his muscle. He had at first, in the genial and easy atmosphere of the loom shop, shot rapidly out of his previous stunted form of the Refuge and into the style of a lad who, as his mistress Betty said, needed 'a guid deal o' fillin' up'. Latterly, he had grown more slowly and was now as fair a sample of humanity as one could wish to see. Happy and contented with his lot, he wist not that it was fairly soon to suffer eclipse.

CHAPTER VII

*The pressgang and its victims – making the harbour of Kirkcaldy – Orrason
in the hands of the pressgang – life on board the King's ship.*

It was the year of Waterloo – though that great battle of the nations
had not yet been fought. The feverish anxiety of the midsummer
month was not yet vibrating in the brains of thoughtful men, but the
earnest and purposeful gathering together of the European military
forces had already commenced. Napoleon had broken from his prison
house in Elba, and the port of Frejus [21] had welcomed the great military
genius and emperor in the closing days of February.

By the 1st of March 1815, he had reached Cannes with 1000
followers. Soon the whole of France was inflamed with the presence
of the man who had brought so much glory and such vast misery upon
her people. Every capital in Europe seemed, too, as if smitten with the
virus of war-like feeling, and fired with immense activity in preparation for hostilities. Our own government was early in possession of
intelligence regarding every movement made by the escaped emperor,
and entering into a solemn compact with Russia, Prussia, and Austria,
prepared for the final struggle with the terrible Corsican. Her army,
never numerous, was yet made up of veterans trained and inured to
the hardships of campaigning and the vicissitudes of battle. Her fleet
had full command of the sea, though the long twenty years war with
France had drained her naval resources and thinned the ranks alike of
her blue-jackets and marines.

To recruit and maintain these at their necessary complement,
government and the naval authorities had sanctioned and maintained
in constant activity a system of forcing seamen of the mercantile
marine into the Navy; this was the pressgang system which proved
such a terror to our fathers and such an oppressive engine of force and
suffering to all classes of men finding a full or even partial living on

the sea. Every man who could handle an oar, rope or sail could be made useful on board a man-of-war, and the government held that the first duty of these men was to serve their country – and to risk both life and limb in that service.

The pressgang was known and hated in every fishing village and shipping port in the kingdom and, as the east coast was replete with the class of seamen best suited to the navy – hardy, skilful and fearless – so was it made the most frequent hunting ground of the pressgang. In the Firth of Forth the appearance of the ships called tenders had become a common though always undesired event, and the people of the sea-faring community were ever on the alert to note the skulking movements of the unwelcome visitor, and specially to keep an eye on the gliding oarcraft with which she was always accompanied.

It was about the middle of March 1815 and the month was, as usual, passing her nights and days in blasty storms of wind and rain with passing gleams of cloud and sunshine. At Kirkcaldy the day broke from behind the Bass Rock and Berwick Law, above a bouk of dense purple cloud masses, and in a long streak of bronze-yellow light, that glittered on the moving waters and played upon the sails and hulls of the fishing and trading craft that lay at anchor or bore away eastward to the North Sea.

During the night under cover of darkness, a sharp-lined, rakish-looking, square-rigged craft with tall and tapering masts had crept up the Forth to a quiet and partially-concealed anchorage on the south side of Inchkeith, with her topgallants visible over the headlands of the island. Her suspicious position, if it tended to conceal the vessel, also encouraged closer observation and enquiry. Her purpose was soon divined, and the younger men among the sea-going denizens of the shore either made rapidly off to sea or found a reason for making a journey inland. It was an old visitor, and every practiced eye detected His Majesty's tender *Bittern* in the vessel so closely anchored to the south side of the Inch and knew it carried the ancient disturbers of their peace – the pressgang.

Very early in the morning, some four eight-oared gigs had left the mysterious ship and landed at different places on the south and north shores of the Firth. With only one of these are we concerned. Lieutenant Thacker, with a well-armed company of blue-jackets, had been deputed to `rake the harbour of Kirkcaldy and bring on board the *Bittern* as many men as he could clap his flippers on`. He had run in to the east side of Ravenscraig and there, under the shadow of the high, wooded shoreland, had waited the advent of opening day. As soon as the day was fully up and crews, as he believed, would be busy at work on their ships in the harbour, he and his men broke from their concealment, clambered up the rocky barriers and gained the highway – then much nearer the shore than now. Here he quickly formed his men, bade them see to their cutlasses, and started off with rapid pace through Pathhead and down to the cove.

Ere the crews of the half dozen vessels lying there could have the least warning of the approaching enemy, the pressgang was upon them. As none of the ships was of large tonnage, and as not one of them was preparing to set sail, most of the men were lodged in various parts of the town and beyond the reach of search. With those in the harbour, however, there was scarcely the possibility of escape. Rough, immediate and brutal was the attack of the gang. For each of the vessels in the harbour, two men were detached from the company. These, drawing their cutlasses, rushed on board, made their way by unerring knowledge and instinct to the quarters of the men, gave a quick look round and, pushing aside the old men and boys, laid strong hands upon the younger able seamen, and demanded immediate surrender. These young men were dragged forcibly ashore and, by frequent use of the rattan and threat of the cutlass, were driven to the lower end of the east pier. Here a small coasting sloop, having received severe damage to her hatches and deckhouse on her homeward cruise, was undergoing repairs. She had only one seaman on board and one carpenter, but that carpenter was our hero John Orrason. He, with the solitary seaman, was at once seized and, with tremendous chorus of oaths and curses, driven along with the others.

The gig had been quickly and quietly been brought round from behind Ravenscraig, and the prisoners – some seven in all – were forced, with worse usage than ever was inflicted even on cattle, into the rocking craft. The spirit of the prisoners rebelled at the treatment to which they were subjected, but the resistance they offered only resulted in blows and wounds from the sticks and cutlasses of the King's men. A crowd was by this time gathering in the street, and numbers of men and women were running down the long east pier. Fearful of an attempt at rescue, the men from the tender now used their cutlasses with merciless severity, and the victims of kingly rage were compelled to enter the waiting boat. No sooner were all on board than the oars were plied, the mast and sail rigged, and soon the swelling waters divided – in most cases for ever – the enraged townspeople from their departing friends.

If Orrason felt himself harshly and cruelly treated in the *melee* on the pier-head, he had no less cause to denounce the treatment he received on board the tender. When the boat in which the Kirkcaldy contingent was conveyed reached that vessel, its inmates found that the other three boats were either already returned or close at hand. All the prisoners – for prisoners they really were – were hustled on board and crammed by force into the 'tween decks. Meantime the anchors were hove in, the yards squared, the sails set and, in a surprisingly short space of time, the ill-omened ship was hull-down beyond the Bass.

The wretched inmates of the 'tween decks were now, and in peculiar fashion, attended to by their captors. Their wounds were roughly bound up. Each man was presented with a glass of grog and compelled to swallow it, under immediate drastic penalties. The guard of the marines placed over them knocked them about in a cruel and heartless manner. The officer's rattan was never at rest. Whoever happened to be nearest him, as he moved towards or returned from the companionway, was sure to receive a blow. Poor Orrason had received a rather severe scalp wound and both his hands were bleeding from the harsh treatment of his captors. The others were nowise in better plight. Some indeed were stretched out on the deck in a state of semi-insensibility from loss of blood, or the stunning effects of heavy blows. Others attempted to find seats on the deck itself, while the larger number simply stood around, half-mad, half-dazed with the situation and, while inwardly cursing the ships, service and methods of the navy, wondered what was next to happen. While they wondered the hours sped on and, as they passed the Ferne Isles, kindly night spread her dull grey mantle over the scene. Supper was served to the hungry men, lamps were lighted, hammocks slung, and the guard of marines being placed, the blessed forgetfulness of sleep closed to Orrason his first day on board the *Bittern*.

Seaman, The Royal Navy, c1815

CHAPTER VIII

The castaway's life at Sheerness – The lieutenant on duty – Letters sent but no reply – On board the Impregnable, now the Caledonia Training Ship at Queensferry – A `pirates` den`.

Carried to Sheerness, the hapless pressed men were handed over to the naval authorities of the station. Here memories of the famous mutiny of the Nore of 1797 [22] were still fresh, and the improved and more humane discipline and treatment of our seamen, which that event induced, made a residence in the floating mansions of Blue Town (the sea) an agreeable contrast to the barbarities of the *Bittern.* The pressed men were received on board the *Brancepeth,* a 74-gun frigate of the second class, stationed here to serve the purposes of the fleet, where they were listed and described.

Lieutenant Blundell scanned the list as he surveyed the men ranged before him on the quarter-deck. A second survey of the names induced a running commentary of questions and statements all of which – after certain verbal difficulties had been overcome – were deemed satisfactory. When he came to Orrason, however, his progress was abruptly stopped.

'So far as I can make out, my man', said the scrutinizing officer, turning to Orrason, 'your name seems to be Orrason. Is that so'?

'That, indeed, is my name', replied our hero, 'though sometimes people shorten it to the milder one of Orson'.

'What? Milder did you say? A denizen of the woods was Orson, nursed by a bear and the ruling terror of his time [23]. And your name is Orrason'?

'Yes, sir'.

'You come from Scotland, do you not'?

'I do, sir'.

'Well, I know something of Scotch' the officer continued, 'and cannot understand why one born north of the Tweed should have the word *orra* in his name at all. Anything orra is extra or uncommon, and anyone being orra must be out of the common line, unexpected or unneeded'.

'Or possibly undesired', observed Orrason somewhat sadly.

'Just as Orson himself was possibly. However, your name should not be changed from Orrason to Orson at the whim of every indolent speaker', and the officer was about to pass on when Orrason observed:

'The one name has an equally good attachment to me as the other'.

'What'! broke in the officer, 'do you not carry your father's name'?

'I have no idea who my father was, and cannot tell whether or not I received his surname', and Orrason spoke with an increasing evidence of feeling.

'Possibly you were treated to your mother's name', observed the officer, gently touching a subject he evidently did not wish to pursue.

'That may be, sir. But my mother's name I never heard mentioned, and do not know whether I bear it or not'.

The Lieutenant was more puzzled than ever. 'Were you a foundling – if I may ask the question'?

'I do not think so, sir. My fate seems to be that of one who was more lost than found'.

'You come, I see, from the town of Kirkcaldy'?

'I lived there for some four or five years'.

'And you lived before that – '?

'In Glasgow', said Orrason.

'And you came to Kirkcaldy some five years ago'?

'Yes', answered Orrason, deepening the puzzle, 'but I was carried the final part of the journey to Kirkcaldy by a man I did not then know, and know little of even now apart from his name. He is no relation of mine in any way. Indeed', he continued, 'I have no relation that I know of in the world, and the only name I know and am known by is John Orrason'.

The officer, now clearly comprehending that a haunting mystery encircled the man before him, pursued the interrogation no further.

Weeks and months of routine duties passed by at Sheerness, and our hero, with a facility born of sudden and changeful experiences, was rapidly adapting himself to his new life. His carpentry experience proved of great value to him here. His commander, finding him an excellent workman, readily promoted him to a place among the 'chips' as the carpenters were called. Soon he proved himself a man of thorough trustfulness and skill and, though still young, was given charge of the shifting squads of men sent to different ships in the docks and down to the river for important or urgent repairs.

Nearly a year passed in this new form of life, and in this new quarter of the world. He had not forgotten his friends in the Lang Toon, and he had no sooner fully recovered his health and settled down to the work than he wrote to his weaving master Peter and to his employer in the joinery business. To these letters he never received any answer, and even one he wrote to Mary Seaton, full of expressions of grateful friendship and warm attachment, remained without a reply. Somewhat of his old sadness of the Refuge came back to him as he waited with fruitless patience during the weary weeks and months that followed the dispatch of his letters.

Meantime he was going more and more on distant duties – to ships at Gravesend, at Tilbury, and at the Nore. He was at length, when fully a year at Sheerness, transferred to the *Impregnable* – a three-decker of 98 guns, destined to form one of the squadron which, under Lord Exmouth, was ordered to the siege and reduction of Algiers.

The *Impregnable* of 1816 is no longer in the category of our ships of war, but the fine, firmly-built old vessel is still with us and, as a training ship at Queensferry, under the name of the *Caledonia*, serves a splendid purpose in the economy of our naval forces. If peace can show a record of deeds no less renowned than those of war, so can she set forth a list of utilities no less essential to our safety as a nation than the more heroic and daring activities of the actual campaign [24]. But few of the hundreds of visitors to the becalmed training ship of the Forth will be able to figure in their own minds the terribly different scenes these decks presented on the 27th of August of 1816.

The incorrigible little sovereignty of Algiers had long – indeed, since the beginning of the sixteenth century – been a mere nest of corsairs and pirates. This plundering state on the southern shore of the Mediterranean had for ages maintained an existence by robbing the commerce of other nations, preying on their commercial industry, imprisoning merchants and seamen and exacting enormous ransoms for their release, and by keeping in captivity vast numbers of men and women seized on the high seas and putting them to labour as slaves. Treaties and arrangements counted for nothing with these bandits; the laws of might and cunning were alone their rules of action.

These prowling sea-hornets infested the shores of all southern Europe, the Mediterranean, and the Eastern Atlantic, and Algiers, their great stronghold on the African shore, was ever a safe and protecting retreat.

The city of Algiers, rising like an amphitheatre on the eastern slope of a steep hill, was defended by batteries and casemated buildings on both sides of the harbour. Immense numbers of guns, carrying shot of nearly every possible size up to eighty pounds, kept guard over this pirates' den.

In the Dey's noisome dungeons in the city, and on his settlements inland, were imprisoned tens of thousands of Christian slaves [25]. Most of these were kept in chain-gangs, guarded by armed Arabs, and goaded on in their labour by drivers who were never idle in the use of sticks and whips. Gangs of these were harnessed to ploughs and forced to till the land. Others were fastened like animals to the rude carts and vehicles of the country, and treated as mere beasts of burden. Others again, in drilled and driven squads, laboured on the works at the harbour, their bodies stripped almost naked, and exposed to the heat of a broiling sun.

Old Algiers

CHAPTER IX

The Siege of Algiers – An `impressive sight` – The `Christian dogs` on the move – The Impregnable under fire – The `lurid light of destruction`.

In May of 1816, a fearful and wholly unprovoked massacre of seamen, fishers, and workers engaged at the pearl fisheries of Bona [26] and protected at once by treaty and subsidy, was perpetrated by the Arabs. This seems to have been the last straw which the patient camel of the Christian nations could bear. Such deeds could no longer be suffered to continue and the system under which they had become possible must be, at once and finally, put an end to. Intimation was made without delay to the Dey, and preparations made to attack and destroy the stronghold of this enemy of peace and progress.

Early in the summer, a British squadron was rapidly fitted out, placed under the command of Lord Exmouth, and sent to sea – Algiers being the destination. At Gibralter, the British fleet of five ships of the line and eight smaller vessels was joined by the Dutch squadron of six ships, under Admiral Capellen, and the whole reached the doomed city by the latter half of August. On the 27th a summons of surrender was delivered by the Admiral in command and, as no attention was given to this, the bombardment was opened on the following day.

Looked at from the deck of the *Impregnable,* the city and its surroundings was indeed a grand and impressive sight. To Orrason, who had never before looked on the shores of this great middle sea, the view was entrancing beyond description. The city itself, as it rose tier upon tier in flat-roofed dwellings, shining white and brilliant in the midday sun, was suggestive of anything but war or rapine; while all round, on every vantage point, rose the scattered residences and far-spreading vineyards of the rich and powerful, conveying the reassuring ideas of peace and repose.

With a light and variable wind, the attacking fleets moved inwards to the harbour. The slow progress of the huge vessels seemed to have deceived the Arabs into the notion that we were unwilling or afraid to begin the action. They crowded in vast numbers on the moles and harbours – soldiers, sailors, marines, and unarmed citizens – waving defiance and shouting contempt on the `Christian dogs` that threatened their avocations of robbery and murder. This feeling gradually died away as the vessels fearlessly sailed under the batteries and proceeded within shot distance of their greatest defences, and the exulting shouts sunk down into ominous silence as the war ships began to enter the harbour.

The *Princess Charlotte,* the *Albion,* the *Superb* and the *Impregnable* were the first to enter. The admiral, with a keen and anxious look out, had no sooner seen the smoke of the first shot fired from the defying batteries than he issued the command:

`Now, my fine fellows, fire away`.

The signal at the mast-head told to every other commander the intent of the admiral, and, as if by one vast overpowering impulse, the whole fleet poured in a broadside of such terrible destructiveness as to astonish and appal even the officers on board. Dismounted guns, wrecked batteries, and falling masses of masonry were seen on every side, while no less than five hundred human beings were killed or rendered useless for fight on the moles and harbours.

The shrieks and cries of the sufferers were soon drowned in the deafening roar of the cannonade that now set in – for the battle between sea and land had now fairly begun. The *Impregnable*, partly because of damage to her rigging, and partly because the light breeze had almost died away, was at an early stage in the fight placed almost entirely as the mercy of the batteries on shore. Swinging gradually and fatefully into a position between two of the strongest defensive works, she suffered losses in men and material far beyond that of any other ship of the fleet. Unable to keep her place in the moving order of battle, she was compelled to anchor in the very teeth of the batteries which, in a short time, had told with fearful effect upon her hull, deck gear, and rigging, and, worst of all, upon her gallant crew.

Men fell thick and fast upon the upper and main decks. Now a shot would strike the woodwork and send hundreds of splinters in all directions with messages of destruction or death. Now a gun or carriage was struck and the gun itself sent tumbling to the deck with danger to life and limb. Now a raking shot would carry off, in its wild rush, a whole gun's complement of men.

Algerian Felucca

Orrason had never before witnessed the horrors and devastation of war and, though at first the destructive shots of the enemy had an appalling effect upon his mind, the sight of the maimed and shattered bodies of his comrades roused him to a species of madness – a madness in which he was proof against all sense of danger, and which only stirred up a fierce passion for vengeance on the foe. Like most of his comrades, he had cast aside every stitch of clothing that could impede the freest action of the body and limbs, or add to discomfort by increasing the heat. He was naked from the waist upwards and his feet and ankles were also bare.

What a horrible and awful sight these men presented on the deck of the *Impregnable*. During two hours of fierce battle and agonizing suspense, the ship had lost by wounds and death 150 of her crew. The rigging hung in a tangled mass of ropes, sails and spars. Her bulwarks were shattered in many places, round shot had penetrated her hull, many of her guns were useless and, while here and there on her decks the mangled remains of the dead were hustled out of the way, others who had lost limbs and were in agony, waited their turn to be carried below to the rough hands of the ship's surgeons.

From the cockpit came the shrieks and cries of those under the knife of the operator, and all round the groans of the suffering and dying made the air hideous with the music of agony. Even when the worst of the fight was over in the bay, and the *Impregnable* was drifting slowly out to sea, she seemed to be a target for all the guns of the enemy, and gladly everyone on board hailed the moment when the shot of the batteries began to fall short and merely to lash the waters of the sea.

The attack had opened about three in the afternoon. It raged on from hour to hour until about eight in the evening, when the batteries had, one after the other, resigned their position as active combatants in the awful scene, and looked like mere masses of brick or stone work, though mixed with fallen guns and tumbrels or ablaze with fire.

Darkness came with the close of the fiercest part of the struggle, and as the mantle of the night fell, the clearness of the heavens was also overspread, and the rain began to descend. Signs were already abundant that the close and well-directed fire of the ships had told with terrible effect in every part of the city. The defensive works, placed all over the slope as far up as the dominating Casbah, had drawn the fire of the ships and, with it, destruction to the civil as well as to the military part of the city. Orrason, when a fitful moment of chance afforded him the view, could see smoke and flame rising in ominous and turreted clouds on the suphureous air, and observe proofs of vast destruction and signs of spreading conflagration on every hand.

But the fleet did not come out of the dreadful encounter without acknowledging – in nearly universal loss and damage – the effects of the fifteen hundred guns, handled with less or more deadly effect by the trained Arab gunners in the city. Every ship had suffered, but possibly the *Impregnable* worst of all.

As the night clock neared the hour of eleven the ships were ordered to withdraw, and slowly the disabled hulls obeyed the order; hours passed by ere the entire fleet could be said to be again at sea.

By this time it was in the small hours of the succeeding morning and while Orrason, as yet unwounded, and his brave comrades, still worked the ship's guns and trod her decks with undaunted hearts, they must have felt her planks slippery with the life's blood of brave men, and looked on scenes of carnage they never had dreamed of.

In the darkness the ship still floated out to sea. In the distance, and far away towards the land, the ships, warehouses and city of Algiers, were enveloped in flames and lighting up the vast expanse of sea and shore with the lurid light of destruction.

Heaven's lightning shot across the fiery gloom, the rain descended, and the floods came – such floods as only southern or eastern skies can pour forth. The day of reckoning dawned on fleet and city and, though hundreds of the brave and good had given up their lives in the dread holocaust, the piracy of Algiers had, for the time at least, come to an end, and Christian slavery on African shores was a thing of the past.

The Slave Ship

CHAPTER X

The castaway on the Slave Coast – A letter to Mary Seaton – on board the Ardent – Sierra Leone – A hearty goodbye – in the 'Doldrums' – A strange craft – A heavy shot from the slaver – An effective broadside – The slaves under hatches.

The terrible excitement of the bombardment was succeeded on the following day with the lassitude of exhaustion. Ere this condition, however, was allowed to supervene, the commanders made every possible exertion to obliterate the evidences of the previous day's disastrous experience. With the dead this was quickly carried into execution and the blue waters of the great middle sea became the grave of many a brave and gallant seaman. With the wounded the process was necessarily less complete. The bed of suffering must be endured for weeks or months to come ere the stage of convalescence could be reached and, though more convenient quarters would soon be appointed to the sick and dying, they must, in the meantime, remain on board. The wreckage of the decks was cleared away, the red marks of bloody execution were washed out of sight and the tangled and torn sails, spars and ropes of the rigging were restored to workable condition.

To Orrason the reaction of exhaustion came with double severity. Deep and serious reflection on the meaning of the slaughter he had witnessed came to him, accompanied with a relapse into the dull, unhopeful tone bred within him in the Refuge, and for some days after the bombardment, he was in the agonies alike of despair and self-accusation. Time, however, is the great healer and soon brought relief to our hero.

The *Impregnable* was desperately in need of repairs and refitting and, after a patching up of her most urgent injuries, the battered craft was sent home to England and put in hospital. The members of her crew, being no longer required, were drafted to other ships of the line, and destined to other missions and purposes of the navy.

Orrason, with a full sense of the fatefulness of his destiny, was assigned a place on board the *Ardent*, a fast-sailing and well-armed brig of 20 guns which, with her consort, the *Delos*, was intended for the West African station and, with Sierra Leone as their centre of operations, to watch and intercept the slave traders on the coast. The brigs had been fitted out at Plymouth and from here, before leaving for his new post, Orrason, with the pertinacity of his nature, wrote once more to his whilom shopmate of the Linktown.

He felt, though he could not explain how nor in what way, that Mary Seaton and himself would yet, in happier days, meet and fill the seat of joy which was now, he believed, vacant in both their hearts.

He wrote Mary a long account of all he had seen and endured since he had last written to her. He told her of his African destination, and pressed her to write him at Sierra Leone, believing that would always find him.

`Still, my dearest Mary`, he wrote, `whether you answer me or not – whether you speak to me in written signs or refuse to break even the silence of thought – I shall still write to you. If I did not I should sink in despair. I cannot live without a friend, or feel joy without love. You are all that to me remains as the living, breathing emblem of friend-ship and affection. I shall therefore write you still, if for nothing more than to keep alive the flame of life`s purpose in my heart. If you write me – which I hope you will – the flame shall burn with greater brightness. Sierra Leone means the lion-shaped mountain – I shall wait under the shadow of the lion for proofs of the love that lives and dies not between us. Once more, and with even a closer companionship of hope, I subscribe myself, yours faithfully, and for life, John Orrason`.

The *Ardent* and *Delos* being well found in men's provisions, and ammunition – not omitting the all-needful medicine chest – were soon ploughing their way through Plymouth Sound on their way to the English Channel and so to the far south. It would prove an all-deciding voyage for Orrason, and was doomed to be of a more trying and enduring nature than he or any of his messmates could have believed when, with sails fully set and everything taut and trim, the crews received the cheers and farewells of the garrison at Drake's Island in the Sound.

Biscay was in one of his mildest moods, and his gates were passed without trial or mishap. Calpe's towering rock [27] was saluted from the west and, three days after, the peak of Tenerif was passed on the east. The region of their station was at last reached, and life under the line was begun by the crews of *Ardent* and *Delos* and our hero Orrason with the presentation of papers and acceptance of duties at Sierra Leone.

Sierra Leone is to most people but a geographical expression. They have no idea of the active, constant and rationalised social life that marks the settlement from day to day. Here the natives of many lands meet and marketing for all tropical and other necessaries of life is done. Here are churches – established and dissenting – and clergymen in white skins and in black. Social institutions of various kinds are found and even a race-course stretches itself along the green or yellow sward. There are law courts where judges hear and decide cases – not only concerning the slave trade, but in all disputes that break incessantly through the monotony of station or colonial life. In the broad sweep of the river there are islands and waterfowl, and sportsmen find scope for their peculiar energies as they choose, near at hand or up the river and among the hilly regions seen from the shore, and gleaming in wood and wild flowers in the brilliant sun.

The *Ardent* and the *Delos* were welcomed by the residents and, from the governor downwards, everyone seemed pleased at the advent of two fresh cruisers. Both vessels anchored in the river and formally handed their papers of warrant and commission to the governor and his court.

While lying here for the first few days after arrival at the station, the strangeness and beauty of everything strongly attracted Orrason's attention. The picturesqueness of the native costumes and of their tribal and religious rites drew his regard and excited his thought. Ashore the crews were treated with the warmest regard, the bishop himself doing, on more than one occasion, the honours of the host. He provided the forecastle as well as the cabin with a select store of books, and when the two cruisers had been fully refitted, he bade goodbye to all and wished them good luck till their return.

Running into densely shaded creeks, where the still waters permitted the dusky natives to crowd around with their canoes, or hovering outside of some far-reaching river's mouth, were tasks that tried the patience as well as the strength and constitution of all on board. Scudding along lee shores, or picking a dangerous path through the waters inside the closely wooded islands, were no less trying to the nerves and skill of their best seamen. With a good offing and a stiff breeze on the quarter-starboard or port, the men forgot the wasting monotony of their duties and became active, musical and happy. They then sang their best English songs, told their toughest yarns and, if a cooling rain came with the shifting wind, they were able to bless the cook and give benisons to his dinner.

Several weeks had been passed at sea with no engrossing occurrence to the crews of the *Ardent* and *Delos*, and Orrason was concluding that chasing the slavers was a matter much more in name than in reality. There were indeed times, even in the slave trade business of seventy years ago, when nothing came or went to stir the monotony of beating or tacking, of crossing or winning the wind, and returning to quarters when signs of a slaver had proved deceiving.

But changes come sometimes even in the Doldrums. One day, when the sun was climbing into his meridian tower and the ship was running north-westward under close-reefed topsails, the look-out man on the *Ardent* suddenly sang out:

'Strange craft on the port bow, sir', to Martin Schellsey, the lieutenant on board the brig, whose watch it was. At once the long glass was brought into requisition and 'Our look-out's right this time', said the officer. 'Our neighbour's as strange a craft as one could wish to see'; and he handed the glass to the commander, who had by this time appeared on the poop.

Commander Halewood [28], an easy-going, yet brave and capable officer of the old type, turned the glass in the direction of the suspected craft.

'She seems to be in rags, Schellsey', he said, as he again applied the glass, 'and completely done for, at least in her rigging – possibly in her steering gear as well'.

'We'd better run down on her, should we not'? enquired Schellsey, turning to the commander.

'Surely, surely! Whatever she may turn out to be, we had better see what she is'.

Orders were at once given that every sail was properly set and drawing well and, as the breeze was freshening, the clean-going cruiser was soon bearing down on the stranger.

Meantime all eyes were bent in the direction indicated by the look-out and gradually the outline of the strange ship was fully seen. The Spanish pennant showed that the craft claimed to run under that flag, but cruisers on the African main soon learn that pretensions are not always either of truth or value.

Her rigging seemed to have suffered a big breakdown somewhere and her sails had as evidently been sharers in a recent disaster. As she lay rolling about, it was difficult to make out whether or not her steering gear was intact. She seemed as if laying to, yet the forms of such intention were neither present nor possible. The *Ardent* bore down upon the stranger with all possible speed and, as she neared the logged and labouring ship, strange signs of excitement and alarm were visible to every seaman on board.

Close in at last, the unknown one was hailed by a signal; the British flag – the well-known Union Jack – was run up, and the answering signal awaited. To the surprise of the captain and the wild rage of all, a puff of blue smoke heralding a heavy round shot, proved her reply. The shot dashed through the shrouds and, though doing little or no harm, was evidently intended to cripple the sailing sinews of the *Ardent*.

Commander Halewood was an old hand among the slavers and knew that every able-bodied seaman on board these ships would dare and risk a great deal before he would allow his vessel to be taken. The round shot incident, while it proved the character of the disabled craft, proved also the effectiveness of the ruse which the commander and his carpenter Orrason had ere now carried out. The ruse was that of clothing the bulwarks and hull of the King's ship in the peaceful garb of a trading ship. By help of boards and paint her ports were concealed and the outlines and semblance of commerce were substituted for her usual look of preparedness for war; the guns of the brig had been carefully disguised to give its broadside all the appearance of a peaceful and plodding merchantman. These little devices had completely deceived the would-be Spaniard, and hurried her commander into an iron-tongued confession of her mission and character. No doubt remained that she was a slave-trader and floating prison-house of suffering human beings and this conviction carried energy and enthusiasm to every British heart on board the *Ardent*.

With the provocation offered by the slaver, the port-hole shutters were stripped away in a moment and every available piece on the port side was discharged to bring the crew of the 'ragged hypocrite', as Schellsey called the stranger, to their senses. The colours were struck and soon a couple of boats, with some twenty men from the *Ardent*, proceeded through a rough and choppy sea to board the vessel, and soon the whole twenty were clambering over the gunwale. On the main deck everything was in confusion and disorder. In answer to Schellsey's enquiries, it turned out that the vessel, after leaving the African shore and going a day's sail westward, had been suddenly struck by one of those short-lived and furious tornadoes which too often assail the mariner in tropical seas. Her topgallants were completely gone, and even her staysails were ripped to ribbons and were hanging in melancholy evidence of the storm through which the ship had passed.

When the storm had come on, the hatches had been battened down, and the six or seven score slaves confined in the hold below were doomed to all the horrors of death from suffocation in the dark and dismal den. With a celerity only possible to British seamen, and Orrason bearing a leading and guiding part, the hatches were torn open, and the light and air of sun and sky given free passage to the black hole below.

Much has been written of the horrors of the Middle Passage [29] and yet the awful terrors of that death-and-life experience to the slave have never yet been laid bare. When the men of the *Ardent* had cleared away the hatches, the odours from below – odours nameless in their kind and intensity – were unbearable and no-one could face the vile and disgusting effluvia from the sweltering mass of human beings – dead and living – below.

Looking around, the effects of the *Ardent's* broadside were seen on every hand. The deck-house had been completely smashed, the binnacle reduced to chips, while splinters lying in all directions showed how well the guns had spoken. Several of the crew were wounded, and two who had been in the deck-house at the time of its destruction were beyond the reach of all future pain. A number of the Negroes who had been working with the crew had also been severely hit. One with a leg torn in a dreadful manner was evidently sinking fast, and another, whose breast had been lacerated beyond all chance of healing, was evidently doomed to follow his friend.

The crew, it was found, were made up of several nationalities but, though the Spanish colours had been flown, the ship and enterprise were, strange and dishonourable as it may appear in every respect, British.

CHAPTER XI

The Middle Passage – Liberating the slaves – A letter from Mary – Pursuit of a retreating slaver – Escaped!

Relays of men from the slaver's crew were told – both by their captors and by their own captain – to look to the state of the imprisoning hold below. Soon a score of gasping and half-conscious creatures were laid out on the decks. The entrance of light and air had revived a large number of the suffering beings – men, women, and girls – crammed into the narrow prison house. These were assisted up the ladders and others managed to clamber by themselves to the deck. Every one of them was drenched in perspiration, and most of them daubed or covered in filth, as nameless as it was revolting.

All of the living having been brought on deck, the more gruesome task of disposing of the dead had to be undertaken. Most of these, it was found, were females who, weaker than the men, had been trampled to death, or crushed out of life in the more distant and airless corners of the den and during the first paroxysms of suffocation. A port-hole, large enough to admit a man – the doorway indeed by which the dusky captives had at first been thrust into the hold – was opened and, one by one, the ghastly victims of a horrible death were committed to the deep. The straw and dried leaves and grasses intended for the sleeping accommodation of the slaves, and which had now become as repulsive as the dead bodies, were also thrown into the cleansing waters. The den, thus roughly cleared, was left for a while to the purifying offices of the sea winds playing between hatch and port.

The men from the *Ardent* were not idle. Rapidly, and with the handiness of British sailors, a cook's galley, the most needful of necessary things now, was fitted up, and as the slaver had been provisioned for a long trip across the Atlantic, there was soon an abundance of simple but reviving soups to regale the sickly and hungry captives. All of those laid out on deck, or who had reached the upper air by their own efforts, gave rapidly increasing signs of returning strength, and the warm products of the cook's galley set them up as if by magic.

The ship's papers were, of course, seized and, though these were intended much more to deceive than to instruct, they were held as of important use and value in what might afterwards happen. The master and crew were made prisoners, and the whole property of ship and cargo confiscated. The *Delos*, which had got far out of hailing distance when the attack began, had now come up to the *Ardent*, and the two crews were not long in fitting up a set of such sailing gear as enabled the slaver to be carried into the port of Sierra Leone, and handed over to the British courts there.

There was often in these short capture-voyages from the high seas to the port of Sierra Leone more difficulty and danger than in the capture of the ship. The time occasionally occupied several days and, though the prize was manned with a crew from the decks of her captors, there were often more desperadoes on board than King's men. The hands hired to man a slaver were only paid at the close of a voyage so that capture of their ship meant the loss of everything. For this reason, they usually fought desperately and, when captured, schemed constantly to escape. On this occasion, Lieutenant Schellsey made such disposition of his men, and such arrangement as to relays, that the vile traffickers in human flesh had no alternative but to submit to their fate. They were carried – ship, men, papers, and slaves – into the station port and the poor blacks set free.

Orrason was overwhelmed with a joy he could not describe when he found, waiting for him in the little post-office in the official residence, a long and precious letter from Mary Seaton. It was full of her personality, of her surroundings and experiences, and told the story of her life since nearly four years ago she had learned the terrible news of his capture by the pressgang.

Mary wrote: 'Dear Mr. Orrason, you must forgive me. I have been long, long in answering your ever-valued and kind letters. This I admit and deeply regret but I will tell you someday how and why this was so, and then you will see that it was not that I had forgotten you or ceased to think of you, but hoped for the time when I should see you back again. When the news came west of the Links that you had been carried off by the pressgang, we were all thrown into grief and confusion. Your joiner master came along to Peter's house, and, running breathless into the shop, cried out that the pressgang had been in at the harbour, carried away all the sailors they could find, and you among them. He was in great consternation how he was to do without you, and swore himself half mad on the shop floor. Betty came but the house and Peter stopped shuttling till they heard the story to the end. Neighbours from all the lands round about quickly filled the place, and we soon had a hundred different stories of the event. In a wee while, the hail neighbourhood were doon to the sands watching the boat of the tender, wi` you on board, rowin` awa` up to Inchkeith. Willie Robb had his long glass brought oot and, when I looked through, I felt sure I saw you in the midst of the blue-jacketed sailors, casting a weary look towards the shore. The boat was soon oot o` sicht, and ere the afternoon had weel begun, the tender an` a` her boats were by the Bass. I couldna work for days after, wonderin` whaur ye would be, and what they were doin` wi` ye.

Peter and Betty werena lang in getting ower their trouble, and your master, east the toon, never cam` again to speer about you.

But I maun tell ye that about three days after you were ta`en awa`, a little dark, black-a-vised man, that naebody kent hereabout, cam` into the shop an` speered everything aboot your wa`-gaun. He gaed yont to your joiner maister an` to the custom-house and ilka ither place whaur he could learn onything aboot ye, and mark`d it a` doon. He was seen gaun awa` up by the Raith, and wast by Boglily [30], but whaur he cam` frae naebody hereaboot kent. He was surely something to do with you, or your folk or your forebears`.

Mary concluded her half-Scottish, half-English letter by assuring her `dear Mr. Orrason` that no-one knew of the letter being written, and finished by reference to Peter and Betty.

`To some extent, these two and most of your old acquaintances in the Links will soon forget about you, but there will always be one who will not lose the memory and image of her old shopmate. For good or for ill, yours faithfully, Mary Seaton`.

For the *Ardent* and her consort the *Delos*, more weeks and months of dalliance, of waiting in port, of lying becalmed at sea and broiling under the tropical sun, or of running under bare poles before the rushing storms of the tropics, followed the capture of the *Ardent's* first slave prize. The two crews had almost again given up hope of anything in the slave-ship line that might break the monotony of their existence. The unexpected, however, generally happens and, when the grumbling ABs of the *Ardent* and *Delos* had finally resigned themselves to imagined perpetual inactivity, they were suddenly recalled to the severer duties of their life at sea.

The morning had dawned in thick, cloudy fogs, and for about an hour after the sun was above the horizon, the distance was completely hid from view by dense and hazy mists. When these, however, cleared away – rising like a rapidly raised curtain from the rolling sea – an object of the deepest interest was seen by everyone on board. A dark-hulled, suspicious-looking craft, which was at first under easy sail but piled on every stitch of canvas when she found she had company, was an object of the most absorbing regard to a cruiser on the African coast. Whatever the character of the new acquaintance, her business was evidently neither legal nor honourable. Her look-out had seen the *Ardent* and *Delos* as soon as they had detected the sails and hull of the stranger. That vessel was already bearing away and bent on running out of reach of the cruisers. Pursuit was at once determined on, and all the extra canvas that could be hoisted on top-gallants, spars, and gaffs, was crowded on the creaking masts of the *Ardent* and *Delos*. For a long succession of hours the chase was kept up with unyielding spirit and by every device and contrivance open to the practiced seaman. The *Delos* – not so keen a sailor as the *Ardent* – gradually fell astern, while her sister ship steadily, though slowly, gained upon the retreating slaver.

Under the glass, the barbarous and inhuman crew was seen to be throwing her cargo of innocent Africans into the sea and these, after a momentary struggle with the waves, were seen to sink, one after another, out of sight. The strange ship was clearly in terror of being overtaken, and the crewmen were thus striving to conceal all traces of their guilt by getting rid of these living proofs of their traffic in human beings.

The breeze now freshened up with the approach of noon and, as the slaver was a splendid sailor, she began to widen the distance between herself and her pursuer. This was perceived on board the flying galleon at once, and their work of drowning their living cargo ceased. A stern chase is always a long one, and every man on the *Ardent's* crew were now more than ever convinced that this was true.

The hours of the afternoon only served to augment the distance between the chaser and the chased, and with the sudden advent of darkness the vain pursuit was over. When the morning of the following day broke, the vast floor of shimmering waters presented no speck of far-distant sail that might be likened to the runaway of the night before.

CHAPTER XII

*The castaway studying navigation – A happy deliverance – Loving epistles
– A welcome promotion for Orrason – The `degradation of the cat` – The
sailors` new benefactor.*

A dull period followed the excitement of this vain chase. To Orrason,
who was always active and always needed, life on the African
shore was mixed with strange variations of pleasure and disgust. The
sea and sky, and the shore and vegetation of the tropical regions,
were ever to him the subjects of deep thought and interested, though
necessarily unregulated, study. The sea-going library consisted only
of the few books accessible on board and the commander`s little store
and had all been devoured by him, some of them several times. In the
long idle days in port, the *Ardent*, in turn with the *Delos*, lay under the
shade of Banana Island, or lolled in lazy inaction in Yawry Bay [31].

The Bishop of Sierra Leone had a greater and fresher stock of books
on shore and, being a kindly-disposed man and easy of approach, he
soon gave consent to shift not a few of his volumes to the bunks and
awnings of the cruising brigs. In this way, and by means such as I
have indicated, our hero found the time spent on the hot African coast
was not wholly unprofitable. He studied carefully the ever necessary
science of navigation and, with such help as Commander Halewood
readily afforded, he worked out long series of problems. Besides
frequently testing his own knowledge, he often had the commander
in action as his interrogator and examiner. Other subjects relating to
the natural history of meridian regions he made as fully his own as
the want of illustrations and specimens would permit. Novels and the
light literature of the day he was also, by the kindness of the bishop,
permitted to read; and saw in some stray copies of the London *Literary
Gazette* the first poems of L E.L., who, many years after, as the wife of
Governor Maclean [32], was destined to a strange and mysterious death

on the same coast on which he was now spending a sometimes weary, sometimes wishful, but on the whole a happy and profitable life.

Two or three years sped away ere the *Ardent* and *Delos* were permitted to leave the station and return to Britain. The order of recall was a happy deliverance to everyone – from the commanders to the cook`s boy – for all were anxious to see once more the shores of old England. But it was the era of peace – the `piping times of peace`, as the more discontented and fire-eating officers called it – and life at Spithead or Portsmouth to the ordinary seaman, and even to the petty officers, was but a round of daily repeated dull and irksome duties.

It would have been so also to Orrason had he not been determined on the pursuits of other objects than the mere discharge of his duties as a man-o`-war-man. The knowledge he had gathered at Sierra Leone he could not allow to waste or fade from remembrance now that he was in England. But, being in the old land (though not sadly his Scottish homeland), and seeing and hearing British people, he recalled his youth and felt, as he had often felt before, the intense longing to know more of himself come rushing back. All the ancient queries returned to him; all the old questions as to possible parents, brothers, sisters, connections, came floating through his brain. Sometimes the anxiety became so strong as to almost drive him to despair. He felt for a time compelled by some dominating force to leave his ship, his duties and his prospects, and devote himself to the search for his hidden parents but, in the end, more moderate counsels prevailed.

He wrote once more to his now shadowy Mary, shadowy because he knew she must be changed, greatly changed, from the girl he knew in the Links of Kirkcaldy, though real and substantially the same to his emotional remembrance. He wrote and told her of all he had seen in the wonderful woods and shores of the tropical lands, where he had lived during the past years, and his experiences, even his thoughts, when afloat on the wide waters of the South Atlantic.

This done, he gave himself once more to study, and to the acquisition of what was certain to be of service to him in future years. Thus in one port or another – in the Solent, the Tamar, or the Thames, in the English Channel, the North Sea, or at the Nore – he counted the months as they passed away, and watched the seasons as they came. At last the *Ardent*, under Halewood her old commander, was ordered to the West Indies station – to the Carribees and Antilles – there to take up her old business of watching and hunting and, by every possible means, putting down that wholly indefensible form of commerce, the commerce in human bodies and human souls.

It would be unjust to Mary Seaton were it not here set down that her letter from the Links, which had reached Orrason at Sierra Leone, had been followed up by others. These marked a steady increase in elegance and some falling off of the homely dialect of the Lang Toon. Orrason accepted the one as only half a make-up for the other, and felt that the new style hardly seemed to fit her retailing of the local doings and local gossip of those who had known him in his former days.

To read these loving epistles in the quietude of his bunk was pure delight to John Orrason and, when the bustle and preparation for leaving port was fairly on, the letters were carefully folded and locked up in his chest for later and repeated perusal.

The passage out was a long and dreary one. Head winds, perturbed skies, storms and hurricanes delayed their course, exhausted their provisions, and threw everyone on his stock resources either of good nature, patience and courageous endurance or of petulance, injustice and tyranny.

Orrason's position was now greatly improved. His patient study of scientific seamanship had recommended him to the notice of Commander Halewood who had so exerted himself on Orrason's behalf as to have him appointed navigating lieutenant in the expedition to the west. Orrason's new position gave him wider opportunities for observation and, by bringing the most important part of the ship's business before him, made him feel that confidence in his own powers which is so essential to success. It also saved him from much of the petty tyranny, and sometimes barbarous cruelty, which the commanding lieutenants exercised on the men. It will hardly be credited by the modern reader that these officers, some seventy years ago, had practically the life or death of the men in their own hands, and it must also be confessed that they sometimes exercised that power with a remorseless frequency that would now be esteemed as both barbarous and unwise.

In the voyage to the Antilles, Orrason saw more in the way of punishment – of imprisoning and flogging – than he could have believed possible. One of the acting lieutenants seemed to take a positive delight in the torture of his men. On the slightest pretext, and sometimes even in the absence of pretext, he would have his men strung up to the shrouds and subjected to twenty, thirty or up to fifty applications of the cat. Scarcely a day passed without this disgusting exhibition and the sight became so painful to the just-minded Orrason that he suffered nearly as much in soul as the poor wretch under the lash did in his body.

The commander was a just but an easy-going and somewhat indolent man. By the rules of his office he was bound to watch the conduct of his officers, and see that no one acted in a tyrannous or cruel manner to the men under them, but this duty and many others he conveniently laid aside, as he expected them to be attended to by Orrason and the other subordinate officers. John Orrason`s ceaseless activity and constant attention to all his duties – even to those the phlegmatic commander had thrust upon him – brought Orrason frequently into contact with that officer.

In these meetings he often thought of his fellow seamen subjected to the cruel scourge and degradation of the cat and, by careful and guarded reference to the facts of the cases he had noticed and known, he managed to rouse the officer to action on behalf of his hands. The commander was careful to shield Orrason from suspicion or resentment but, adopting the method of personal and quiet observation, he became convinced that his navigating officer had not exaggerated the gravity of the situation.

On the second day after he had taken this course, one man had fallen from the m`zzen yards to the deck and was killed on the spot. The weather was quiet when he fell, and there was no reason that he should have lost his hold but that he was weary of life. Another had recently fallen from the mainyard into the sea and was lost. Both of these men had been, the commander ascertained, flogged on several occasions, and for delinquencies of the most trifling nature. Their life had become a burden to them, and their existence a mere degradation.

They died, but their deaths proved the salvation of their shipmates. The commander was difficult to rouse but, when once `on his feet`, he spoke with firmness and decision. The offending lieutenant was called to the cabin, the facts of the two cases laid before him, and the conclusion remorselessly deduced that their deaths were due to undeserved punishment. The offending officer was dismissed from the interview, and the others enjoined as to the future treatment of the men.

The voyage and cruise continued; and though the men did not know who had acted as their benefactor, they felt as though under a new and blissful *regime*, as compared with their earlier months in the *Ardent*.

Reaching Antigua, the *Ardent* was joined at English Harbour by a small ten-gun sloop named the *Badger*. These, in company, proceeded at first round to St. John`s, and were there fitted, provisioned, and otherwise `found` for a cruise of uncertain duration.

CHAPTER XIII

British slave-drivers in the West Indies – A Negro rising in Antigua – British cruelties – Flogged to death.

At the station in Sierra Leone the object aimed at had been to intercept the slavers as soon as they left the African coast and to set the Negroes free on a British settlement. In the West Indies it was not so much a question of preventing the slave ships getting out with their living cargoes, as of preventing the cargoes being profitably landed.

Everyone caught red-handed in the fiendish traffic could now, by the force of legislative enactments passed in the British Parliament, be treated as a felon, and deprived of all the property he had held or employed in the trade. These recent heavy penalties affixed to complicity in the forbidden traffic, together with the conditions under which every man engaged in it was bound, made the seizure of slave ships a task of ever-increasing difficulty.

Besides, the countries on the opposite sides of the Atlantic – Sierra Leone and the West Indies – were wholly different in character. The new western station to which the *Ardent* and Orrason were sent was made up of a vast number of islands, of innumerable intricate channels, and of deep-winding and indented bays – in many places a mere hiding ground for law evaders and law defiers. Thus the *Ardent* and *Badger* had duties assigned which, to the commanders and crews, were far more irksome and dangerous in the carrying out than fell to the seamen on the Sierra Leone side of the ocean.

As the consorts left the rocky shores of Antigua and in the immediate neighbourhood of St. John`s, Orrason could not help remarking to Lieutenant Schellsey, who was then in command of the men, that if all the islands were as rocky and forbidding as Antigua, he could not understand the eulogies he had often read as to their beauty and fruitfulness.

'You are apt to be deceived by appearances', said Schellsey, 'Antigua seems to have girded herself with a framing of rocks all round outside, but inside the rocky barrier, the island is filled with rich plantations, the hills and woods and road sides are garlanded with flowers, and the soil is the most productive out west'.

'And what is the population made up of'? queried Orrason.

'They are mainly slaves, nearly all Negroes. The whites are made up of the planters, their chief hands and the drivers'.

'That is the slave-drivers, you mean'? queried Orrason, wishing to be precise.

'Yes, the slave-drivers', replied Schellsey, somewhat indifferently, not observing the look of absorbing interest with which Orrason had put his question. Then continuing: 'The slaves in Antigua just now may number thirty thousand, and there may be one or two thousand more made up of whites and half-and-quarter colours, who do as they fancy with the big droves'.

'Then here, at least', Orrason observed with a smile, 'It is the case of a minority being in power and the majority obeying'.

'That is so, and that is nearly always and everywhere so', and the philosophic Schellsey turned to give the final directions to his men as the good ship made her way westward into the open sea; then, turning back and resuming the theme:

'Yes, it is the minority that rules everywhere, and over all these western islands especially so. Here the Negroes are twenty to one, and yet the twenty supinely bend their necks to the one – and he, as firmly, puts his foot on them and drives home his demands'.

'But I should suppose', put in Orrason, going somewhat against his own knowledge, 'that in British colonies the driving you speak of will be more in name than in reality'.

'On the contrary', hurriedly interjected Schellsey, 'we, that is the British, drive and tyrannise and punish with a severity not surpassed even by the Spaniards, whom we are constantly holding up to reprobation'.

'Well, I admit', said Orrason, 'we are not immaculate examples of consistency, but surely our slaves here are treated with more consideration than those in Cuba, for example`?

`You think so`? and Schellsey turned to his fellow officer. `I do not. Our people talk a great deal, and profess immense philanthropy for the `poor black` , but no sooner do they come out here and pick up a plantation than they pick up also the goad and the whip. Man alive`! he continued, warming up. `We had a rising a rising among the Negroes in this same island of Antigua – a rising forced into shape and activity by our own barbarous treatment of the workers – and how did we punish them? We crushed the rising by balls and bayonets, and then we proceeded to burn the leaders alive, hang them on gibbets, rack them on wheels, and otherwise torture them to death for our own satisfaction. We compelled the others to give evidence against their fellows and if anyone refused, we hung them up by the hands or the heels till he consented to say what we wanted. Some of them were noble fellows, and chose a Roman death [33] rather than betray their leaders or their cause. We threw others into fires and pulled them out again, and hung them up and pulled them down again, till we were weary, to extort the evidence we wanted; and when we failed, we left the half-burnt and half-hanged wretches to shiver slowly out of life, dying in agonies no man could ever describe`.

`This is horrible`, sadly observed Orrason, as he gazed eastward on the fast receding contour of the island they had just left.

`I admit`, interrupted Schellsey, `that these things are not done so much now – at least in Antigua. More humane treatment of the patient Negro has banished the causes of revolt; and the more humane form of our slave laws, and the sentiments they breathe, have taught us to look with a kindlier eye and a warmer appreciation on the hard-working, cheery-hearted native of Africa`.

`Yes, that is true` said Orrason. `We owe in this respect no little to the exertions of Buxton, Brougham, Clarkson [34] and others, who have fought for the rights of our black brothers with a pertinacity and eloquence and sacrifice beyond all mere verbal praise`.

`And yet, despite the fine words, cruelty still exists in some places under British law`, said Schellsey. `Step ashore on the island now rapidly going down on the horizon, and what do you find? We find the Negroes brought out in gangs from their huddle-up lodgings, ranged up in the field – each gang under its own driver. The men, the boys, the women, and the girls, even the old and weak, are selected and ranged in rows. It may be digging or hoeing, or weeding or trimming, in the cane or tobacco fields, that forms the task. At the word of command they start at one end of the field and painfully proceed to the other. The driver comes on behind, delivering himself every now and then of harsh, horrible, indecent and profane interjections; and whenever any weak or sick or weary one falls a foot behind, the lithe whip sweeps over his bare back, he utters a scream of pain, and bends himself with renewed energy to his exhausting task. That is a sample of how we go on just now in these, the Leeward Islands, while the welkin rings with the cry of right and justice for the Negro – in London`.

This was a long speech for the usually taciturn Schellsey to make, but he evidently felt keenly on the subject of the captives` wrongs, and spoke at first nonchalantly as one that desired to speak with caution; but, finding that Orrason breathed the same spirit as himself on this keenly debated subject, he spoke without fear or restraint.

`I will say more`, continued Schellsey excitedly. `We allow our treatment of the slave to degenerate into mere brutal atrocity. Some strong-minded, strong-bodied brother in a dark skin excites the wrath – and more so, the fears – of his driver. He is strung up, and the strongest flogger on the plantation is set to the task of flogging him, till he (the man with the lash) is worn out. Another takes his place and he, too, goes on until his arms fall helpless by his side. Another and another still succeeds! We go on flogging the living body until the blood streams down to the heels. We flog on until the back is one mass of tortured flesh. We continue the fiendish process till his bones shine out in the light of a burning sun. We go on long after the last spark of life has deserted the agonized and quivering frame. We do this under British law and British sanction, and still we prate of the humane conditions under which the slave in the Leeward Isles lives and moves and has his being`. And Schellsey, as he concluded, turned a deep contemplative gaze on the shimmering seas beneath and the vast majestic skies above him.

CHAPTER XIV

A sharp encounter with a Spanish slaver – A storm at sea and its results.

To Orrason, the statements made by Schellsey served partly to confirm and partly to reveal. He had read and studied the general aspects of the slave question and knew that Schellsey had spoken only the truth as far as he knew it, but the details of the slaves` past and present condition were all as new, as they were painful and repulsive to his mind.

Schellsey had left the poop, where he and Orrason had been standing. He came back, however, and seemed desirous to put himself right with the actual facts:

`I have indicated`, he went on, `that things are shaping into kindlier channels for the poor slave, and signs are multiplying – if I read recent accounts rightly – that public sentiment in the islands is now undergoing a real, possibly a radical, change and, as the cruise proceeds, we may learn more and better`. Stepping down as he spoke, he was soon lost to Orrason`s view.

The *Ardent* and *Badger* were still within fair signalling distance, and both were borne away with a fair breeze on the starboard quarter towards the Guadaloupes [35]. These soon rose to view, and the ships took in sail as they neared these possessions of France. Entering the narrow channels of the Salt River, which divided the two islands, they ploughed their way with gathering caution through the strait. Beyond it at last, they were making for the French island of Marie Galante [36], when the tapering top-masts of some waiting-on craft were descried just over the shoulder of the land.

As the unknown craft lay, the look-out on board could not possibly have seen either the *Ardent* or her consort. The channel of the Salt River was not deemed either suitable or safe for cruisers and evidently the hiding ship, keeping an open eye to the west, had not thought it possible she could be discovered from the coast.

Rounding to the east, and opening the view on the strange sail, both Orrason and Commander Halewood, who had now mounted the poop, became convinced of her true character. No sooner did the stranger discover the cruisers' colours and nationality than the French pennant was run up and, at the same time, hurried efforts were made to home the anchor and spread sail. It was, however, too late, and when the make-believe port shutters – for these were now in constant use – were quickly drawn on board the *Ardent*, all attempts to get away by the run ceased as soon as they had begun.

The distance being shortened to almost speaking reach, a boat with a well-armed crew was at once lowered from the brig and sought acquaintance with the stranger. She proved to be the *Feliz Ventura*, and hailed from some unknown or fictitious port in the south of France. On the papers being demanded, a refusal was promptly given, and the anchor being by this time on board the *Feliz Ventura*, the hands were again busied in anxious activity to set sail and crowd the masts and yards with canvas. At a signal the boat withdrew, and the *Ardent* sent a shot across the bows of the *Feliz* to bring her to reality. The *Feliz Ventura* was, however, moving off, and as she bent in graceful style to the whistling breeze, she sent a goodbye in the shape of a volley of small shot among the crew of the retiring boat. One of the *Ardent's* men fell at the discharge, and several others were wounded.

The whole scene was witnessed by Commander Halewood, Orrason, Schellsey and nearly everyone on board the *Ardent*.

'Give it to her now', shouted Halewood, thoroughly roused by the injury to his men, and the contents of several heavy guns went crashing into the rigging and across the decks of the *Feliz Ventura*. The shot or two in the rigging proved a rapid means of shortening the sail and lowering the pride of the slaver, and the messengers of death that swept along the deck had not visited the planks in vain.

By this time the *Badger* had come up, and evidently all hope of resistance had died out in the hearts of the foreigners. The *Ardent* bore closely in, followed at a short distance, and with a clear outlook, by the *Badger*.

Two boatloads of men armed with cutlass and pistol, rapidly clambered aboard the *Feliz Ventura* and soon verified her purpose. She was a slaver pure and simple, and was provided with Spanish and Portuguese as well as with French colours, in order to hoist whatever might prove most suitable.

She had left the Gold Coast some months before, got clear away, and was now waiting a chance to bear down on Martinique, where a market had been provided for her cargo of blacks. The Middle Passage had been long, arduous, and stormy, and the ship's papers, one way and another, indicated that a large cargo of slaves had been put on board – stowed away probably in every possible corner of the ship. Of these, only some sixty-five miserable, half-dead wretches still breathed below.

The commander and officers of the *Feliz Ventura*, with such of the crew as could be spared, were put in irons. A prize crew was put on board and, convoyed by the *Badger,* the ship with its cargo of slaves and tropical products (the poor blacks being brought on board and cared for) were sent back to St. John's, Antigua.

The *Ardent*, now left alone for a time, proceeded westward in the direction – easily marked by the towering peaks and volcano ranges – of Dominica. Here, after a few days, the crew was gladdened by the sight of the *Badger* bearing down under easy sail upon them. Leaving this location, and still proceeding to the Windward Isles, the two ships had measured their second day out from Dominica when, as it drew towards the close of day, Orrason observed, far away on the horizon, a sudden change and agitation in the sky.

'What means that? There is something coming from that quarter', he said, turning to Lieutenant Schellsey.

'There may be', was the reply, 'and it looks as if we were to have a rusher'.

Both men agreed as to the coming of a storm, and hardly had the words been uttered when the wind fell suddenly away, and the ships were enveloped in so profound a calm that every man looked a picture of alarmed expectation. The extreme quietude brought the captain on deck and he, taking a look around the sky, at once pointed to a cloud out of which flashes of lightning were frequently breaking, and which spread rapidly over the heavens.

'Shorten sail at once', he shouted, 'and get the ship under close-reefed fore and maintop sails and fore-staysail. You had better also send down the upper masts and yards – and do so without a moment's delay'.

The order was instantly obeyed, and signals were made to the *Badger* to follow the example. Sails being thus shortened, the guns were breached, ports were barred, and the hatches all firmly battened down. The threatening cloud had already spread over a large portion of the sky and, when the sun went down, the entire heavens were covered as with a pall. The darkness was so deeply intense that even the nearest objects were completely invisible. This, with the complete silence and stillness of the evening, became at last utterly unbearable.

At last, a few faint, flickering fires played in and outside of the cloud, and a few faint breaths of air came to them through the gloom. Then intermittent and irregular puffs followed, and then came a roar of such vastness and depth that the long swell of the ocean breaking upon the shallow surfy shore only faintly conveyed the idea of its force. A vast sheet of lightning now broke in brilliant flash across the sky, and a peal of thunder that seemed to shake alike the hulls, masts and riggings rolled and rattled above them. Then the rain rushed down in such force and quantity as we never see in temperate zones, and compelled every man on deck to hold on by rope or shroud to prevent his being beaten down with its weight and force.

It passed away as quickly as it had come, and left the ship again – but only for a few moments – in the prevailing unnatural silence. The roar of the waters, at first far away, and faint and low, now burst upon their astonished ears, and this time, the line of a white and rolling breast of foam peered out of the deep, dense darkness, and told the storm was now upon them. The hurricane fell upon the ships with terrific force; for though each had been prepared for the terrible visitant, both vessels suffered tremendously in the moment of attack. The *Ardent* was thrown on her beam-ends, and the fore and maintop sails were blown out of their fastenings, and rent with a report like a bursting cannon. This, however, finished the disaster to the rigging. The ship soon righted and, bending over to the fury of the wind, paid off in fair style, and ran away before the storm. To steady her and carry up her head, the men, by immense labour, got fixed up in the mizzen rigging an old and disused yet strong piece of sail-cloth. This had the desired effect, and the men now knew so long as they had sea room they were safe. The sea had been breaking clean across the decks, and the boats and spars were washed from their lashings and swept away. The storm continued during the whole night, and when daylight came and the sun had risen, the crew was able to survey and count the damage done.

The *Badger,* from the appearance of her rigging, had suffered even more heavily that the *Ardent.* Her jib was entirely gone, her staysails were fluttering in the wind, while her topmasts, not having been sent down as those of the *Ardent,* were hanging down among the ropes and gear of the mainsail while that, in turn, though it had been well secured, was wrenched from its lashings and split in pieces. The confused condition of the *Badger's* upper stories evidently prevented anything like rapid handling of the ship – the last essential in such a storm as was now in progress. This was forced on the attention of the *Ardent's* crew by the effect of the next sudden and treacherous squall. This did no damage and had no evil effect on the *Ardent,* but the *Badger* was caught aback and driven, for a space, furiously astern, and everyone was apprehensive lest she might founder beyond the reach of help. As the day brightened, however, the storm began to abate, and both crews had time to secure the most vital points in the broken and torn parts of the rigging.

The sun had risen about two hours when the wind fell away as suddenly as it had come. The sea, however, was wild and choppy, and seemed to be running from all directions of the compass at once. The strain on the timbers of the ships was trying in the extreme, and had either of the ships been less firmly put together, or less fairly trimmed, the bursting of a leak or the final disaster of foundering must have been expected.

Looking at the aspect of the *Ardent* after the hurricane had died away, Orrason saw at once the nature of the storm, and an explanation of the condition of the slave-ship they had met with some years before when on the station of Sierra Leone. These tremendous tropical storms come as sudden as do the changes from light to darkness, or from darkness to the morning light. They come with the same sudden celerity, rival both in intensity, and pass away with the same astonishing rapidity.

English Harbour, Antigua

CHAPTER XV

The castaway leaves the navy – Life and love – In shipping commerce for himself

It is no business of mine to describe the change of nature in the Gulf of Mexico, or to tell how men, their doings and their lives, shrink into littleness, and are dwarfed into pigmy proportions in face of the forces of nature as seen in the tropics. Everywhere these forces make the gravest among us wonder, and the boldest tremble. Here around the Windward and Leeward Isles, where ocean currents boil and whirlwinds germinate, the greatest of man's works dwindle into insignificance, and even man himself appears but a winged yet helpless insect, to be tossed out of life and smitten and marred as the plaything of an awful and unseen Power.

Orrason spent two more years of his chequered life amid the reeling seas and sunny lands of the west. With occasional incidents of chase or capture, of dangerous reef entanglement, of sailing with the steady trades or shivering under rushing storm winds, the days, and weeks, and months sped on – time spurring on for ever the horses of his wearyless chariot.

The peace of exhaustion still happily continued with the European nations, and was felt as a breathing and happy time by every people in the world, and in every clime. In the Leeward and Windward Islands, and all through the West Indian colonies, the blessed influences of peace were felt in every part. The growing sentiment of opposition to slavery and the slave trade also tended to calm the often turbulent features of social life in these far western colonies of Britain.

Orrason's life during the years spent with his cruiser was one almost without personal incident. Were it indeed possible to give interest to the watchful jottings of an observant man, to a student's careful sifting of assertion and observation, or to the fleeting dreams of each passing mood, in the mental and emotional life of a good and brave yet dissatisfied soul, we might indeed fill in many a chapter of pleasing excursion in the vagaries of human life – but metaphysics never mix well with adventure.

Tired at length of the restraint of – to him – unnecessary discipline, and warned also of what he had seen in the earlier part of this cruise, he made up his mind to leave the now dull routine of the navy, and seek the freer air and more varied experience of life in the commercial marine.

The *Ardent* was lying at St. John's, capital of Antigua, when he sought and obtained his manumission as a servitor of the Crown. He based his claim on the fact of his being a forced or pressed man, and that the object for which he had been pressed had now been completely served. He received his discharge, and left the *Ardent* with the best good wishes and deepest regrets of the friends he left behind. The men mounted the rigging and cheered him off and the officers, one and all, felt they were parting with one whom, though sometimes quiet and fitful, was yet a true and strong-souled man. With Commander Halewood the parting interview had been long and of evidently serious import.

That Halewood had penetrated the secret of Orrason's life story, at least in the main, may be granted, without suggesting that our hero had made the mysterious incident of his life the subject of gossiping, or even of passing conversation. But, while Commander Halewood desired to know sufficient of Orrason's life and origin as would enable him to appreciate his conduct and motives, he was careful never to probe those secrets of his career which our hero had resolved on maintaining inviolate. But Orrason had learned to respect, if not indeed to love, his commander, and he accepted as of value more than gold, the running commentary of advice which the easy-going, yet at the bottom, brave and honest man, offered him at his leave-taking.

The commander had, like his lieutenant, Schellsey, been in the west before. He had 'hugged and hunted', as he expressed it, nearly every island in the group, from the Bahamas to the Grenadas, and he had learned not only the ways of cruising, but the ways and tricks of trade and traders, as manifested among the dealers in rice and spices, rum and tobacco and mahogany all over the Gulf.

Orrason had made no secret of his intention to substitute the mercantile for the naval marine, and while Commander Halewood guessed and appraised the motive of his navigating lieutenant, he no less praised the resolution to try, and promised success to every fair enterprise in which Orrason might engage. As he descended the side of the *Ardent*, his heart swam, and a joyful sadness oppressed him, as his ears drank in the rough, honest cheers of his old shipmates.

Orrason had not been three years in the Great Gulf [37] without learning something. He had picked up much of the ways of commerce and of men in these western islands and seas during his many voyages to every port and bay and creek in the far-distant and wide-spreading groups of islands. With this knowledge and that of his skill as a practical seaman, and science as a navigator, he believed he could hold his own, do well for himself and also do well for others.

With a Scotchman's proverbial economy he had steadily and regularly saved from his wage payments, even from the time when, as a junior 'chip' at Sheerness, he was put on the pay list of His Majesty's forces. With these savings, now largely secured in the banking and commercial houses at St. John's, and available when wanted, he made himself the owner of a fast-sailing topsail schooner of some 250 tons – a vessel he had marked long before, and which had proved alike her staying and going qualities. He called her the 'The Mary', though no-one in this far west region ever learned why such a name was painted on her quarter.

At that time, as now, the principal trade of these islands was in spices, gums, woods, rum and tobacco. Not confining himself to these, John Orrason soon made himself one of the best-known and best-trusted of men and traders in these ever fruitful, long abused, and neglected islands of the west.

He has no sooner determined on his new way of life than he again wrote to Mary Seaton. Somehow he still thought that Mary should know all the leading changes in his life. He would have made her familiar with every detail indeed, had it been possible to reach her ear. This could not be, but he believed it necessary she should know always where he was, what he was doing, and that he was still keeping her pleasing image in his mind.

Her pleasing image! It was far more than this if he measured the greatness of her influence, of her power over his life's whole tone and every action. In all his dangers, Mary's image stood beside him; in all his little plans of life Mary was ever present to advise and decide and, as he rose in the world and grew in wealth, his happiest thought was that Mary was rejoicing with him, and would yet live to share and enjoy it with him.

A strange passion this of Orrason's, I hear some of you more fastidious readers say. How was it he could nurse the soul of love for woman without that being's inspiring presence? How could he ally his whole existence with a shadowy being that showed itself even less than ghosts do to his aching apprehension? Hardly any word of explanation will do. As those born blind cannot be instructed in the beauty and nature of light, neither can men or women who demand at all times only the living reality be taught the mystery and radiance of an ideal. The ideal to Orrason was the existence of a power he was bound to acknowledge. If it could not be grasped with his living arms, it laid hold on him and bent his every action and coloured his mind.

It was to him no evil fantasy or hindering enchantment. It was a joy and help and purifying influence, like a steadying keel in his ship of life and his thought. It kept that ship level amid the yawning seas of that sad contemplation that would at times haunt his otherwise happy and cheerful soul.

With this inspiring idol in his inmost heart, he saw the duty of life clearer and, under its soft silver radiance, the ways of the world and of men and of things were laid bare as in the sunlight of heaven. A halo of wandering effulgence it might be but if so it did not burn without to distract or mislead him, but glowed within to direct his steps. Ever happy and blessed is the man who, like Orrason, carries the main guide of love in his heart.

That Orrason succeeded in his new and self-reliant enterprise among the western islands may be accepted as a natural consequence of his fitness for the task he had assigned himself. His trade connections and correspondence lay in all the islands, from Kingston in Jamaica and Havana in Cuba to St. John's in the Leeward Antigua, and he always sailed his own ship, and would never risk either his own good craft or the goods of other people in the hands of another. He had a wholesome dislike of hirelings and, so far he was able to penetrate the surface of the seeming fairness of commercial transactions, and find the actual motives of the actions of men in these islands, he was more and more driven to trust to himself alone as far as circumstance would allow.

Fort James, Antigua

CHAPTER XVI

Life as a shipowner – `Who am I`? – The soul`s Arcadia – `Happy were his dreams` – Sold out – `Home, Mary, and kindred`.

This policy of individual action bore the fruits of satisfaction and contentment from the very first. His vessel always sailed well and wore well. His men knew they could trust him implicitly and he, in selecting his assistants, was always able to take on and keep those whom he could as thoroughly rely on. His variable cargoes made the art of stowing one of first importance and, as he had his hands carefully taught, it came about in due course that he learned to trust, with unfailing result, the men who served him.

Every merchant who commissioned John Orrason knew that, if damage was done to his goods, it must be from causes no human foresight could prevent. Steadily his business grew and as steadily his field of operations extended. From the Gulf, he followed the coast northwards to parts on the New England seaboard, as well as finding the needs of those in the far western depths of the Gulf, and on the shores of the Mississippi.

As his business grew in bulk and stretched to more and more distant quarters, he had at length to resign the resolution of always sailing his own craft. He became possessed of one ship after another, and he could not be the master in each, but he kept a careful and vigilant eye on every ship and on all proceedings, and as he had become a keen and ready judge of character and fitness, his captains came to be, in fair measure, but duplicates of himself.

Thus years passed on, and the far-away wanderer, now come to the maturity of manhood, seemed also to be nearing the crisis of his life. In every step of his progress, he had written out his thoughts to Mary Seaton, and at every lull in his activities he had felt the recurring and overpowering force of those self-centred questionings which, from his earliest years, had haunted his imagination.

Who am I? Whence have I come? Who are those that should have loved me, yet wilfully have deserted me? Shall I ever know them? Shall I, the wanderer, have the dreary task of speaking my identity into the ears of those who would rather shun my presence, who would find no comeliness therein nor music in my voice? These, the ancient enemies of his peace, *would* come back to him, and whisper eternally their suggestions in his heart.

He had built himself a light and airy house on the heights above St. John's – for Antigua had more charm for him than any of the Golden Horns [38] of the west, on which he had yet rested his eyes. From this bright sequestered spot he sallied when going to sea, and to its inviting shades he gladly retired on his return. From its gladsome heights he could hail the rising and bid adieu to the setting sun. He looked from this eyrie over a wide expanse of shimmering sea, and could mark from afar the approach of each sail-wafted, winged denizen of the deep. Sitting in his verandah in the cool of the evening and when the sun spread a trembling glory over the wide waters, he would watch each approaching ship as it crossed this shining trail, and he would speculate to himself as to its cargo and its passengers. Who might *they* be? Would *she* be one of them? Would not some good and great power waft her over the far-dividing seas and bring her loved form to him?

Oppressed with these strange questionings, he would yet think them over and nurse them into strong personal vitality, and feel lonely when they left him. Such imaginings were yet the balm and solace of his empty hours, and if they came at his bidding and vanished at his wish, he was none the less bound to obey their sweet whisperings.

The hard-pressed, common-sense business man of the present day will find in all this abundant reason to smile derisively at John Orrason, and his dreamy lapses of thought. A man who could guide himself in siege and battle, who could be fearless in storm and danger, and kindly and just even to his enemies, who could calculate the chances of gain or loss, and provide himself with the means of making gain certain – such a man could never to his own injury carry a dreamy love in his heart, nor bend his mind without reserve to the pleasure of unsubstantial imaginings.

How little indeed do we know of each other, and how apt we are to judge amiss because we judge from external appearances put on to suit the hour and because, unthinkingly, we assume that all men are like ourselves. John Wilson, the dear 'Christopher North' of old, was a strong man and the defiant athlete of his time, yet who can deny the dreamy sweetness of his *City of the Plague* [39].

> How bright and fair that afternoon returns
> When last we parted! Even now I feel
> Its dewy freshness in my soul! Sweet breeze!
> That, hymning like a spirit up the lake,
> Came through the tall pines on yon little isle
> Across to us upon the vernal shore
> With a kind, friendly greeting

So swelled and grew the dreamy love of John Orrason and happy were his dreams. He would, at times, resign himself wholly to their influence and imagine the time when he would run with swift feet down the hillside to the harbour as the white-sailed barque from the homeland ran over the bar. And he felt himself in imaginary delight, grasping *her* by the white-gloved hand, and leading *her* ashore.

He would then banish his flying fancy and tie himself down to realities, but he began to feel all the same that, while the world of reality would come to his bidding, it came with ever-growing reluctance. His fancy increasingly fell – amid the sunlight of enchanted land – like ripened oranges around him, and tempted him with delights he could not resist. It was the *Ranz-des-Vaches* of the heart driving him to the homeland, and he must obey.

He was still a young man, and most of the world – the best part of it – was still before him. He had no wish – never had any wish – to spend the days of his years, or to lay at last his nameless body far from the graves of the kindred who – even though they had deserted and disowned him – were still the authors of his life and formed the magic circle of his being.

'I shall, and must know who they are', he said, 'and I can only do that by going – home'. And then after a pause, 'And Mary will be with me in my search for the roots of my life and being'.

His mind made up, Orrason sold out his possessions in ships, stores, houses and holdings – all but his first and favourite schooner, *Mary*. She had borne him o'er many a rough sea, borne him in safety and borne him to many a rich argosy. Now she would do him a greater service still, carry him to the fairest of all lands – to the richest of all argosies – to his home, to Mary, and to his kindred.

CHAPTER XVII

In Antigua – The Symes and Grahams – A big bargain – A letter from Mary Seaton – Homeward bound.

Yes! He – Orrason – sold out as completely as circumstances and the far-reaching connections of his trade would allow. His ties with the western world could not all be snapped asunder even when he, the tied one, should decide. There were claims to meet and debts to satisfy as the one or other matured, and the maturing process – so irritating to resolute, and more so to impetuous men – must go on for months or years after he had ceased connection with the region. He knew all this, and had weighed its possibilities and consequences in his mind – and weighed them to such good effect, in his own way, to fix and settle them wholly.

Among those with whom he had, in the sordid language of the Exchange, `done business`, there was no one for whom he had a greater or happier regard, or to whom he could more implicitly trust the holding of his fortunes, or settlement of his affairs, than to his trading and personal friend, Robert Graham of Falmouth, Antigua.

As the name would indicate, and as the warm friendship of the two men proved, the merchant planter of Falmouth was a Scotchman – one of that numerous, and nearly ubiquitous, clan called the `Scots abroad`, who had an intense love for the old home but found that fortune smiled more blandly and more continuously in lands beyond the seas. Fired by the spirit of adventure, the wish to see new lands and to face new circumstances, and not less by the desire to `mak` mair`, Robert Graham had come out to the Western Main, and found, as well as founded, a home in Antigua, the same little island as that in which Orrason had found the finest elements of beauty and society the Leeward Isles could show.

Young Graham – for he was still a young man, the junior of Orrason by a year or two – had come out to the colony to try his fortune a few years before, indeed, about the period at which Orrason left the Navy for good. Fortunes were being made in the products of the islands, in the trade among the Gulf ports and in the plantation business. Young Graham had heard these whispers and, as no opening appeared to make itself for him in the old country he had made up his mind to try some settlement in the new.

He was determined in his choice of Antigua by the fact that he was recommended to a member of the little Colonial Legislature, James Syme, a man who was known to all in the settlement, and who had formed trade ties with several of the other islands in the Leeward group.

Robert Graham was, in a trade sense, lucky, and in a higher and more important sense, happy in the person selected for his guide in colonial life. James Syme was, when young Graham first met him, a man beyond the keystone period of life. He was a comparatively small man and a decidedly thin one with grizzled hair where he had any. He had possibly suffered from his colonial experiences; he had been dried and shrivelled by the sun and his skin was puckered into innumerable crow feet round his eyes and curled in wrinkles round his hard, bony temples. In comparison with Robert Graham, good Mr. Syme must be made to suffer, for Graham was rather above than below middle height and full, fresh, and strong.

Mr. Syme seldom ventured out of Antigua and was, indeed, not often out of his chosen town of Falmouth and it was here in the fall of a year in the early 1820s – to put things on a chronological base – that Robert Graham, Esq., had presented himself in the office of James Syme, planter of Antigua, merchant, and shipper.

Mr. Syme had received his new acquaintance not only with a friendly greeting, but with all the ardour which, as Graham afterwards found out, characterized the man. As Graham had brought a fairly well-filled purse with him, in the shape of notes, gold and parchment securities, his colonial mentor advised securing the whole lot against loss or misfortune by a simple banking investment.

I should inform the reader that, before this, Mr. Syme had introduced his young ocean tramper to his family, consisting of a wife and two fair daughters – neither of the latter married, though of an age to be so. This, in a strange country, and with an absolute scarcity of acquaintances, was rather dangerous for an ardent young man, and the danger of the situation was soon proved by the young man becoming absorbed in the Syme family by marriage with the younger daughter. His choice of the younger over the older daughter was slightly and jokingly resented by the mother but, as it met the heartiest commendations of the father, young Graham considered himself `in clover`.

Robert Graham found that his money was not only safely lodged but quite available whenever he had occasion to spend it. This occasion turned up with amazing alacrity in the form of a plantation in the immediate neighbourhood of the holding claimed by the Symes. In this way, it appeared to the sanguine young man that his cards were turning up nearly all trumps and he, metaphorically, rubbed his hands and stroked his chin with pleasure.

There is, however, no end to that last weakness of great minds – ambition – and Robert Graham had no sooner got his sugar vines and his vineyard, and his tobacco and rice plots in good condition and working order, his slaves looked to and his books arranged, than he began to look around for other areas to conquer. He had already made some money – by himself as well as by his marriage – and he had a desire to let it run and be multiplied.

It was at this time that he heard of the change of location our hero planned. Graham and Orrason had met and thirled each other before, had beat down values and hitched up prices, and generally gone quite often through that mysterious operation called bargain making. That, however, which now loomed in the near future, was a bargain of bigger dimension than any which Graham had yet faced and, he frankly acknowledged, more than he could yet manage to grasp.

In this little strait he had recourse to his accommodating father-in-law, and then there was a grand *tria juncta in uno*, or parliament of three. The upshot of a session lasting one hour was the passage of an act or pledge, bearing the colonial and imperial stamps and effigies, and setting forth that certain warehouses and ships, with goods and stores therein, and pertaining thereto – and of which a full inventory had been made out – had now passed from the hands of John Orrason and become the property, or trust holding, of Robert Graham. And then the several parties drank tea with the ladies – and parted for years.

Before leaving his western home – the scene of his mental and emotional expansion as well as of his successes in the material walks of life – Orrason received the last of his foreign-stamped letters from Mary Seaton. In it she recalled the usual rounds of her experiences in the Links, filled in and spread out before him her own thoughts, hopes and fears, and wished him all the good than man can or could enjoy. The letter was beautifully written and picturesquely composed. The appearance and altered tone of the letter set Orrason thinking and building afresh the image of his love.

It is said that a lady`s letter has always the most important part pressed quietly into the postscript, and when Mary closed her letter by stating that she had accepted a situation in another part of the country – for which non-sanctioned act she would account in her next letter, and asking him to send still to the old address – Orrason felt that there was truth in the statement.

Still the idol of his fond imaginings carried him captive, and made him the willing prisoner of an imperative hope. Yet, he did not forget himself. As we have seen, he sold prudently and secured well. He also bought wisely and, having found a good freightage for the City of Glasgow – the great emporium for the products of the Western Main – he wrote his usual letter to Mary Seaton, enquiring as to her new sphere and form of life, and telling her of his new resolve, his change of fortune, and his new venture – his voyage home.

No thundering storms stayed,
No accidents betrayed,
The *Mary*.

Glasgow Brig in 1820

CHAPTER XVIII

The castaway gets back to the Clyde – The Port of Glasgow – Captain Orrason on board the Mary – In the George Hotel, Glasgow – Interview in the George with Mary Seaton's father – `Yes, John! Always yours`

Spring's first gale had come forth to whisper where the violets lay when the *Mary* reached the Clyde. Looking shoreward as he sailed up the noble estuary, John Orrason was reminded of that gay morning long ago when, bounding along on the top of the Glasgow-Edinburgh coach, he marked the yellow coltsfoot on the wayside and the wind-flower in the woods. On that occasion he was escaping from a chilling and loveless life and moving into an atmosphere of human love and faculties. Now his heart was set and his hope was bent for even brighter days than those that blessed his years in the Links. Orrason felt that, with the exception of one short-lived storm of evil in his childhood, his life had not been in the hands of blind fate (as some believed) but had been a continual brightening of the sky, an opening up of the hand of Providence and a pouring-out of ever-increasing blessings.

As Orrason finally reached the Port of Glasgow and anchored at the Broomielaw, he looked with pride and joy on the ceaseless activity that already marked the fast-growing city. Glasgow was, in the 1820s, a pigmy to its present proportions. The Broomielaw was then but a one-sided quay, and that but a comparatively short one. Ranged on the north side were a few sheds, all the usual arrangements for mooring ships, a quantity of primitive fittings for loading and discharging cargoes, and a miscellaneous scatter of barrels, casks, bales, raw materials in bulk, lying under the sheds or exposed on the open quay. Further off were the warehouses of the importing merchants, the Custom House and other harbour buildings. With the ship fairly berthed and the dues settled with the water bailie, it was time to relieve the *Mary* of her load.

The firm to which the cargo of rum, sugars, tobacco, wines, wool, cotton and spices was consigned, was that of Sproul and Laurie, long and well-known in the city for its long and honourable connection with the West India business [40]. John – or, as we must now call him, `Captain Orrason` – was not long in notifying the firm, whose offices were a little way from the circus in Jamaica Street, of his safe arrival in port. The task of delivering, measuring, and weighing the various portions of the somewhat miscellaneous cargo on board the *Mary* were matters of every day occurrence to the servants of the firm and were quickly put in hand and bargained off with the authorities on the quay. The warehousing, especially that of the liquors, was a matter to which the firm gave the greatest possible attention – having evidently imbibed the lessons of economy and care, for which the merchants of St. Mungo [41] had long been famous.

While the *Mary* was being emptied, Orrason continued his residence on board following out his old habit of seeing his cargo off hand and accounted for before he left the ship. That bit of ticklish work finished, he was prepared to domicile himself elsewhere in the city, see what events might turn up and make up his plans for the future. The firm to which his cargo had been assigned was so thoroughly satisfied with the condition in which its goods had been landed, that Captain Seaton, the only living representative of that long-established house had, in his own mind, prepared a return freight of cotton and linen fabrics, chemicals, etc. to be shipped on board the *Mary* for the port of Kingston in Jamaica. But, although he had met and liked Captain Seaton, Orrason had other plans in view; in the expressive language of the Gorbals, he had 'other fish to fry'.

Having compounded with his mate and one or two of his men that the *Mary* should be laid up for a time at some convenient corner farther down the river, and having put his highly-valued schooner in their care, and giving instructions as to cleaning, painting, etc., he took up his quarters in the oldest of the city hostelries, the George Hotel in George Square.

Here he wrote once more to tell Mary his news, addressing his letter as before to Peter Saunders, weaver, Links, Kirkcaldy. His first and most important purpose to this was to know where his loved one had gone, where she had pitched her tent and how she designed to live. He reminded her that all his past purposes of life had been to make himself and her independent – so far as worldly means were concerned – and gently rebuked her for enjoying herself, and tying herself to any situation without first asking whether he could not have furnished her with one that would have lasted for life. He waited with all a lover's impatience for an answering epistle.

The water bailie of the Clyde at this time was an important person. His authority extended from the Clough [42] to the Broomielaw and he was punctilious in insisting upon the observance of all his aqueous rules. Some point in these had not been observed in selecting a bye-berth for the *Mary* and this affair called Captain Orrason down to the water. Ere he had got the little matter put to rights, he was hurried up again to the city to have a settlement made as to cranage, etc. and further port dues. These trifles occupied our hero with sufficient seriousness – for trifles often do this more effectually than weighty matters – to make him forget for two or three days his letter to Mary and the expected answer. The tea-cup tempest being smoothed down, the situation again cleared itself, and he got finally in peace to the George.

Heroes, like heroines, are generally described to the reader when first introduced but in the case of the principal personage in this story, it would have been evidently unfair to his physical as well as to his mental nature and possibilities of development to have described John Orrason when first he came on the boards and little less unjust to have described him when on board the *Bittern* and not much less so when, thin and sallow in complexion, he sojourned on the African coast.

He has now, however, reached his full tilth of manhood, and the reader ought to know that John Orrason was five feet nine inches in height, was broad and square across the shoulders, and had an abundance of dark hair and a pair of dark brown whiskers. His eyebrows were peculiarly smooth and arched, and a pair of kindly hazel-coloured eyes glanced and shone beneath them. His face was broad, his cheek bones were Scotch in prominence, and his complexion, while browned with wind and weather, was clear and pure as the poet's boast in the *Nut Brown Maid*[43]. He was dressed in blue, with a white, unstarched shirt front, touched into colour with a silk bandana. If the reader will imagine his hair to be extra long, and dressed behind in the fashion of the time, he will then have a fair and full photo of Captain Orrason of the *Mary*.

I have not yet told the reader how Mary Seaton looked, or how other people appraised her beauty. She is now, however, in the George Hotel, Glasgow, and as she moves about in agitation, or rests in an elegant and spacious sitting-room there, putting on an effort to be collected and calm, we can see that she is a woman of the average stature, that she is carefully and neatly dressed, that her face is round rather than oval, that she is fair in complexion, and that her mien and manner are natural, graceful and engaging. She speaks with slight affectation, though with the correctness of the time, and there is at times a flash as of merriment in her eyes and in the play of her lips.

In the room with Mary is an elderly gentleman, one who had rounded the half-century a bit and confesses it in his iron-grey hair and whiskers. He wears the universal surtout on the main part of his person, knee breeches, stockings and buckled shoes – the buckles being broad, massive, silver bands. His broad-brimmed beaver lies on the table. The old gentleman is Captain Arthur Seaton, Mary Seaton's father. He is the same Captain Seaton we have already met as the representative of the firm of Sproul and Laurie, but it is on different terms that he has come to meet once more Captain Orrason, the man who brought their goods from distant lands. From something Mary has confided to him, he feels that this may be an important meeting.

'Shall I ring for Orrason'? Captain Seaton asked Mary.

'Yes, father. Ring for the waiter and make the enquiries yourself. Yet', she said, almost inaudibly, 'I am almost afraid to meet the man whose face I have been longing to look upon for all these past years. It is surely strange, yet not less surely true'.

The waiter appeared.

'Do you know if Captain Orrason is in the George just now? If he is in, will you kindly show him in here'?

The waiter vanished and presently returned with the Captain.

'Good day, Captain Orrason, I am glad to see you again', said Seaton, advancing to the door as Orrason entered.

'I am also glad', said Orrason, 'to meet again one for whom I have so great a respect as yourself'.

'Will you kindly allow me, Captain, to introduce you to my daughter, my only daughter, Miss Seaton'.

Orrason advanced as the lady rose and, bowing low, extended his hand towards her.

The hands met and grasped each other – the small one trembling with an agitation the strong man could not comprehend. He looked in her blue eyes, and he saw that these were suffused with tears and could not look in his again.

It was his turn now to feel the agitation of the moment. He dropped her hand for an instant as he heard the door of the room shut behind him and, on looking round, he found he was alone with the lady.

For a moment he was utterly bewildered. All his thoughts seemed to be rushing into chaos. There was something about the lady, something in the tone of voice, the look, the manner, that touched his emotional nature into flame yet gave no reason why the flame should burn.

The lady, with downcast eyes and warmly blushing, handed him an open letter. An instantaneous glance sufficed to show it was his own – his last one – to Mary Seaton. It was thrown down as quickly as it was received.

'Are you Mary – my own Mary Seaton'?

'Yes, John – I am yours, always yours'.

There was some explaining to do but that could come later. In the meantime, let the young imagine, and the old remember, that there is in human joy a sacredness as intense as that which attaches to the deepest grief. Orrason had obtained at last his long cherished love and unalloyed happiness, and Mary felt now the pure and trembling joy for which she had waited in undiminished faith through the long years of their separation.

The Trongate, Glasgow, c1820

CHAPTER XIX

*Life's glad moments – The lovers meet – From a weaver girl to a lady –
A derelict ship in the North Sea – A good stroke of fortune – A `grey-
haired father and a swankie lover`.*

You would have to see or experience the heartfelt joy of the loved
and loving who, after long years of yearning yet steadfast love in
separation, meet at last and melt in each other's arms, to know how
hallowed is the scene.

The two were left alone. The father of Mary had done his little
yet essential part in bringing them together, and now they were alone.
Yet company were they to each other, more real and acceptable than if
crowds of angels and men stood witnessing around them.

`Forgive me, Mary, I did not at first know you. You are so different
from yourself in the old days. How have you fared since then, and

how have you come to be so changed since we last saw each other in the Links`?

`It is a long story, John, and some of it you have had in my letters – though other parts I purposely concealed from you – partly because I thought it imprudent on my part to parade my good fortune – for good it has been – and partly from a woman`s ways – a wish to make you happier with a surprise. Your last letter was sent on to me and I knew that this was the time to reveal all`.

`You know, at least, dear Mary, all the important, all the real changes in *my* life. The smaller events will keep, and if we live for each other – as I know we will – there will be time enough to tell them all. But tell me, dearest Mary, how you have become what you now are – a sweet and gentle lady`?

`I might also ask you, John, how you have become what you now are – so accomplished, so learned and (I have no doubt) so wise`? Then after a pause: – `I felt you would be changed, but I could never have pictured to myself – even in my wildest imaginings – what a great and strong man you have become`.

`Ah, Mary, God has been kind to both of us. He has blessed me with health, protected me from danger and withheld me from degradation. And you – He has surely made you the favourite of His care`.

`Yes, indeed, John, we have cause to be grateful, both of us – to me has surely come the best of fortune`s gifts`.

`But, tell me, Mary, how you came to be what you are – how you changed from the weaver girl to the lady I now see beside me`?

`Well, John, I will try to tell you, but as my father will probably be waiting for us, let the main events suffice. You know that when you worked with me in old Peter`s shop, my father was at sea in charge of a North Sea barque, mainly in the coal though sometimes in the general shipping business. He was counted a trustworthy man and was entrusted, not only with the ordinary duties of a sea-going commander, but with the transaction of many delicate and important matters in the Baltic ports. He was a careful man and had laid aside a fair round sum to meet the chances of the proverbial rainy day. You had been away four years when he had an extra piece of good fortune.

He was returning from the Baltic in the month of November on what was expected to be his last voyage for the season. The usual North Sea storms had just blown their fiercest over those wild waters and father was returning in the rear of the chasing gales, when his ship fell in with a valuable derelict vessel. She had been abandoned by her crew in the North Atlantic and had drifted round the north into the track of the Baltic-leaving ships. She was laden with a cargo of tobacco, rum, grain, a miscellaneous collection of machinery in boxes, cased liquors and other things. Them ship and cargo were valued at £30,000 and one third fell to father`s share.

The contents of the derelict vessel seemed to change his ideas as to the best lines of trade. He gave up his charge in the Baltic ships, and with the help of the late Mr. Laurie – of the same firm of which father is now a member – he bought a very serviceable ship for the West Indian trade. He commanded it himself for a good many voyages and was very successful – so successful, indeed, that Mr. Laurie, getting old and frail, and wishing to retire, adopted father as a member of the firm, and put the whole of the sea-going part of the business in his hands. Mr. Laurie having died since then, and his partner Mr. Sproul having died many years ago, the whole of the business has fallen into father`s hands`.

`Your father has been very fortunate`, said Orrason, `though not more than he deserved`.

`As regards my share of his good fortune`, continued Mary, `I was taken from the weaving shop and, after some training in the finer forms of hand-sewing and dress-cutting, was sent to an institution in Edinburgh, where I was taught those things – useless and silly some of them, though others are, and will always be, valuable – which are called the accomplishments of a lady. It only remains for me to say that, when the late Mr. Laurie died, and father was compelled to take up his residence in Glasgow, I was bound to come west with him. I told you in my last letter that I had got a situation in another part of the country, and I put it this way for the same reason that, in my former letters, I said nothing about the better fortune that had come to us`.

Then, after a breathing space, she added, `And now I think, John, you have got the substance, if not the detail, of my life since we parted so many years ago at Kirkcaldy`.

She rose as she spoke, and Orrason rose too.

`I had thought, dear Mary`, he said, looking into her eyes and drawing her to his breast, `that I should have had the happiness of providing for you the means of attaining a higher life – higher in social position (forgive my loving vanity) – and now it seems this happiness is to be denied me. Yet the joy shall not be lost, I shall turn it unto love, and add it to the bonds with which I am bound to you and you to me`. As he spoke, he pressed a kiss upon her lips as if to seal the ardent expression of affection he had just made.

As if by mutual consent both left the room and sought that occupied by Captain Seaton. As the happy pair entered, the father laughed a hearty welcome. Orrason smiled in joyous confusion and Mary, beaming her happiness through tear-dimmed eyes, bent tenderly upon her father's breast and imprinted a kiss upon his cheek.

`Well Orrason`, said Captain Seaton, when all were again seated, `I suppose you two`, and he glanced towards his daughter, `like other selfish people – and that means nearly everyone – will have settled matters between you, without any thought or consideration of the old folks you will have been conspiring to desert`.

`On the contrary`, said Orrason, `our first thoughts and steps are towards yourself. I believe I can speak for Mary as I can for myself, that we desire to arrange nothing without your consent and blessing`.

`It is a curious, indeed a mysterious, business this all through. I have often been at sea, but never more so than in this case. I had no idea, and could have none, when I freighted your barque, and engaged yourself, to bring that cargo from the St. John's that I was engaging the familiar correspondent of my daughter; and I had still less any suspicion when, within the past two weeks, we were concluding that same West Indian transaction, that I was dealing with one who has the most serious designs upon my family. No, Orrason, until very recently, I had no idea of these things`. And Captain Seaton cast a look of pleased interrogation across the table.

'Well, well', replied Orrason to these serious avowals, 'if you did not know, if you were in ignorance of all this, you will admit it was impossible for me to instruct you. I did not know when writing to you some months since, nor when speaking to you the other day, that you were the father of the lassie I loved in the loom-shop of the Links, and whom, after long separation, I hoped to meet and make my own when I came back to Scotland'.

'And then, father, 'interrupted Mary, 'you were so much from home, and John's letters came so very seldom, that it was nearly impossible to remember things, and keep you posted up with the latest news'.

Old Seaton smiled as he answered this last. 'You could easily have done the remembering, Mary, had you been set on't. You did not forget the man who was a great deal further awa' than I was but I admit at once there's a great difference between a grey-haired father and a swankie lover', and Captain Seaton gradually dropped into the vernacular of the Lang Toon as he proceeded –

'It's a hiddlin' way o' gaun on! Here's a young fellow I have scarcely seen between the een when, as I may say, he comes in as a life-long acquaintance o' the family. I canna say but it's a queer sort o' business', and Captain Seaton laughed as he pushed the glass towards Orrason.

'But it could not be otherwise', the latter replied, after he had simply touched the liquor, 'I could not write you since I did not know you, nor where you were, nor whether you existed even, though, doubtless, the correspondent at your end would have the best of reasons for keeping matters *in retentis*, as the lawyers say'.

CHAPTER XX

The castaway and the Seatons – At the George Hotel, Glasgow – Mary's mother – 'A trio of blessed mortals'! – Captain Seaton's house in 'Tradeston' – Mrs. Seaton at the tea-table.

'Well now', Mary interposed, 'what else could I do? Just think of it, John, and you think of it, father – I could not seriously inform you about a man who I had never seen since he was a boy, and who had been carried off by the pressgang; and who after tracking slave ships in the tropics, had taken up the West India trade, and might have married a planter's heiress at any time. Had I spread my little store of letters before you, and taken you into my young, innocent confidence, and the heiress had at last caught him, how foolish I must have looked in your eyes, father. Ah no, it was better to wait and see, lest the calm might kythe into a storm'.

'In other words', returned Mary's father now grown somewhat jocular, 'you preferred to keep dark till you were able to give me a real shock of surprise – you thought you micht as weel hae a little fun oot o' your auld father, ere you finished the conspiracy', and the Captain Seaton laughed heartily at his wild conception.

'No conspiracy', hurriedly interjected Orrason, somewhat tickled with the joke. 'We were both at first too much simpletons to become partners in any scheme, and we have both always been too straight, and too serious to concoct even the meekest of arrangements to hide and conceal our connection and intentions'.

'Nae doot, nae doot', said Seaton, 'you were aye open as day wi' a' your contrivances – though it maun be confessed there's a want o' evidence – an baith your mither an' me, Mary, will just be compelled to tak' your ain and Mr. Orrason's explanation in what is conveniently ca'd guid faith'.

'Forgive me! Do forgive me! Captain Seaton', cried Orrason with anxious warmth. `You mentioned just now Mary's mother. I am ashamed to think I should never have referred to Mrs. Seaton. You will excuse me since you will know I have not yet seen the lady since I came to Glasgow, and my life and manner of life have almost banished the notion of motherhood from my mind. Can we not see her'? – and he looked at Mary and at her father with a look of interrogation in his eyes and on his face.

`Mother, no doubt, will be waiting for us, and wondering at home what keeps us all so long at the George Hotel', Mary put in.

`She'll be in a peck o' troubles, an makin' a' sorts o' guesses as to the cause of our lang stay here', said Captain Seaton, and then continued, `I gave her an inklin' o' what was up when Mary an' myself left the house to strike up this new acquaintance wi' you, Captain Orrason, at the George. And now since we have said all we can here, we had better seek our way across the water. Just a word before we go. You, both of you, have all the consent I can give, and all the good wishes I can bestow upon you. Make up your own minds, do well and be happy'. He then opened the door and the trio of blessed mortals sallied into the square.

The house selected by Captain Seaton was one of those erected on the lands once belonging to the trades or incorporations of the city. The entire settlement was then as now called Tradeston [44] and the village was made up at first mainly of houses suitable as dwellings for those who, in the subtle slang of the city, were `able to pay' for them.

Captain Seaton's house was of two stories and self-contained, had an open space in front, and a larger courtyard, with patches of cultivation, behind. The party of three, who have just left the George, chatted gaily along Queen Street and Argyle Street, and swept past the green open spaces and warehouses in Jamaica Street. This brought them to what was then called the New Bridge [45] – a structure of seven arches, and with parapets sufficiently low to give long-extending and charming views of the river and shipping.

There are times, however, when even the grandest of landscapes lose their charms, and there are moods of the minds – moods of pre-occupation – when Nature's most entrancing displays shine out in vain before the unperceiving eye. Our hero, Orrason, and the woman by his side, might be excused if at this moment they missed the beauties of the Clyde.

The house to which they were bound occupied a site which gave the merchant-captain a fine view of shipping on the opposite bank, and that in great measure compensated this lover of the waters for his banishment from the deep.

They reached the first floor and were met on the landing by the anxious Mrs. Seaton.

Mothers, as a rule, have a firm belief that their sons are always able to choose, and to chose properly, their own helpmates in life, but a daughter is ever regarded by *materfamilias* as a weak and enticeable creature, who cannot be trusted to select a husband and arrange her own marriage and who will always need her parents in her life. As the ancient saw has it:

`A son is a son until he gets a wife,

But a daughter is a daughter all the days of her life`.

Mrs. Seaton was clearly a victim of this old hallucination.

She shook her new acquaintance warmly by the hand – holding his great fist in both her own – and she looked anxiously into his face as if to read the heart within and at his external appearance to see how he looked in a woman`s eye. Mary was not a little troubled while the scrutiny lasted but divined, by a single blink of her mother`s glance, that the man and the hour were alike a pleasure and welcome.

`An` hoo am I to name oor new friend, did you say, Arthur`? queried Mrs. Seaton, when the company had found their places at the cosy tea-table.

`John, did you say? `Od, John is the name o` most o` the men folk I ken, sae it`s mair than likely I`ll be mixing him wi` ither folk, an` making fuils o` some o` them. Fill up the cups, my lassie`, the last being addressed to the lassie or maid servant who, in her finest array, moved about in a deft and quiet way, to the convenience and taste of the four all-important people she had now to serve. She took many a look at the stranger, and had formed, no doubt, her own conclusions regarding him. The old lady had, however, been `arranging determinations`, and when the fragrant tea cups were filled and set, the lassie crept out of the room with the same silence with which she had glided round the table.

`Noo, John, mak` yersel as free and at hame at this table, as if it was your ain – I`m no speakin` o` what`s on the table sae muckle as o` the few folks that`s round aboot it`. It`s wi` them I would hae ye mak` yersel at hame, an` feel nae mair restraint than if ye were sittin` at your ain mither`s fireside`. This was a long speech for Mrs. Seaton and after her unusual efforts, she drained her tea cup ere she laid it down again.

The reference to a mother seemed to waken an uneasy chord in Orrason`s breast, and he looked first at Mrs. Seaton and then at Mary, as if in enquiry. As yet neither of Mary`s parents knew ought of his strange history, but Orrason himself did not know this fact for certain and, while he was desirous that they should know everything about his birth and fateful experiences, he could not tell whether and how far his Mary had revealed his history.

`It is just possible, mother`, said Mary, `that Mr. Orrason has not the experience to which you refer. There are people, you know, in this world, who have not known a mother, and therefore cannot recall anything concerning her table`.

The old lady was quick to perceive that there was more under Mary`s remark than belonged to a casual observation, and Mr. Seaton looked as disconcerted as if his hospitality had been put in doubt by some remark of undersigned rudeness to his guest.

`I hope, Mr. Orrason, my gudewife`s weel-meant remark has not in any way put you out or recalled unpleasant thoughts. You may depend nothing was further from her thoughts or from mine`.

`I know it, I know it, my dear friends. And now, since I perceive that Mary, who knows as much of my life`s story I could tell her or write her, has not made you partakers in her knowledge, the best thing I can do now – and it is due to you both – is to tell you what I can of my origin – birth I cannot speak of – and of my curious history. Forgive, if you can, the seeming egotism of the task, and believe me when I say it is only undertaken that you may know who and what I am`. When Orrason was silent, Mary relieved the position by quietly explaining.

`Let me be allowed, dear father and mother, to say here that John`s whole life is, and has for years, been known to me. But I never could see how a revelation of his life and connections might affect his future prospects, and deemed it best to wait his return ere anyone, outside of himself, should know how he found himself in the world, and how the world dealt with him`.

`Ye`re a wise lassie, Mary`, said Captain Seaton, ` nearly as wise as your mither, wha`s never tired telling me that `the least said is sunest mended`. But I am interrupting you, Mr. Orrason`, he said, as the company of three prepared to listen to story of John Orrason`s life.

That story is already known to the reader, so far as it has been told, in all its essential features. No doubt Orrason recited details, peculiarities and matters personal, which give themselves more readily to the living voice – especially when it is the voice of the chief actor himself – than when dropped from the pen.

CHAPTER XXI

A betrothal – A `witch for wisdom` – Lovers` secrets – Mary`s mother relieving her mind.

When Orrason`s strange dislocated story had been heard to the end, and heard with breathless attention, the narrator – in a voice pitched in low, solemn tones and trembling with emotion – turned to his two chief auditors and said,

'And now you have heard the story of the social castaway, of one who has neither kith nor kin that he knows of, who may, for ought he knows, belong to the poor and needy, or to the vile and depraved, who has no great one to commend him, or deeds of valour to lift him up. This forgotten and disowned one now comes to seek connection with your family, to claim the hand of your daughter – shall that loved hand be given me`?

The answer came at once with clear and rapid utterance from the father.

'You have my answer already, my dear Mr. Orrason. Your story, wholly unknown to me until now, only serves to raise you still higher in that high esteem I have entertained for you since first we met. We are bound to speak of a man as we find him. I have hitherto found you an honourable and faithful man, one good and true in all his dealings, and if you and Mary desire to possess each other, I will only say as I said before – do well and be happy – my blessing shall go before you`, and the captain was silent.

'It`s a wonderful story`, said Mrs. Seaton, as she played nervously with the ties of her cap, 'an if e`er there was a sign of God`s ain hand in the guidance of a man – that sign has gone forth and abiden with you. Providence has been round aboot ye, and nae doot preserved you for a brichter an` happier future. It`ll be a sair trial to pairt wi` Mary, but since ye`ve been brocht thegither an` kept thegither by sae mony shining marks o' heavenly favour, it would be a sin to stand in the way o' your marriage. Wi' a' my heart I gie consent, an' may the blessing o' a kind an' protective Providence watch o'er ye baith', and the kindly old lady, wiping a tear from her eye, assumed again her former cheerful manner, and pressed the good things of the table on their attention, and bade them mind – in 'a' their wonderin' thochts' – the needs of the body.

Orrason, having expressed his thanks, and Mrs. Seaton having refilled the steaming cups, Mary, looking from John to her father and mother, interposed:

'It will be best in every way, I think, to keep this story of the castaway – as he calls himself – as far as possible as a piece of exclusive family property. Let us keep the history to ourselves. It can do no good to spread it abroad, and possibly the keeping of the little secret may prove of benefit in the future'.

'Ye're a wise lassie, Mary', said her father, 'an' nae doubt ye'll live to be a wise woman, too. The course ye suggest is at aince the best an' safest, an', though ye're the youngest among us, we know that wisdom has been perfected in the mouths of babes and sucklings'.

This inroad into Scripture raised a hearty laugh all round, and when the old lady had observed that Mary 'wis jist a witch for wisdom', the story of John Orrason became from thence an accepted family secret.

If the young and ardent couple were found, shortly after this, enjoying the sweetness and entrancing joy of their first chapter of unfettered speech in the woodland resorts of Paisley Road and Ibrox, we need not wonder. However glad their hearts had hitherto been, there was a mine of personal communion deep down in each of their souls that had not yet been reached. So they walked beneath the pale shadows of the great old trees, just then – for it was March – acknowledging in opening buds the life-giving breath of spring. Coltsfoot and dandelion peeped out from the hedge-roots and, if he saw not here his never forgotten wind-flower, he knew it was blooming, unseen, in the beauty, in the depths, of distant woods.

'How suggestive spring is of renewed life', said Mary, breaking into the silence of their gladness.

'It is, indeed', said Orrason. 'And may it be to us both the token of a revival of a long-buried joy'.

It was afternoon of the short but lengthening days, and the mavis, in woods across the fields as in the tree-tops near at hand, sang his hymn to the evening with such lusty power as told of exuberant joy within.

'All nature rejoices in the returning signs of life after the decay of winter and seems to speak hope and confidence to us both', said Mary.

'Yes, Mary, though to you and me the season of despair never came and we seem to be alike in the possession of a nature of endless trust. You in ever-loved and bonnie Scotland and I amid the burning tropics cherished the same plant of trustful assurance and now appreciate the glory and fragrance of the blossom'.

And as Orrason ceased he looked into Mary's face which was pensive yet radiant as his was glowing and earnest. Their eyes met, and their hearts were entwined in these viewless bonds which loving eyes alone can frame.

Thus they conversed with each other, breathing in each other's ears the old, old, yet ever fresh story of the loving, trusting heart. Hour after hour flew on – their flight unnoted – till the falling darkness called the lovers home.

In that home we left the father and mother of Mary Seaton. These, sitting on each side of the cosy fireplace, were privileged to discuss the changed condition of things which they must face since their daughter had decided to enter a new partnership.

'Isna that John Orrason a maist wonderful man, Arthur? He's sic a gude-looking and stalwart man, an' yet sae quiet an' wise in a' he says', said Mrs. Seaton, trying to relieve her mind of the floating and ill-defined impressions that filled it.

'Yes, Janet, he's a most uncommon man – so exact an' methodical in his business, so animated with honour and the principles of fair dealing, and yet so calmly enthusiastic, as if he were an apostle baith of philosophy and religion. Yes, he is a rare and uncommon man', said Captain Seaton, as he meditatively lighted his pipe.

`His voice is sae stoor and deep-set, an` his words sae carved and shapen to the purpose in hand – he looks, when he`s speakin`, mair like a minister than a sailor`, said Mrs. Seaton, holding on to her first thesis.

`His origins, his life at the Refuge and his methodical way of thinking, have all tended to make him the man he is. With most people the circumstances of life practically make the man, and, it is only here and there, as in the case of John Orrason, that we find one whose thoughts rise above and, to some extent, defy his surroundings`. This incursion within the ethical line was too much for Mrs. Seaton, and she observed:

`They`ll baith be thinkin` nae doot tae get by wi` the marriage as soon as possible an` for my pairt I see little use for ony aff-pit o` time. They`re made for ane anither if ever man and woman were sae they may weel get married soon as late`.

`I do not think`, said Seaton, `that Orrason has any inclination to waste time in pursuing a courtship which has already lasted so long and though both are pleased to be fancy-free in each other`s company, yet I believe, from certain words he let fall at the table, that he has some project on foot, in which he desires the help and advice of Mary. No, I do not think the marriage will be delayed`.

They took the theme up again and again and looked at it from all sides, as people will do when the subject, as in the present case, becomes wholly absorbing because of a deep personal element. Variations were played in, in the form of future domestic relations, and of present financial provisions – `For Mary, ye ken`, said her mother, `can ne`er be allowed to leave the house either with a toom hand or a toom pooch`.

CHAPTER XXII

Mrs. Seaton's wisdom – Preparations for the marriage – A 'couthy and canny' wedding in Glasgow.

The lamp was lighted on the landing, and the newly-introduced and new-fashioned gas-light in the parlour, when the door opened and the willing wanderers returned. The duets on economics inside and on vows and visions outside were now brought to an end, and a 'foursome' crack took the place of both for one more happy hour.

Time again, however, took flight for the inmates of Seaton House, and the long hours were drawing near the longest one when Captain Orrason bade them all good night, and took himself to the George.

Most of the next day, and many of the following ones, were spent by Orrason in the house of the Seatons. Weeks sped on, the day of the marriage was fixed and its character decided. Then Mary and her mother became entangled in a maze of details regarding the house in which the young couple would set up, the furniture and general 'plenishin'', clothing, dresses, etc., until, as Captain Seaton said, they 'nearly lost their heads, and aince or twice fairly lost theirsels, in running through the city, lookin' and seekin' for things he ne'er heard tell o' before, an' would likely forget a' aboot, as soon as he had the chance'.

Though the Captain spoke in this somewhat disrespectful manner of the ladies, he had to admit that he did a good deal of the running about himself; and even Orrason could not be allowed to be idle or, as Mrs. Seaton put it, 'to gang aboot wi' his hands in his pooches when a' the rest were sae sair put till't'. The new home – which was also fixed in the new Tradeston village – had to be looked at, and approved by all the four concerned, and most of all by the two who were to start with the responsibilities of house-keeping within its walls.

But 'It's a lang lane that has nae turn' – at least, Mrs. Seaton said so – when 'the buyin' in and the payin' oot had a' been got through wi'' and the new house was filled and fitted to the taste and pleasure of all. In the execution of this running contract, common consent had been arrived at that the house should have all that taste and comfort required with superfluity, for its own sake, carefully shut out.

'It's a fine house for twa sensible folk', said Mrs. Seaton, when the newly-furnished dwelling was being finally surveyed by the critical quartette, 'an' since nane o' you twa', turning to Mary and Orrason, 'are chickens o' the first year that disna ken a shinin' chuckie frae a boil't bean, ye'll hae wit enouch to ken the gude o' a house that provides a' ye want an' wish for, without botherin' ye wi' extra rooms and useless articles o' show, that cause mair loss o' temper in keeping' them richt than gain o' pleasure in looking at them, or showin' them aff to ithers. The hoose is real weel, an' muckle luck may ye hae in it'.

'I suppose, Orrason, we may simply chime in here and say amen to the women folk', spoke out Captain Seaton.

'Any other course, I am afraid, would be unwise', Orrason answered. 'There are some things in which one may risk to cross the ladies and make suggestions, but in the furnishing of a house all male interference is rigidly excluded – and happily so for such a wandering Mother Carey's chicken as I am'.

'The house is very well', said Mary, 'and mother deserves a round of thanks for the trouble she has taken and the taste she has shown'.

'Agreed, agreed'! shouted both the men, and all laughingly departed for the night – one to the George, the others to the warm fireside of the Seatons near by.

The wedding came off in the following week, and I will try, for the sake of the lady readers, and for sartorial antiquaries among the other sex, to describe the dresses and adornments worn by those present, and the procession of events by which the grand and mysterious ceremony of binding a man and woman together was finally accomplished.

It is only three quarters of a century since this little social function came off, but in that short space we have experienced a whole host of social revolutions – a good many of them, almost without our knowing, have passed over us. In dress the changes have been less violent than in many other things and, though both men and women have oscillated between older forms and newer absurdities, the dress of seventy years ago differed less from the present with the females than with members of that sex which is continually twitting the ladies with being slaves of fashion.

With Mary, the skirt was shorter than prudes would now approve, but the pretty sandal-shoes would stir the envy of our gayest Princes Street belles, and the closely-knitted patterned stockings would no less call up the approval of their critical eye. The bodice, square and close-fitting, and the head gear, always the crowning part of a woman's apparel, were and would be deemed pretty and becoming in the highest degree. Gloves were worn and other nameless adornments of the lovely and good, but there was no long veil or train. Mary had come to do a deed of consent and consecration, and she brought to it, not the attractiveness of rich apparel, but the charms of a lovely person and a pure and noble mind.

The mother, in the freshness of well spent years, and the serenity of a restful contentment gave – in her harmoniously coloured silk gown, bracelets and lace necklet, her brow-band and white lace cap – a tone of mingled gaiety and serious enterprise to the company.

The men I have on a former occasion described, and if newer and gayer suits were given to each, if flowers or favours be found in their lapel buttonholes, if white gloves be fitted to their hands, and an air of earnest preparedness be given to both, the old description will still suffice.

The wedding guests were few, and for good reasons. Orrason had no relations and no friends except his faithful seamen down the Clyde, and the Seatons concluded that, for his sake and the family compact, it would be better to have a small rather than a numerous company.

The old notion that it was right – if not absolutely necessary for future good luck – to have the marriage ceremony in the bride's house, was scrupulously observed. There were suggestions of going elsewhere than Glasgow with the day's doings, and a hint also of having it in the George, but Mrs. Seaton would have none of these proposals.

'When my lassie gangs oot into the world, let her gang frae her mither's ain door. I'll hae nae o' yer far-awa' junkettins afore the marriage take place; an' as for marrying Mary Seaton in a change hoose, I could never think about it. Na, na, let the business gang on at oor ain fireside, and let the lassie step oot into the world frae oor ain door cheek. It's by far the maist couthie and canny and decent way o' passin' twa folk oot o' single into married blessedness'.

This was a long speech for the good lady to make, and the uncommon effort showed how very decidedly she had made up her mind. She was queen – and deservedly so – in the Seaton household and, on this occasion, her majesty's opposition did not exist. The marriage took place as Mrs. Seaton would have it – at home.

The company consisted of the original four, the mate and the steward from the *Mary*, Bailie Bullions and assessor Dryflats from Kirkcaldy, officiating minister Mr. Law [46], also from the Lang Toon, the pastor, Mr. William Kidston [47], of their own church in Glasgow, and the two Misses Ford, close friends to Mary and visitors at the house, who were eager to witness her marriage ceremony.

CHAPTER XXIII

The marriage and its `festivities – The great ministerial `breach` of 1747 – Bailie Bullions proposes the health of the newly married couple – Mr. Law has his say on Kirk matters in Dunfermline – Music and dancing.

It was a simple Scotch marriage. The Rev. Mr. Kidston was the last to arrive and, though he was late by only a few minutes, an uneasy nervousness was at once evident on more than one face until he arrived.

Introductions over, Mr. Kidston offered up a short and, in the fashion of the time, a somewhat doctrinal prayer before a portion of scripture waled from Matthew and First Corinthians was read. Rev. Mr. Law then vised the `lines` and, being satisfied with his inspection, he asked `the parties about to be married` to stand up. This done, he addressed to them a pretty long list of injunctions touching the commonest and also the most private affairs of life.

Hands were joined at his bidding and, after the usual preliminaries, Mr. Law pronounced John Orrason, bachelor, and Mary Orrason, spinster, husband and wife, concluding with the words, `What therefore God has joined together, let no man put asunder`. A benediction followed, and the signing of the lines brought the simple ceremony to an end.

All present congratulated the bride and groom and then, Mr. and Mrs. Seaton leading the way, the company followed into the dining-room. Here a simple, yet substantial, repast was prepared. Wine was offered to and partaken by all. There was then no social ban on the use of liquor and none was needed, for certainly no more abstemious people ever gathered to a marriage feast as those now enjoying each other`s company under the roof of Arthur Seaton. Nearly all were known to each other and, having much in common, had much to say, and jokes, anecdotes and reminiscences of other days flowed on wings of mirth and joy round the table.

Mr. Law had been known, loved and appreciated for over twenty years in the Langtoon. He had been placed as pastor in the Bethelfield Church of Associated Seceders in the last year of the previous century, and the Seatons had all their lives been seceders of the school of the Erskines and the Browns [48]. Mrs.Seaton was strongly persuaded that no one should have the honour of marrying her daughter but her own minister and herein was found a sufficient reason for bringing a clergyman from the `kingdom` of Fife to tie with his tongue a knot which no one else could loosen with his teeth!

Mr. Kidston was of the same seceder persuasion and as the captain's family now `sat under` the reverend gentleman, he, too, must be at the marriage for, as Mrs. Seaton said, `he micht no` be pleased ye ken, if he wasna bidden, an` thae black coatit gentry, either craws or priests, are kittle cattle to deal wi`, an` maun aye be strokit wi` the hair`.

The two clergymen being experienced with all sorts and conditions of people became, by their ready wit and reference to bye-gone times, the soul of the gathering. They also touched on more serious subjects of interest to the company, such as the `healing of the great breach`. That breach had occurred in 1747 when the anti-burghers shook the dust off their feet against the burghers, and the burghers stood apart to let them go but, after nearly three-quarters of a century, the warring parties had come to terms, smoked the pipe of theological peace and dubbed themselves the `United Presbyterian Church`. In this great schism both Captain and Mrs. Seaton, the bailie and the assessor were deeply interested, and even the younger members of the company knew sufficient of the quarrel to follow with interest and understand all that was said on the matter.

The discussion dried up, the stories finished and the jokes exhausted, Bailie Bullions rose to propose the health of the newly-married couple.

`I have not`, he said, `the honour of the acquaintance of the young man, Mr. Orrason, who has – who has – yes, made off – with the daughter and only child of my honoured and honourable friend,

Captain Arthur Seaton. But I am bound to admit, and to conclude, that this young man is a good and noble fellow – 'Hear, hear', from the assessor – and I am sure I only require to mention the name of Miss Seaton to excite the regard of everybody in the company, and to arouse the enthusiasm – yes, the enthusiasm and devotion of every gentleman present. I will say no more – I had no intention of saying so much, but when a man is on his feet, and feels he has got a really splendid subject (here the bailie slapped his white vest) and feels himself warming to it, there is no saying how far he may go and to – to – to what degree of eloquence he may rise. On this most auspicious occasion – and in the name of our host – I ask you all to drain your glasses to the health of the bride and bridegroom'.

The assessor, accustomed all through his life to see things done decently and in order, deemed it necessary to 'second the motion of his friend, the bailie'.

When he rose, he pulled out a gorgeous turkey-red handkerchief, unfolded its glories of colour and wiped his nose; then, solemnly taking three pinches of snuff he began:

'I am more accustomed to bargain-making than to speech making, but this remark reminds me that it really *is* a business of bargaining – a most important bit of adjustment and agreement – in which we have been engaged to-night, and I am in the happy position of being able to witness that the arles have been paid, and the high contracting parties bound thirl to each other. I believe, with the bailie, that both parties are fully aware of the conditions and responsibilities they have under-taken; that they will pull together and in the fair way of the harness, and so bear the load of life equally and justly. I believe all this, and therefore invoke long life, happiness and health, to both'.

Captain Seaton, as host, rose and proceeded in a quiet style to thank everyone for their kindness and good wishes. He referred to his former intimacy with the worthy magistrate and his life-long friend the assessor. In serious vein he touched on kirk matters and grew warm over the various doctrinal and ecclesiastical fightings they had seen in the congregation gathered and made and kept together by the practical and prophetic Robert Shirra [49].

This called up Mr. Law who continued the history and wandered into reminiscences of his own young days in Dunfermline, with quaint items of forgotten kirk-lore in connection with the Macfarlanes and Dr. Black of the anti-burghers, and the 'worthy divine' Ralph Erskine with his fiddle, the bapteesement o' the bairn and his praise of tobacco [50].

But at last everyone had had their say and even the sober seamen from the *Mary* were drawn out, while the Misses Ford became earnestly attentive and broke into peals of laughter at every amusing point the seamen made.

The stories, the jokes and the discussion tapering to an end, the two clergymen took their leave, Mr. Law going with Mr. Kidston for the night and both being escorted all the way home by the host.

The tables were then redd up, the room cleared and the gay spirits of the young and the happy hearts of the old went gaily into a lively dance as, for some hours afterwards, the music of a 'wicked little fiddle' was warmly replied to by the music of the feet.

Somehow the bride and bridegroom got lost on the floor, or by some means unknown had gone out by the door. They were sought for below, they were sought above, but the bridegroom was off with his bride.

How long the jaunt of the honeymoon lasted we need not too particularly enquire; where it was spent we need not be too curious. Orrason and Mary returned in a few days, were warmly welcomed by the old folk and installed for good in their new home. With house-warming observances over, and visits from friends over too, the young couple were free to set about the Orrason's settled purpose in life – to find out who had brought him into the world and then abandoned him to his fate.

CHAPTER XXIV

The birth search begins – Wilson's Charity School – Interview with the Dominie.

When the newly-married couple – the young man and his younger wife – sat at breakfast on the first clear day after all the necessary duties to friends and neighbours had been discharged, their conversation, if it had not changed from `lively to severe`, yet had acquired the tone of a definite business colour.

Mary had long known the calmly-resolute determination of her husband to search and find the name of his parents and the time and circumstances of his birth and, as his partner in life, she was no less anxious and no less resolved, to probe the mystery to the bottom. She had always believed that John Orrason was not only good but wise. He had always been, and was now more than ever, her hero – a hero she would gladly follow whithersoever he led. The search might be a long one and tantalizing, disappointing, and expensive, but whatever the nature of the hazy enterprise, however circuitous the labyrinthine road they had to travel, both were equally devoted to the journey, both equally ready to give their best talents and most enduring energies to the task.

`How do you think, Mary – for I know what is in your mind`, said Orrason, `we should begin this queer enquiry of ours`?

`The only thing I can say`, Mary replied, `is that we must begin where we are`.

`Ah, no doubt, if we intend to proceed and end well in this mystery of my birth we must begin where we are, but possibly we had better `clear the coast` of certain unconnected matters before we proceed to sea on our voyage of discovery`.

`And what other things have you on your mind`? returned Mary.

'Well, don't you think it might be as well to have the schooner brought into harbour, and fitted out for Kingston or Falmouth West, and freighted with the cargo your father formerly spoke of? It would keep the hands busy and out of mischief, the vessel in profitable occupation and your father's interest promoted'.

'Surely, surely, John. That is a very thrifty proposal, and as we have no plans fixed for the day, we might as well be doing something that will be a benefit all round'.

No differences of opinion existing on the point, the details were quickly settled. Mary called upon her mother, and Orrason was soon at the business premises of Sproul and Laurie meeting Captain Seaton. The ground of the visit was soon laid down, the propriety accepted and the men instructed to bring the *Mary* into harbour. The mate was elevated to the command and the commercial arrangements left solely in the hands of Captain Seaton. On the next day, when Orrason and his smiling wife were packing up to begin *their* voyage of discovery, the *Mary* was being carefully stowed for one which – though on the uncertain waters – had a purpose and goal far more definite and certain than the one on land.

'I think you said', observed the husband to his wife, ' that we should begin our search from our own door'.

'That indeed was what I said', replied his wife, and I still hold to that opinion'.

'Well, as we shall not run far off the first day, our travelling gear may be left at home, and if you are ready we shall sally forth on our foray'.

'But whither away'? enquired Mary, for Orrason had not as yet indicated where he had resolved to begin his search. But he knew himself and replied:

'To Montrose Street – to Wilson's Charity School for boys, across there! Ah, Mary, I think I see you wince at the proposal of charity schools! Ah! These institutions have no romance about them'.

'Now, John, that is hardly fair. You know that romance in itself has little allurement for me and I will say more. Wherever the threads of your life's story lead, there will I find the most real of all possible romances. So now lead on and I will follow. We seek a speirin` fortune, and by speirin` we shall find it`.

Discoursing on possibilities, the seekers after truth soon found themselves in Montrose Street, and at the door of the humble academy, founded by the good Maister Wilson, London merchant, some thirty or forty years before.

The voice of the dominie was heard within, breaking clear over the hum of juvenile voices, and calling frequently to silence and order, where indeed little of either was to be found.

When told that a lady and gentleman waited outside, he was immediately in motion and when, in square cap and spectacles, he appeared, flipped his whiskers and looked at his visitors, he led the way to a side room where, gravely, he turned and waited. The card with which he was presented contained – in the taste of the time – the figure of a ship in full sail with the words `MRS. AND JOHN ORRASON` on the exposed quarter.

`John Orrason, John Orrason`, muttered the man of the ferule. `Infinitely pleased to see you. Can I be of service to you? The name is rather a strange one in these quarters, though, is it not`?

`Somewhat uncommon, no doubt`, said Orrason, `though you had once, at least, that name upon your daily list`.

`Indeed, and is that of verity? But surely not for many years, Mr. Orrason`?

`No, sir, not for a good many years, but there was once a pupil of that name in the Wilson School, and my object in calling today is to find the date of entry and exit. Can you help me`? the visitor asked, looking carefully at the teacher.

`Can you, Mr. Orrason, give me an approximate date of either event – for that will help *me*`.

`Well, I think you will find the entry in the year 1802, and the exit possibly in 1810`, and Orrason waited as the good dominie turned to a shelf of brown-skinned, dust-coloured volumes, ranged in rows upon shelves rather out of the little man`s reach.

`Eighteen hunder and twa, eighteen hunder and twa`, he continued in low tones, as he pulled out and replaced one after another of his registers. `Eighteen hunder and twa – the year o` the peace – Napoleon First Consul for life – great London docks opened – Toussaint L'Ouverteur [51] surrenders – Toussaint the Opener declares himself – at last`, and as he finished this curious jumble of phrases, he flung down the register for 1802.

`Orrason, Orrason, Orrason`, he still muttered as he flipped over the leaves. `Orrason, Orrason. Yes, here is the entry full and correct – John Orrason, from the Refuge, aged five, April 27th 1802`, and he turned the page to his visitors.

As Orrason made a copy of the neat and formal handwriting, the ancient schoolmaster was again amongst his volumes.

`Anno Domini, eighteen hundred and ten, did you say`? looking over his shoulder to Orrason and Mary. `Eighteen hundred and ten – year of great events, sir – riots in London, processions in London – Burdett liberated, Cobbett's imprisonment – the King goes mad – *Times* printers sent to jail – Battles of Busaco – Torres Vedras [52], and general upset of everything in Holland, Turkey, Russia, and France.`

Orrason could not avoid laughing outright as the busy little man plied his search and rattled off his history at the same time. `Eighteen hundred an` ten – there you are again, sir`. As he dashed down the book and raised a cloud of dust round his grey locks, he kept muttering, `Orrason, Orrason, Orrason. Here you are again, sir, and the exit is as faithful as the entry – John Orrason of the Refuge, age 13, March 10th 1810`.

While again Orrason made a careful copy, the ceaseless speaker addressed himself to his lady visitor.

`Busy here today, Mrs. Orrason; our annual turn out, you know, in a kind of way, our *gaudeamus*, you must understand`, and he smiled briskly towards Mary, as he continued `We are all in gala dress today, even the charity children have got something fresh`. Then he stopped as having exhausted his topic. It was only for a moment, however. `You have called early, Mrs. Orrason, and no doubt you are right. Early prayers – Matins, you know – always most effective`.

Then, turning to Orrason, who had now completed his copies, `quite satisfied, sir`? If there any other matter of personal or material import that I could help you with, command me. Did you say you were once a pupil here? Oh, indeed, then possibly you might like to see our grand procession. Today is general Founder's Day – comes round every 26th April – we'll be in the streets within half-an-hour, and then you may witness the procession' [53].

The little, lively man, being now tired out, leapt inside the school just as the uproar was becoming unbearable, and left his visitors in possession of the *sanctum sanctorum*. The din was soon quieted, and the noise of tongues gave way to the shuffling of feet and to the shifting and falling of seats. Stentorian words of command had soon apparently got the little crowd into order, for suddenly the door opened and the long file of rosy and pale-faced boy bairns sallied forth into the street. Orrason watched them with interest, and, as each little feature of the annual turn-out revealed itself, the whole came back to his memory with a freshness and vividness that surprised him. The small party-coloured banners with their curious and rude devices, were all once more made familiar to him, and he felt himself unthinkingly looking in the faces of the boys as if to discover in them the companions and confidants he had chosen during the eight years he had been at the little academy.

Boy from Wilson's School, Glasgow
(background, St. Andrew's Church)

CHAPTER XXV

A charity procession in Glasgow – A church service – A needle in a haystack – The lost son.

The solemn procession moved off, finding its way from Montrose Street into Ingram Street. The gathering was guided to the old site of the Hutcheson Hospital at the corner of Ingram Street and John Street where vast crowds of school children, from all the charities in the city, were forming in regular array. At their head were the city officers, watchers and others; then came the magistrates and council, and these again were followed by the city clergy, the teachers and professors. At the head of each section walked the officers of each particular school – each distinguished by its own halberds, ensigns and banners. When all were fairly in order, the procession moved into Hutcheson Street, Wilson Street, Brunswick Street, along the Trongate to the Cross, and then down the Old Saltmarket into the ancient Church of St. Andrew's. Impelled by old associations, by an influence that he could not explain and by the sentiments of mere curiosity, Orrason led Mary in the wake of the queer, many-coloured procession and with it entered the church.

Why our forefathers should have sought to make the lives of the little ones so dull, so cheerless, and often so sad, it is now bootless to enquire. As the crowd of children thronged into the seats, and gradually filled every corner of the great building, a look of solemn reserve seemed to subdue even the bubbling vivacity of their childish nature; and when the hard-voiced precentor, reading and singing alternately each line, rang out –

Few are thy days and full of woe

O man of woman born,

– the thin tremulous voices seemed to respond to his lead with a tone of pleading despair. The prayers were of extraordinary length, and weighted with doctrinal references no child could understand. The petition sought the descent of blessings utterly beyond a child's capacity to comprehend, and the long-drawn out and frivolous implorings on behalf of the powers-that-be, from His Majesty on the throne, down through all the officers of state, the magistrates of the city, ministers, elders and officers of the church, must have proved a string of meaningless jargon and wearisome repetition to the pleasure-hungry crowds of children who were listening. More psalm-singing was followed by unmerciful exhortation – unmerciful in its length and in its nature. The half-hour sand-glass which stood on the edge of the pulpit had already run through two measures, and was far on in its third, when the preacher, having got through all his forty heads and particulars, had reached at last the application, and struggled on through mere sounding phrases to the final Amen.

To Orrason, this last word came as a relief in the greatest need. To Mary the trial was less severe because less uncommon, but even to her the close of the service was long desired and warmly welcomed. How they pitied the poor wee things that filled the square and high-backed pews. Many of them were asleep, some had woken up from terrorizing dreams and were crying, and all were worn out from severe fatigue and an exhausting task.

This was the last act of the grand annual charity school turn-out in Glasgow of seventy years ago. How far the native might be pleased with the exhibition it might be perilous to say, but the foreigner must have held it as a proof that we, as a nation, take our pleasure sadly.

As they left the church door, Orrason and Mary met the little dominie once more.

'You have been very lucky, sir, and you too, madam, in having called today just when we were about to turn out for our *dies mirabilis* – our day of wonders. Lucky you were indeed, both of you'. Then, turning to Orrason, 'You must, sir, have enjoyed the tuition of my predecessor in office – a good teacher – a really capable teacher, sir; but classics and history were not in demand in his time, and he knew next to nothing of these sublime subjects. Pray make it convenient to call some other day; and now, good lady, good afternoon, and you, sir, and in the meantime *au revoir*', and the little animal of activity vanished in the juvenile crowd. Thoughtfully Orrason and Mary left the scene.

'Weel my bonnie bairns, an' did ye get a' ye gaun a-seekin' for'? said Mrs. Seaton, as Orrason and his young wife entered that lady's hospitable door. 'I thocht when ye set oot on your traivels in search o' truth, in fact it was like seekin' a needle in a haystack, or lookin' for fine feelin' among the tobacco merchants at the fit o' the Candleriggs'.

'We got all we expected to pick up', said Orrason, 'and we were offered a great deal more than we had any use for'.

'That is so', said Mary. We were offered a potted edition of the 'History of Europe' in addition to an extract from the precious brown books as to John's entrance into and exit from the Wilson School. The teacher, the dominie, was indeed a vastly learned and garrulous little man, and quite bent on making us as learned as himself'. And Mary laughed in concert with her husband as they recalled the curious exhibition of the little dominie, and related it to Mrs. Seaton.

''Od, that maun be the same man that comes down to Mr. Seaton's offices o'er the water, an' spiers a' sorts o' questions aboot foreign pairts, as if he were bent on writin' a book o' traivels, without journeyin' abroad'. And, as she busied herself with the tea-urn, she went on, 'A wee wick o' a cratur wi' a snuff-brown coat an' knee-breeks o' the same material, an' a waistcoat a' jaupit wi' ink. He keeks o'er the tap o' his spectacles when he speaks, and glowers through them when he's reading'

`Well, I should say that is exactly the man`, Orrason observed, `and your description does credit to your powers of observation`.

`He`s ca`d the `Dainty Dominie` – though for my part I see nothing dainty about him. Open the door to your faither, Mary, I hear his fit i` the stair`. And, as Mr. Orrason held the door open, the worthy captain entered.

`We were just speaking, father, about the schoolmaster we met at the Wilson Institution today, and who gave us the extracts of John`s time in the academy. Mother was telling us he comes to the office sometimes on spiering excursions to learn of far foreign parts`.

`Oh, yes`, said the Captain, as he seated himself comfortably at the table. `That`s the Dainty Dominie and we all know him well. He has a son out in the west – the West Indies – from whom he never heard cheep. And, somehow or other, he seems to think that by coming often enough to the office, he will at last learn of his long-lost son. His dominie peculiarities have run to seed, but the fatherly affection within the man is stronger than all, and though he seldom mentions the name of that son, we all know what he so earnestly seeks. The dominie`s name is Donald Fraser, and his son will have to be Donald Fraser of that ilk`.

CHAPTER XXVI

A visit to the `Refuge` – An interview with the Laytons – A touching scene

With family talk of plans and ways and means, the evening hours were spent, and when Orrason and his wife found themselves in their own house again, they felt that their search had begun in fair style and with fair augury of success.

The early hours of the succeeding day were devoted to following up the lead given by the extracts from the dominie's books. The Refuge in the vicinity of the Rotten Row was evidently the next house of call. Here the couple found themselves knocking for admission some hours before noon. Their call was answered by a tall dark woman, long past the meridian of life, and obviously still further past the meridian of her strength. She beckoned her visitors to an open door in the hall. They entered and found themselves in a dimly lighted and musty-smelling apartment.

Having ascertained the purpose of the visit, the ancient matron – known in the place as `Mistress Emily` – stated with expressions of regret that she could not aid them in their quest as the governor, Mr. Layton, was at the time so poorly in health she doubted if anything could be had from him on the subject.

This intimation raised at once, in the breasts of both visitors, a strong feeling of anxiety, and the old lady was soon made aware that it was no idle curiosity that had induced the visit, but an unflinching desire to learn the time and manner of Orrason's introduction into the institution.

Retiring for a time, Mistress Emily returned to say that the `maister` had now got up, and would try to satisfy the lady and gentleman who had called.

Leading the way, the old lady, her white cap ribbons hanging loosely over the shoulders of her black silk dress, led the way through several passages and rooms and, by a wide partially-carpeted stair, to the private apartments of the institution.

In their passage thus through this part of the establishment – all of which was familiar to Orrason – little of the life led by the children within could be seen by Mary, who was anxious to have a clear object-lesson in the manner and treatment to which her husband had been subject in babyhood. Beyond the familiar sight of the dry-nurse with her diminutive charge and numerous cots with numerous occupants, she had neither time nor opportunity to see more of the crowing infants or the romping boys and girls in the playroom or the back court.

On reaching the last landing their guide stopped short, tapped on the nearest door and entered, followed at once by Mary and Orrason. On a large, somewhat rickety reclining chair, propped up with pillows, was stretched in a half-sitting position a thin, cadaverous-looking man. His breath came in short laboured bursts; his eyes were deeply sunk and he displayed a constant desire to close them against the light, which now streamed in through the curtained windows. He raised his head as the visitors entered and signed them to seats.

He was attended by his wife, a woman in a coloured dress and hastily donned cap and ties, with fragmentary additions in collar and lace bands. She was evidently of fewer years and in better health than the sinking man she carefully attended on the couch. The guiding lady, Emily whom, it was now found, was chief authority in the rooms and among the servants below, was also desired to be seated, and Mrs. Layton waited to hear the desires of her visitors.

'We are troubling you over much, Mrs. Layton, and we must be a trial to Mr. Layton, whom I see, to my sorrow, is now in that condition when quietness and rest is most desirable'. So spoke John Orrason to the woman who had once known him well, but who could not in the bronzed and broad-shouldered man she saw before her recognize any likeness to any boy she had ever known in the place over which she and her husband had long held rule. She glanced curiously at Orrason and awaited his queries.

`Do you remember the name John Orrason as that of one who was once an inmate here'? our hero asked Mrs. Layton.

One could see that the sick man heard too, and divine by the closely pressed eyelids that he was trying to recall the strange name. Multitudes of the unknown had passed through the institution – and many – far too many – of these had been desired by all connected to pass out into utter oblivion. All had indeed been named, but the name had too often been given by chance selection, with a clear design to cover and conceal the child`s identity. In this way, the names of the consigned children – for consignments they were, and nothing more – became to the mind of Mr. Layton like so many mere numbers that, as in the case of prisoners and convicts, served a useful purpose so long as the holder was present, but could not, and need not, be remembered when absent.

`The name is a strange one`, weakly whispered the sick man, `and yet there seems to be a faint impression on my mind that I have heard it before`.

`If I might be allowed to help you`, said the guiding governess quietly, `I think a child with that name was brought here many years ago, by a middle-aged man and a woman`.

The latter part of this intimation was eagerly seized by Orrason, and both himself and Mary made notes of all that passed.

`Can you charge your memory, Emily, with anything like near the time'? queried Mrs. Layton, turning to the speaker.

`It is difficult to be precise as to dates from mere remembrance – but it must be over twenty years since then`, answered Emily.

Here Mary interposed – `It must be fully twenty-five years, I believe. I have some little means of knowing, and I believe my husband will agree with me as to the time`.

`I may say now in a word`, broke in her husband, ` that I am the John Orrason we are enquiring about, and I agree with my wife that the time must be about twenty-five years ago. So far as I can make out, I was a child under three years then, and at that age a child`s memory is weak and wandering`.

During the delivery of this little speech, the sick man raised his head, and looked with wonder and admiration on the developed boy of his early care.

`You, Johnnie Orrason`? he gasped, with all his power of breath, as he reached out his claw-like fingers by way of welcome. `God bless you and keep you! Take my hand in yours and let me feel your own. Yes, I remember you – your name. Yes! It was a man and a woman brought you here`. But the effort was too much for the poor sufferer's wasted strength. He was seized with a fit of coughing, and streaks of blood were seen on his lips as, more in semblance of death than life, he sank back in his chair.

Mrs. Layton was by his side in a moment and Emily, smoothing the pillows of the sufferer, laid him gently down as the sorrowing wife bathed his almost rigid features with the delicate touch of a loving hand.

CHAPTER XXVII

Emily and the dying Mr. Layton – The book of names – An important entry – Guess work – 'Dunfarlin' make'! – Comparing notes.

Slowly, and as if in agony, the waning Mr. Layton returned into the area of conscious existence. 'Get the book of names', he said, after a while, 'and look up Orrason'.

The books always carefully kept by the now fast-sinking Mr. Layton, were brought by Emily, and Mrs. Layton, placing the volumes on a table near the window, invited Orrason and his wife to help in the search.

The reader knows already that the entry was carefully made, and he knows also what the entry was. When the volume containing the names for 1799 was at last reached, the name in its order, and under its letter, was duly found.

'Here is the entry you are in search of', said Mrs. Layton, and she read out in the hearing of the exhausted occupant of the chair:

'John Orrason, nearly three years old, full grown, healthy. Mole or dark spot under the right breast. Left by C.G. and his wife, C. – 25th October 1799'.

'Left by C.G. and his wife, C' said Orrason, looking at Mary with a touch of disappointment, if not, indeed, dismay on his face. 'Who could C.G. be? In a world of possible places for my origin, there may be or may have been thousands of men who could answer to the initials C.G'

'The range is, however, limited by the C. of his wife', said Mary, 'Not every man has the privileged of marrying a Catherine, the most likely name under this initial, and even if it should turn out to be Christian, the range is not wide. No, John, let us be thankful for the C' she continued, as she and her husband resumed their seats.

'This then, Emily, is the man and woman you spoke of'? queried Mrs. Layton.

'Yes', replied the lady, 'and I think I said they were middle-aged persons'.

'There again, Mr. Orrason', suggested Mary, 'C.G. was middle-aged and so was his wife Catherine or Christian – another limit to the wide field of enquiry'.

'Is there any circumstance', enquired Orrason, 'by which the two persons could be distinguished by coming from or going to some particular place? Otherwise the information received must prove of little use. We are bent on discovering my connection – my parents, if they are alive – and, at any rate, to find out how I came and where I came into the world. If you can help us with any remembered scrap, we shall feel deeply grateful', and he waited his answer.

'The man, if I remember rightly', said the governess Emily, 'remained in the lobby while his wife brought the child to my room. She handed me a parcel of linens for the child, some of it very fine, and patterned in a way rarely seen on such things. And this minds me', she went on, 'that I have in my possession one of the finer towels which the woman left with me'.

'Kindly fetch it here, Emily', said Mrs. Layton, in a voice of authority, and the servant turned towards the door and disappeared with greater alacrity than she had yet shown.

Meanwhile, poor Mr. Layton, gradually recovering himself, had his pillows readjusted and, sitting up, he viewed the company now assembled. Reaching out his attenuated hand as the governess Emily returned to the room, he looked carefully at the little piece of linen damask – for such it was – folded it up again and, handing it to his wife, uttered the words, 'Dunfarlin' make!', looking into his wife's face as he did so.

'I believe it is, Andrew', she returned, 'Do you remember if there was anything said about Dunfermline, Emily, when the child was left'?

'One thing suggests another, 'replied the governess, ' and now I do remember that the woman, while taking tea with me in a hurried way before going, talked once or twice of that town, and I felt convinced that she and her husband had come thence`.

`The same memory dwells with me`, added Mrs. Layton, `though I had no speech with her except when parting; and then it was only some remark made by yourself, Emily, as to her getting back by the Canal, that made me think at all of Dunfermline. And now, Mr. Orrason, allow me to congratulate you on the success, small though it be, with which your search has already been crowned, and allow me also to thank you for the visit you and your wife have made to your early home. I feel proud to see a son of the place grow to such stalwart proportions. Mr. Layton hears all that is going on and I am sure he approves of all I am saying`. As she ceased, she turned to the sick man and, as he smiled a tearful approval, he stretched out his fingers once more, and shook hands all round as a signal for good-bye.

Before leaving the Refuge, Mrs. Orrason had made a bargain with the dark lady, Emily, for that piece of damask linen and Orrason had pressed on Mrs. Layton a number of gold and silver pieces to give a treat to the children within. With many warm expressions of friendly attachment, the visitors said good-bye and found their way to the village of Tradeston.

On the way the partners compared notes which were carefully written out when home was reached, and verbally paraded at the fireside of the Seatons later in the evening. The old folks were elated beyond measure, and Mrs. Seaton gave up her theory of the needle in the haystack, and believed now that John Orrason was in a fair way `to come by his ain again`.

CHAPTER XXVIII

Lock 16 on the Canal – The canal boats and how they were towed – Stage coach to Stirling – The poetical host of the Stirling Brown Bear.

The remainder of the evening – spent in their own house – was given by Orrason and Mary to meditation and resolve. The information gathered from the lively dominie and the dying Mr. Layton had determined our two adventurers to retrace, as nearly as possible, the actual drift of fate in the child and juvenile life of John Orrason. They now believed that John had entered Glasgow by way of the Forth and Clyde Canal and a fascination – fateful or fanciful it might be – led them by mutual consent to trace backwards, and by this waterway, the hidden events of twenty-five years before. The next morning found them at Port Dundas, the Glasgow depot for the canal. They were accompanied by Captain Seaton, but he only came, as he phrased it, `to see them off on their voyage along the muckle ditch`.

The advertisements of the Canal Company – for people could advertise then nearly as well as they do now – stated that the passage boats were fitted up in the most commodious and elegant style, and that cabin passengers would find everything on board that could minister to comfort and convenience. The cabins, it was claimed, were spacious and the steerage airy and pleasant, the stewards attentive and the master careful to a fault, all of which Mary and Orrason took with a big grain of salt.

However, having committed their heavier boxes to the tender mercies of the company's track boats for delivery in Dunfermline, they booked themselves for Lock 16, and thence by `coach, chariot, caravan, or wagon`, as the hand-bills had it, to the `town of the rock` – Stirling. From here their intent would lead them by Forth's lovely shores to that ancient town of which the poets aforetime sang:

`Merry were they in the gay, green wood,

When mavis and merle were singing;
But merrier they in Dumfarlin` gray.
When a` the bells were ringing` [54].

They had a fair notion of what their journey would involve and, if it presented features that were not wholly attractive, both were young, strong and itching for adventure. They had read honest John Mayne`s eulogy of the `big ditch` through which they were about to sail, and both laughed as Mary recited:

`Athort the land frae Forth to Clyde,
Ships in a` winds and weathers glide;
An` on the bosom o` the tide,
Wi` gentle motion,
The vessels like a forest ride,
An` kiss auld ocean` [55].

The cabins, so called, were only boxes constructed under the deck, and the steerage was a weather-shaded space for two rows of opposing sitters, where the knees of the one were in knapping distance of the other. The boats were abnormally long for their breadth and, as one passenger said, looked `rather cockery for safety`.

The drawing horses, fresh and lively at first and furnished with a postillion in coloured jacket and cap, started off in fine style, and the long, coffin-shaped water conveyance got along to Stockinfield at what was considered a rapid rate, and the boat – called `a swift` – was deemed entitled to her name. The two rows of steerage folks kept rigidly to their seats and, if Orrason and Mary from the `stern sheets` watched betimes the passing scenery and the rows of rigid and restless passengers, the constant variation of the one seemed compensation for the monotony of the other.

They had reached Windford Lock near Castlecary and here most of the steerage sitters were to land. With a too common impulse they all moved quickly to the side, at the very moment when a gang of Irish labourers were jumping aboard. So many and so much weight at one place brought the gunwale of the rocking craft to the verge of swamping and, when the shifting cargo of people moved off so suddenly, the frail barque, lurching to the opposite extreme, pitched two or three of its deck dwellers into the muddy waters. There was a wild outcry and an effort at rescue. This was soon accomplished – the incident was only too common – and a fresh horse, with a fresh rider, brought our travellers to the end of their watery journey.

They arrived in gay and lively style, for the labourers who had been so incontinently dipped at Windford were in no wise damped in spirits by the wetting outside, but stripped their soaked outer garments, put the steerage seats atop of each other, and making thus a clear place on deck, danced their clothes dry and yelled themselves hoarse, in their efforts to recover their 'good sinse afther the durty trick the ould baste uv a boat had done them'.

The coach was waiting and but a few minutes were spent on Jehu's usual routine, before the vehicle – amid immense cracking of whips, and shouts for halfpence from a crowd of juvenile onlookers – was dashing along the road to Camelon, thence to Grahamston and Larbert, and on by Plains, Bannockburn, and St. Ninians to the grand old gateway of the Scottish highlands – Stirling.

Our travellers were pleased with the sight of the magnificent scenery through which they had passed, but they were unconscious that these fields and hills and plains were sacred to Scottish hearts by their connection with the mighty and unmurmuring dead, who built up the fame and independence of Scotland in the brave days of old.

Night was fast settling down on the 'sons of the rock' when the stage coach carrying our hero and his bride drove into Stirling by the old St. Ninian's Road, turned into King Street and pulled up at the doors of the Brown Bear [56]. Here, mine host, looking carefully after his own business, bustled about with immense activity, directing everybody else, and smiling on the two who had come to test his hospitality.

The accommodation, if somewhat olden, was abundant enough, and the rooms, if just a little stuffy, were soon sweetened by open sashes, and were found, so far as appointments were concerned, to be in excellent form.

Hungry, stiff and tired – for even love and enthusiasm will not ward off these 'plaints of nature – our travellers soon paid their respects to the food mine host placed, smoking and inviting, before them.

``Tis rather cold travelling by stage in these biting east winds, Mr. Snoddy`, said Orrason, handing his card – with its nautical device of the ship in full sail – to the landlord.

The landlord – who had a curious habit of talking in rhyme – replied `Cold it is, indeed, sir, but a joyous fire fulfils desire, and we shall have remede, sir`, and he smiled softly as he scanned Orrason`s card. `Oh, yes! In the sea line, I opine`, he said, looking towards Orrason and indicating the pictured ship. Orrason nodded and Boniface continued:-

`I hope the noble lady here, will find at least some passing cheer, to beit the season of the year`. `Thanks for your good wishes`, said Orrason. `Thanks, indeed`, added Mary, `seeing they are so prettily expressed`. The poetical host laughed and, with a profusion of bows and smiles, he disappeared.

When appetite on good digestion waits, the viands quickly disappear, and Orrason and Mary acknowledged, by their actions, that this saying was true, and both felt better fitted for the work ahead than they did when leaving the coach.

CHAPTER XXIX

An anti-resurrectionist row in Stirling – Wrecking the body-snatcher's house – The Provost and police to the rescue.

Mr. and Mrs. Orrason had hardly eaten when, attracted by what appeared to be an extraordinary tumult in the street below, they looked into King Street and were at once struck with wonder at what they now beheld.

People were rushing in mad groups, now across the open areas, now into Spittal Street, now into Friars Wynd – enquiring, shouting and evidently filled with rage at some real or imagined evil.

'What can it be'? Mary asked and, as she spoke, she pulled up the window sash, and peered into the poorly lighted streets. The ominous roar of an angry crowd surged in at once. 'Some calamity has happened – see! The women and girls are as wild as the men'.

'Something has happened in Stirling to stir even a Scottish crowd', and Orrason, listening to the words floating upwards, leaned out over the sill to catch their meaning.

''The resurrectionists'! I hear them calling', and he turned inwards as he spoke. 'The resurrectionists! Lay hands on them! Pull down their d-d house about them! Smash the doors and bring them out, and we'll soon make an end of them and their horrible deeds'!

Mary looked anxious. 'There is nothing will stir a Scottish crowd to more unreasonable wrath than the thought of a resurrectionist' [57].

'But what does it all mean'? Orrason asked.

'A resurrectionist is what people further south would call a body-snatcher', said Mary in explanation'.

'See, Mary', said Orrason, hurriedly peering into the growing darkness, 'how that crowd there is fighting and struggling. I must go out and see how the whole thing has arisen. Will you find something to do till I return`? But he did not wait an answer. He dashed into the hall and lifted his hat, and a minute later Mary faintly saw his form rushing across the street.

By this time the crowds were surging out of the Bow, and Mary heard their scuttering feet and broken imprecations as they turned into Friars` Wynd. From this quarter came ominous sounds of wild deeds of destruction and Mary expected every minute to see the red glare of fire upon the houses and the sky.

It appeared, too, from the stillness that reigned about her, that she was left alone, if not within the hotel, at least within the room. Uncertain fears, the worst of all fears, began to agitate her breast, and she was cross with her husband for leaving her, even in the excitement of the moment. This mood, however, lasted but an instant, and her next move was to find her way into the street, discover the cause of the wild mob and bring her beloved out of danger.

Mary was a resourceful woman and she had hardly formed the resolution to sally forth when she had fitted herself, in her ancient Linktown fashion, with head-and-shoulder shawl, and was passing through the hall. Here she met the vastly concerned host who implored her not to venture forth, as the crowd was now fairly roused, smashing the houses in Friars` Wynd and `throwing volleys of stone in every direction, though the provost has gone to secure protection`.

`If that be so, if the provost is out, so will I be. Look after our things, we`ll be back within the hour`, and the darkness swallowed her light form as she swept from the door of the Brown Bear.

In the poorly-lit street she was compelled to allow herself to be guided by the same instincts as those which had drawn out almost every member of the crowd. Hurried feet and half-muffled forms ran hastily past her and, as she enquired what was going on, the answer came in hasty, passing form, `Th` croods i` th` wynd are smashin` the hoose o` Clantabber`.

`And who is Clantabber`?

`The villain that`s been liftin` the dead and sellin` the bodies to the cuttin`-up doctors`, and the crowd passed on.

Mary followed as best she could and soon found herself in a

thickening mass of human beings, literally jammed between the buildings on either side of the wynd, and all looking to where fitful and glaring lights marked the centre of the crowd's activity. Determined to know more of the meaning of the fray, to watch results and to know the worst as to Orrason, she forced a way through the dense gathering and was soon in front of a house already completely wrecked.

Doors and windows had been forced from their hinges and smashed to a thousand pieces, even many of the tiles on the roof and the cans on the chimneys – as she could see by the objects projecting against the sky – were reduced to fragments. One stone, better aimed than any other, had struck the owner and inhabitant of the house and felled him at his own fireside, and the sight – or knowledge only – of even the hated Clantabber being now helpless and insensible on his own hearthstone, seemed to mollify the fierce anger of the mob, for the volleying of stones abated, and the cries for vengeance became less tumultuous.

At that moment, Provost Thomson and Sheriff Macdonald appeared on the scene, and the crowd, being suddenly carried off by a new and wilder impulse, turned out of the wynd and, in their stampede, carried our heroine completely off her feet into the freer and more open spaces of King Street and Baker Street. As she stood here, the officers, seizing the opportunity, hurried the wounded Clantabber from his house in the wynd to the safer quarters of the town prison.

Waiting for a moment to catch her wits and her breath, Mary saw the direction in which the crowd was rushing and, undeterred by her rough usage in the wynd, she again followed on the skirts of the maddened mob. The crowd passed into the narrow gullet of Spittal Street and then on to St. John Street, where they resumed the work of destruction.

Anxious not to fall behind, Mary crushed through the eager moving mass and soon found herself again in the centre of the activity.

The cry was not now for vengeance on Clantabber. Not this name but that of Stitchell now caught her ear and the fury which she had seen in the choked-up wynd seemed to be redoubled in the wider area of St. John Street. The same cries, the same wild oaths and the same terrible invocations for death and destruction filled the thickening darkness of the night.

The glass and frames of the windows, the doors and passages were rapidly forced, and every obstruction ruthlessly torn down, till the building in front of the mob was all but wrecked.

Suddenly, a police-officer – with a man Mary did not at first recognize – dashed through the thickest of the mob and, skirting her position, disappeared into the house. The officers of the law had perceived that nothing could save the shrinking and wretched man within, short of lodging him in some other and stronger place, and had called on every law-abiding indweller to render assistance in maintaining order. No one had responded to the call, except the solitary man that Mary had seen rushing into the beleaguered dwelling.

In a few minutes the two had again appeared bringing the prisoner Stitchell with them. Amazed and alarmed, Mary perceived that the officer's single assistant was none other than Orrason himself. She could hardly restrain herself as the officer, with his powerful helper, made a gallant attempt to open a clear space in front of the door, and to extricate the prisoner from the clutches of the crowd. The strange man – strange to the Stirling mob – drew at once their attention and curiosity, and diverted them for a time from their wilder designs.

The two rescuers took advantage of the passing lull, but their united efforts proved in the end wholly unavailing. They had only succeeded in freeing their man from the dangers inside to expose him to the greater dangers outside the house. Within the house he had some short respite from injury but in the street he was open to immediate attack.

Castle Wynd, Stirling

CHAPTER XXX

The 77ᵗʰ from the Castle take part in the melee – A `wild Scotch crowd` – Mine host of the Brown Bear poetically inclined – A Stirlingshire farmer`s opinion of the `collyshangie` and how it happened.

The rescuers had scarcely got Stitchell out of the imprisoning house, when he was wrenched from their grasp, thrown to the ground, and kicked and beaten with the madness of insensate rage. Despite the most daring and desperate attempts of the officer and his helper, the miserable man was reduced to the last stage of exhaustion. Almost blind from weakness, wounds and mud he struggled to his feet. It was, however, only for a moment. He was again seized, his coat torn to ribbons and the rest of his garments stripped from his writhing body and flung among the crowd.

By a last effort of his defenders he, being a man of considerable strength and endurance, got himself free of his persecutors and, making a dash for the door next to his own which stood invitingly open, he got fairly inside and had time to breathe. The crowd, repeating their operations of the wynd, soon wrecked the doors and windows of this house and some of the more daring among the leaders had forced an entrance.

Stitchell had, however, with the aid of his two faithful assistants, escaped by a back entrance to the house, and so cheated, for a time at least, the vengeance of the mob. For, entering a third house in the same row, he there became barricaded and protected till the arrival for the second time of Provost Thomson, who this time brought, not only the sheriff, but Captain Jeffrey and a file of the 77th Regiment, then lying in the Castle.

The crowd had by this time filled all the streets on the eastern slope and but one desire seemed to stir them all – vengeance, dire and effectual, on the men who had spoiled the graves of their dead. The provost and the sheriff, animated with a sincere desire to see the crowd disperse without having recourse to arms, warned the men and women present of the wholly unlawful nature of their proceedings. He told them of the utter folly of their doings, and asked them to return at once from the streets to their homes.

This kindly warning of Provost Thomson was heard in every word by Mary, as she stood – now eager to see the end – within earshot of the speaker. The crowd, as it had collected from impulsive motives, proved still as obdurately unreasonable, and yelled defiance to his words.

A whole Company of the 77th was now brought down to the scene and soon formed a clear space round the door of Stitchell's refuge. On a given signal, the door was thrown open and, in the faint light of the street, the solitary officer came forth with his prisoner, with John Orrason, on the other side, shielding him from the pressing crowd.

Mary Seaton could not restrain a cry of alarm when she saw again her husband in the midst of that wild sea of angry faces, and made a rapid and frantic effort to reach his side. He heard the cry soon as it escaped her lips, and turned round to see from whence the voice had come and saw a fair woman, partly muffled in a shawl, breaking strongly through the crowd. Muffled though she was, he knew the figure, the voice and the manner too well to be deceived.

Letting the unhappy man Stitchell go – for he was now safe within the cordon of soldiers formed around him – he dashed to the edge of the encircling ring.

'Oh, Mary! Why are you here? Why did you leave your room? You can do no good, and you are in danger'.

'If I am in danger, John, how much more are you? And where you are there must I be also'.

The soldiers, moving forward with their prisoner, now compelled the crowd to give way. This they did, but only as crowds usually do – by venting the wildest imprecations alike on the soldiers and their prisoner. Stones were thrown among the former, and not a few of these were bruised and cut on face and hands. So terribly were the men abused by the retreating crowd that several levelled their pieces and fired. The commanding officer pleaded with his men not to aim at any 'son of the rock', to respect the lives of the citizens, and to believe that the morrow would see them in better and more sensible mood. The men and the crowd – still fierce – passed on to the doors of the prison. The portals opened and the man, Stitchell – the cause of all this wild tumult – was hurriedly thrust inside.

'Come, Mary, we have seen the first and last of this wild Scotch crowd, it is no place for you'; and Orrason caught her arm in his.

'Nor for you', said Mary in reply, 'and I can never be less daring than yourself'.

The crowd made way and, though the people cursed the man for aiding in the escape of their intended victim, they could not help admiring and praising them both for risking so much in the discharge of duty and, in the case of the woman, at the bidding of love.

They reached the door of the Brown Bear, and the busy, anxious host was in the entrance waiting the safe return of his guests. 'Welcome as the flowers of May, welcome from this gruesome fray`, exclaimed the fussy little man as he led our heroic two into the parlour, and continued, laughing as he spoke, `why went you forth this crowd to see, and put yoursels in jeopardy`?

Placing seats for the now fast arriving frequenters of the Bear, he whisked round the table, smiling to one, remarking to another, and finally whispering introductions to his two daughters who had just come on the scene.

Ladies, as well as gentlemen, were, included in the company, and the two female representatives of the Snoddy family were much in request.

`This is a bonnie collyshangie an` nae mistak``, said an excited farmer from the bottom of the table. `What in a` the earth does it mean, and hoo did it come aboot`? And he looked round for answer.

`It just means this, Turfhills`, replied the farmer *vis-à-vis* across the board, addressing his friend by the name of his farm. `It just means this – an` ye`ll better pay attention, for ye ken ye hae`na muckle gumption anent thae things – Lord Gillies, ane o` the Court o` Session birkies has been handlin` what they ca` a Circuit Coort in the toon o` Stirlin` to bring to trial a` the biggest rogues i` the place, an` gie them their due rewards`.

`An` wis ye no ta`en up yersel` observed Turfhills, slyly, `after sellin` me that angle-berried broon mare, Towriggs? They shoud`na left you oot o` the coont`.

The whole company laughed at Towrigg`s expense, enjoying the joke.

`Weel, weel, maybe, Turfhills, let that flee stick to the wa`. But I was tellin` ye aboot the real rogues – no` the imaginary kind that ye dabble among – and, among the undisputed vagabonds that cam` before his Lordship, were three o` thae resurrectionists I think ye ca` them. Ane was a young hempie, a student o` medicine named Moods, an` the ither twa were Clantabber an` Stitchell. Moods was in need o` subjects – a genteel way o` sayin` dead bodies – and he engaged the twa` mool howkers to lift the deid oot o` the graveyards – when the moon micht be behint a thick cloud, ye ken – an` bring them to him.

The twa had been weel watched, an' a hail string o' stories – baith horrible an' awfu' – were soon whispered and barkit roond baith toon an' country. Han' me a dram noo', demanded the speaker, stretching his hand in the direction of what was known as the 'tappit hen'.

'Tape it oot canny till he gets through wi' his story', loudly whispered Turfhills, as the landlord poured out a refresher to Towriggs. 'He'll get tongue-tackit an' stupid if ye gie him owre muckle'. Again the company roared in merriment.

'A nailer frae St. Ringan's [58], resumed Towriggs, 'gaun hame wi' a dram in his noddle ae nicht, saw the twa howkers, wi' spades an' shools, hidin' ahint a gravestone. A weaver body frae Bannockburn swarfed clean awa when he met Stitchell wi' a lang soople pock on his back, an' when the kirk bedrall saw baith the unearthly villains loading a powny cairt owre the kirk yaird dyke, he drappit the Bible an' lost the Psalm Book amang the snaw, an' never after that could look up to the laft whaur Clantabber an' Stitchell sat. An' at last when the twa thochtless devils gaed into Lucky Macvicar's change house to get a drap o' the Auld Kirk [59] to wash awa' cadaverous smells, an' smerten them up after their dreary work – leavin' the white powny an' the cairt at the door – that gleg-eyed cratur, Tammy Toddie, frae the Raploch, cam' by an' the game was played oot. Raploch saw in a minute what the sacks in the cairt contained. He juist took the powny by the head an' drove it richt up to Bailie Shoobuckle's door, ca'd him oot an', lichtin' a caunle, bade him look at the contents. That blew the coal a thegether. Clantabber an' Stitchell were surprised in Lucky Macvicar's; Moods' connection wi' the body-snatchers was made clear in a jiffy, an' a' the three were apprehended, made fast i' the jail for a while, an' then examined an' let out on bail. Moods made his heels his cautioner an' fled the country. The ither twa were brocht before His Lordship but, the young hempie being beyond their reach, there was nothing' in the way o' evidence to convict the twa howkers, and they were, this afternoon, discharged frae the bar. The folk were mad wi' rage; they rose in mass to invoke Judge Lynch, the riot ensued – an ye ken the rest'.

CHAPTER XXXI

The `crisis o` the fecht` – A night at the `Bear` – Sunday in Stirling – A visit to Bannockburn – An enthusiastic native`s address at the `Bore Stone` – Historic Stirling.

'Thanks for your explanation, my dear sir` spoke out Orrason, looking towards Towriggs. `Some of your phrases are a little hard to understand but you have made clear most details of this extraordinary outbreak`.

This short remark drew the attention of all present to the speaker. The tongue was strange, the mode of speech uncommon and the dress more that of a merchant seaman that of a commercial man or a farmer.

`Gentlemen `tis only due, that I should introduce to you, Orrason, the honoured name, which should be known and blest by Fame`, announced the facetious landlord.

`Hear, hear, Snoddy`, echoed the company, while Orrason himself rose and bowed.

`If I am not mistaken`, said a perky carpet-bagger at the head of the board, `that is the gent I seen a-helping of the officer to put the body-snatcher Stichell inside of the prison-house. It was a brave stroke, it was, and I honour the gentleman that made it`.

`Hear, hear`, once more from Turfhills, Towriggs and the rest.

`There`s nae doot o` that`, struck in Turfhills, `an` noo, since we`ve got time to cool doon a bit, we may be a` thankful` that naebody lost their lives in the daftness o` the moment. It was as near as onything cou`d be that it didna actually happen. That time the half-drunk sodger fell doon among the feet o` the crood, wi` his loaded musket in his feckless hands, an` the folk began to struggle and wrestle wi` baith the police an` the sodgers – that time was the crisis o` the fecht, an` if naebody was shot dead or wounded, we owe it in great measure to Provost Thomson and to the gentleman now present who so gallantly assisted him`.

`Leave off, gentlemen, if you please`. Orrason observed, `I think it only right in times of fierce excitement to tide the moment quietly over, if possible, so that justice and law and order may be maintained and lawless rule prevented. I had not the least notion of what all the noise and destruction was due to, and I only learned in a very dim fashion the bearings of the quarrel when I had for some time been moving among the crowd but, when I heard that Judge Lynch had been invoked by the good people of Stirling, I felt that a mistake had been made or was about to be made somewhere and – in what I did – simply wished to preserve the good name of the city, and the sons of the rock. But I was sorry I had gone into the sweltering crowd, when I found that my example had drawn at least one other into danger`, and he looked into Mary`s face as he sat down.

Mary blushed and the Misses Snoddy looked for explanations to their father who, looking to Orrason, broke out amid laughter:

`Ah! well, no doubt, that`s very true,

The saying`s very good for you;

But then it is a woman`s right

To back her husband in a fight,

And leave to her what she might say,

If he should fight and run away`!

`Aye, but there was no rennin` awa`, `said Towrigg, `unless it micht be frae the wynd to St. John Street, and frae the croon o` the Causway tae the jail door, an` I`m greatly mista`en if oor friend Orrason is ane o` the kind for rennin` awa` in ony case, an` wi` his wife at his back he waud be waur than daft tae attempt it`.

`Hear, hear, that`s unca true, as ye ken by experience, Towrigg`, and Turfhills winked slyly at his friend.

In this way with jokes and even a song or two, the company whiled away the evening hours at the Bear, till someone suggested retirement for the night. No objection being raised, the host wished them all sound sleep and pleasant dreams, bowed and disappeared.

The Sabbath bells – the ringing bells – awaked our travellers the next morning and bid them realize it was Sunday in Stirling. Needless to say this day was spent as all respectable Scotch people spent it, at the Kirk. Whether the Sabbath was wholly given to devotion may be doubted, for by Monday morning Orrason and his wife had a programme made for the day to visit Bannockburn, return to Stirling and thence move on to Dunfermline by the afternoon stage.

Breakfast over, and their luggage prepared for flitting, Orrason and Mary and a few others from the Bear drove out by an early conveyance to the ever-famous field of Bannockburn [60]. Arrived in the vicinity, they were guided to the Bored Stone by the knots of pilgrims that sought their way to the little height As they reached the gathering congregation, Orrason and Mary they turned their gaze to the south and looked across the plain by which the day before they had reached the City of the Rock.

Orrason had read much of his country's history and thought much and often over its varied fortunes. Yet, while being whirled over that plain the day before, he never once thought he was traversing ground made classic for all time by a thousand memories in the life and experience of a small, but influential people. Now, when the rough region of hill and plain met his eye, thoughts came hurrying through his brain of dead-and-gone heroes, of poor and wretched royalties, of cavalcades and progresses, of invasions, irruptions, and wild death – and – life struggles that raged over and consecrated these fields.

Both Orrason and Mary turned as a voice attuned to homespun Doric, yet having a ring of dignity and force, broke over the heads of the little crowd assembled round the Bored Stone. The voice came from a man clothed in the common lowland garb, whose face was marked with the deep depression and high ridges of the Scottish countenance, whose brow was broad rather than high, and whose head – for the broad blue bonnet was carried in the hand of the owner – was crowned in locks of iron grey.

'Men and women', he said, 'for this is not a place for ladies and gentlemen – we stand here around the real heart of Scotland. Not only of her independence as a nation, nor even of that military renown of which we are sometimes proud, but the heart and life-giving centre of all her greatness in art and science, in literature and philosophy, in poetry and religion, and in all those glowing features of our human nature, which mark and refine the intercourse between man and man.

We are apt to think of Bannockburn as simply a great military triumph, and to forget that the victory here – one of right over might – was not only a subduing of all those forces which go to the making of a spiritless, deceptive, indifferent, or superstitious people, but was, as much and more, the breaking of those fetters which bind down and humble the aspiring nature of a noble race.

Independence in the individual man is the first condition of progress, the first essential element of elevation. In the case of a nation it is no less so. The man who feels that his actions and expressions only echo the will of another, and who thereby loses dignity and self-respect and self-reliance, only typifies the nation which has been subdued, and which has no consciousness of self-impelled enterprise, risk, or research. Both sink in the scale of being, and crawl and cringe as they approach, but are too spiritless to climb the heights of refinement and beauty.

It was a fight in which the forces of tyranny were as three to one, but the arms of the Scots, like those of the prophet, were upheld by a great, if unseen, power because for once in our history there was no division in motive or desire.

There to the front are the rough ridgy banks of the Bannock. There to the left are the undulating heights from which Edward charged. That sloping field yonder marks the place where the Scottish cavalry scattered the English archers. The hollow ground to the left front is the bog of Milton, where pits and trenches were sunk, and where the huge, unmanageable mass of Edward's forces became easy prey to the all-devouring spears of the Scots. Away there to the north-east and to the east and south are the knolls and gullies and swampy meads where the forces of tyranny devoured each other by their very bulk and numbers; and far away, beyond the reach of sight, are the fields and haughs and woods, where the bodies of the slain, for miles and miles around, lay scattered and torn`.

The speaker ceased his discourse and, donning his cap, he strode downhill, inviting all who would to follow him over the historic field of Bannockburn. An hour or two spent here amid the grey mists of the growing day, and under the guidance and of their genial and inspiring guide, sufficed to gratify the rising patriotism alike of Mary and Orrason.

They drove back to Stirling and to the Bear and dined there under the auspices of Mr. Snoddy. They visited the Castle and gazed upon that wondrous contrast of winding river and receding plain to the east, of towering mountains to the west, and of blooming fields and rough isolated hills. They entered the Hall of Parliaments, the old Palace of the Kings; they gazed on every stone and thought of long past scenes enacted in the Douglas room.

And peered into the dangerous dark and deep,

Where ghosts, imprisoned, wail and weep [61].

Well satisfied, they returned to mine host and got ready to leave for the Grey City.

The Spire Inn, Dunfermiline

CHAPTER XXXII

*The castaway and his wife at the Spire Inn, Dunfermline –
A conundrum – Rankine, the Master of Song in the Old Abbey –
An important interview with him.*

The road by which the stage and mail coaches of the 1820s measured
the distance between Stirling and Dunfermline started from the
former place by crossing the Forth as it does now, running north to
Causwayhead and then striking east by Cambus, Alloa, Clackmannan,
Kincardine, Torryburn and Cairneyhill.

The region is a delightful one for quiet, rich, far-stretching views.
The level reaches of the carse of the Forth on the way to Alloa, are
rendered to the highest degree inspiring by the near vicinity of the
towering – yet soft and undulating – outline of the Ochil Hills, while

the broadening river and Firth have the charming variation of finely wooded backgrounds to the east, and hills and straths further west. The quiet villages, and quieter waters of the bays and creeks at Culross and Kincardine, delighted our travellers, while the quaint, red-tiled cottages of the nestling towns, with their weaving populations, recalled to Orrason and Mary alike similar scenes in the Links of Kirkcaldy of many years before. At Newmilns, the weavers, with white or coloured apron, enjoying an afternoon pipe at the shop door, presented a picture so like Peter Saunders as almost to belie the assertion of difference.

The view westward from Torryburn was – as it still is – one of the finest and grandest of its kind to be seen anywhere in Scotland. The ancient woods at Craigflower formed a happy contrast to the long, weary-looking village of Cairneyhill, although the plantations at Pitfirrane and the gardens of Crossford restored the feeling of pleasure and satisfied the desire for natural beauty. Climbing Kate Simpson's Brae [62] over the bridge and up through the ugly cut at Urquhart, Orrason and Mary, having seen the spire of the Abbey glittering above the trees in Pittencrieff Glen, soon found themselves in Dunfermline – the City of the Crooked Stream – and at the door of the Spire Inn [63].

Received in mine host Laidlaw's effusive style, our travellers quickly made themselves at home in the upper chambers of his hostelry. Reared on the highest point of the High Street, the Spire – now (in 1896) the County Buildings – over-topped all the southern part of the town, and Orrason and Mary's windows opened on a view of such magnificence as is rarely to be matched anywhere. The peaks of the far-receding Pentlands were touched with the crimson rays of the setting sun and sinking into the grey of the evening clouds, as our weary wanderers endeavoured to shake off the fatigue of their twenty miles drive.

Supper had been discussed, and the introductions to landlord and guests got over, when a letter – forwarded from Captain Seaton – was handed to the arrivals. The gallant captain expressed his warmest good wishes, and his confident anticipation that Mr. and Mrs. Orrason 'would find out all they had gone forth to seek and discover', and the good Mrs. Seaton was fully persuaded that her 'twa bairns, in the matters o` seekin` an` speirin` would neither come back wi` a toom hand nor a thowless account o` their pilgrimage`.

Enclosed was an intimation of the death of Mr. Layton of the Refuge. The note was written by Mrs. Layton herself and stated that her husband had died on the day succeeding the visit of Mr. and Mrs. Orrason. His death came swiftly at the end but not before he had added something to the story. The two women had been talking in whispers of the visit, and trying to recall the incidents of twenty-five years before. Mr. Layton, with eyes closed, had been listening to the conversation, and suddenly he turned himself in the bed, raised his head and said:

`The man`s name was Charley – for his wife, I remember, said `Charley, we`ll hae to go – let us catch the next boat – they`ll be waitin` on us at hame`.

Further speech, wrote Mrs. Layton, had been stopped by a severe fit of coughing, from which Mr. Layton never recovered.

Next day broke over the Auld Grey Town as one of the opening days of summer. The sanguine omens of the night before had spoken truly:

`The evening red and the morning gray,
Had kythed in the light of a golden day`.

Breakfast over, and the preliminaries of the day`s proceedings settled, Orrason rang the bell.

`Kindly send up Mr. Laidlaw, will you`?

The servant at once disappeared and the tall form of mine host was soon in evidence.

`Can I be of any service`? he said, as he bowed to the lady and looked towards the gentleman.

`That remains to be proved`, replied Orrason, smiling and beckoning to a seat, `are you good at conundrums`?

`The very poorest hand you could possibly find`, and host Laidlaw smiled in return. `No, no; conundrums are not in my line, sir`.

`Will you try`?

`Certainly, sir. Will you propound the puzzle`?

`There, Mr. Laidlaw, is the cryptogram I want solved`. And

Orrason handed a slip of paper across the table. `You see thereon the initials `C.G. and C`, conveyed in the words `Left by C. G. and his wife C. 25th Oct. 1799`.

`Now the first two are the initials of a man`s name – and we now know that the man`s first name was Charley – and the single letter that of his wife. You will see the date runs back over a quarter of a century. What I want is the man himself to whom these letters belong – the single initial of his wife might help us. Can you do anything`?

`No, sir, I fear I cannot – I presume they are both Dunfermline people`?

`Ah! Yes, I forgot to say so, but doubtless both of them are, or were, resident in Dunfermline. We – my wife and I – want to find them`.

`Well, I am sorry to say the date of the slip is some eighteen years before I came to town and, though I know a good many people in it, I don`t see how I can help you in this puzzle, though I should be glad to do so`, and the landlord was about to retire.

`One minute, Mr. Laidlaw` – it was Mary who spoke. `It strikes me we might at least get the first step of progress in our wild goose chase from yourself`.

`Command me, my lady, in any way I can help`, chimed in mine host.

`Is there anything in the idea of calling on the registrar, and scanning his marriage list, do you think`? questioned Mary.

`Yes – well, there might be – and if anyone can help you in the matter, it must be the man who keeps the people`s name-books. He is James Rankine and he is also the master of the song of Dunfermline Abbey`, replied Laidlaw [64].

`The notion is a good one`, said Orrason, `and points the way we must proceed, while being aware that the least expected quarter may also furnish the clue we need. Mr. Laidlaw will tell us where we may we find this recording angel`.

Orrason stopped suddenly for the landlord had broken into a burst of laughter.

`Excuse me, sir, and you too, madam, but I could not help it. The idea of James Rankine being likened to an angel was just too strong for me`, and the great hearty man laughed loudly as before and with such effect that that both his guests laughed in chorus with him. `But don`t mistake me – he is a good, honest man, and if singing to please the heart and the ear could make an angel, Jamie will take first rank`.

`Well, of course, we can only guess what makes you laugh so much, but you have roused our curiosity to such an extent, we must see this worthy without delay. Can you direct us`? and Orrason waited a reply.

`Certainly; everyone knows where the master of the song lives. When you are ready to go, a messenger will be ready to guide you`, and Mr. Laidlaw turned and disappeared.

In a short space the guide appeared at the door and led the Orrasons from the Shire to a house, now no longer in existence, in North Inglis Street. Admitted and seated, they were quickly joined by a young man of the middle height, strongly made, with brown hair, a smile on his face and a lurking air of merriment in his fine blue eyes.

James Rankine was in his day one of the best-liked men in West Fife, and as a singer of the auld Scotch songs, loved and appreciated everywhere [65]. His easy, happy manner, his sanguine countenance and his open expression endeared him to everyone.

The outburst of laughter of Mr. Laidlaw at the Spire might have been natural if Rankine was held only as a boon companion, but must have appeared impious and misplaced to anyone hearing the master of the song on a Sunday rendering the inspired lays of Israel`s royal bard. The sacred lays of the royal David were never treated to musical interpretation with such grace and faithfulness of expression as by the master of the song at Dunfermline Abbey, yet as a free-and-easy, cheerful, even a jolly man, there were few to rival James Rankine.

`Good day to you both`, said the master of the song as Orrason and Mary entered, `how can I serve you`?

`We want your services in a somewhat curious way, Mr. Rankine, and possibly your patience may be exhausted even in the telling of our errand`, said Orrason, apologetically.

`You had better risk it at any rate, till we see what we can pit up wi`, the singer-recorder observed smilingly. `Sae mony folk come here on thieveless errands that ane has to be sharp sometimes when they wou`d rather be easy`.

`Will you oblige, Mr. Rankine, by reading that slip of writing`, and Orrason handed the registrar the mystical ribbon of paper.

`Weel, I can mak` that oot no sae ill, but I maun say the sense or meanin` thereof is mair in the way o` mystery than explanation. Can you mak` it clear`?

`Only this far`, put in Orrason. `These initials are those of a man who – we are bound to believe – lived in Dunfermline at the date given, that is twenty-five years ago, and he may be living still, and we are here to-day to try whether it were possible to find who C. G. is or was`.

`Aye, man, but that is a puzzle! For mysel`, it would tak` me back to aboot the time o` my comin` into the world, and I wasna then in the toon. It is only some four or five years since I cam` to Dumfarlin`, and canna ca` up onybody among my acquaintances bearin` sic initials. Then, as for seekin` through the books for a man initialed by C. G., and his wife lettered by a single C., that looks to me like seekin` through Moss Maurin for last year`s thistle taps [66]`. And Rankine looked a picture of humorous despair.

`Indeed, is the case as bad as that`? asked Mary, somewhat alarmed. `It would only be the marriage register you would require to run through`.

`Nae doot, my good lady, but ye maun keep in mind that the man who carried thae initials twenty-five years syne micht be married, wha kens, mony years before that`. An` then wha can tell whether he was married in Dumfarlin`, or in a parish maybe a hunder mile awa`? Do ye no see what a wilderness o` possibilities begin to open up when ye look fairly athort the question`? And the good-natured Rankine looked comically serious over the matter.

`We found out only last night that the man`s name was Charley. It is but small help, I admit`, observed Orrason; `but the enquiry, if successful, must in the long-run be made up of a host of little things`.

Here Mary and Orrason explained something of the circumstances connected with their enquiry and, though they did not as yet disclose the personal interest they had in the matter, they showed that their motives were of the highest kind and of the deepest interest to them.

'I should like to state further', said Orrason, 'that twenty-five years ago the man, C. G., and his wife, C., were said to be of the middle age'.

'Which may mean', retorted the man of song, 'that the parties micht hae been married twenty-five years before that, or, indeed, now running well up to their jubilee'.

'I would take it that C. G. and C. – supposing her to be his first wife – were married about 1770. A few years before or after that date will limit the possible period of the marriage', observed Orrason, looking towards Rankine.

'I think you're right about the time', said Mary.

'Aye, man, but that hint aboot the second wife is a sair thocht, an' suggests the possibility o' twa or three different letters taking the place o' C as ye gang backwards. However, there's my books up there i' the shelf and, though it's a tapitless kind o' a job, I'll arrange to hae the marriage register run through, an' gie ye a list o' men named Charley G. and his wife C. Of course, if the folk be dead and gone ye'll hae nae use for the names'? Rankine laughed.

'No, no – no use in that case', chorused Mary and Orrason.

'Weel a weel', said Rankine, rising. 'If ye ca' back in a day or two – or in a week or twa – we'll see how far ye've got towards your ettle'. And the genial master of the song and session recorder bowed out his callers with a grace and *bonhomie* rarely met with in officials of parochial routine.

CHAPTER XXXIII

A drive to Limekilns and Charlestown – 'A weird mystery of memory' –
The cottage at Rosythe

Whether it was that Orrason and his wife had concluded that Dunfermline, in some way, had a special claim upon their respect and affection, it was difficult to say, but we know that both of them lingered among its quaint and awkward-looking streets, its queer broken-up site, its ancient, royal, and ecclesiastical ruins and the beauties of its glen, for days after all ostensible reasons for stay had been gone. They had thought over the difficult task undertaken by the registrar, and had come to the conclusion that any search in the local name lists must require considerable time and they would not hurry that part of the enquiry.

Orrason was delighted with the aspect and the environs of the old grey toon, and every day found him and his wife walking or driving in the vicinity.

They had climbed the hills of Saline, and gazed on the flowers and fruits of this garden of West Fife; they had familiarized themselves with the literary and polemical shades of Carnock [67], and mused among the tombs and sylvan beauties of Abercrombie [68].

Gladly would they have lingered in this latter place, but other points of attraction awaited them, and the great business which had called them forth must still be pursued. In the end it was chance that came to their aid.

In their easy goings to and fro, they had driven one day to the prettily situated village of Charlestown, where the shipping operations going on there, small though these were, proved a pleasant surprise to Orrason. No less were both enchanted with the quaint, picturesque village of Limekilns and its finely wooded and towering rocky background. The shore road, winding north and eastwards, led through hay-covered, crop-clothed fields till, running down on Rosythe, it opened to the astonished eyes of our travellers, the wide, far-stretching eastward panorama of the Forth. There was then no Forth Bridge to intercept the view, and the nearer islands seemed like floating emeralds on a sea of silver; while those receding into the dim distance seemed to be resting on the airy horizon.

The scene made the eyes of both the wanderers dilate with wonder, and their hearts to expand with joy. To Orrason, the sight of sea and shore, with the huge mass of Rosythe Keep frowning from its sea-girt rock, seemed to call up a strong yearning desire and feeling of a coming revelation that he could neither understand nor explain.

When passing the farm of the Castle, a comely woman with a white cap over her silver hair leaned over an embowered gateway and looked smilingly on them as they passed. The mysterious agitation in Orrason's heart warmed up as they hurried on and, as the horses spieled the rising ground at Orchardhead [69], and ran down the slope that winds again round Castlandhill, he became more and more oppressed with unutterable emotions within. Round the hill at last, he leaned over the side of the carriage and gazed with awe-struck and affectionate wonder on the enclosed sandy beach, the stretches of soft, smooth turf, the old keep, the rocky heights east and south, and most of all on two small houses almost on the shore rocks and the toll-gates that barred the roadway.

`What ails thee, John, do you feel unwell'? enquired Mary, with a shade of alarm on her face.

`There is nothing wrong with me, Mary; but there is something about the scene before me which affects me in a way I never felt before. I feel as if it were all known to me, and that I am now passing through a land I knew in some former state of existence`, and he turned restlessly in his seat as the horses paced slowly forwards.

`That is a strange kind of feeling, John. How do you, or how can *we* account for such shadowy thoughts'? And Mary looked first at her husband and then at the shimmering, silvery sea.

`The thought or notion, or whatever you may call it`, answered Orrason, `is not so much shadowy as it is foreboding something we must presently learn. I can abide the feeling no longer. We must stop and get out`, saying which, he leaned forward, spoke to the driver, and at once the carriage drew up to the roadside.

The halt was made just to the west of the present cross-roads, where patches of common ground gave verge and scope to the horses and vehicle. Orrason, pressing his hand upon his brow in an evident mental effort to recall some faintly acknowledged past, took Mary, as one child would take another, by the hand and led her forwards.

`I know not`, he said, `where I am going, but I know – for knowledge comes by strange pathways – I feel I am treading a familiar path`.

Mary knew not what to make of this mystery of memory. She had sense and feeling enough to hold the hand that pressed her own, and walk in silence, and she was rewarded, for presently Orrason let go her hand, turned towards the sea, and looked for a time steadily towards the west. The huge bulk of Rosythe was shining inverted in the waters of the bay, the wooded heights rose far above to the right, and the sandy beach with its little well-spring and streamlet was immediately beneath his eye.

`I have been here before; I have lived here before – I know it. O! Who will tell me what I then was`? And his eyes were full of enquiry and mystery.

`Do you recognize the two houses`? queried Mary.

`Yes, both of them, but one more, far more, than the other. My mystery sleeps inside the distant cottage`. He turned towards it.

As he and Mary approached, the door was opened, and the woman who came into the little porch looked curiously puzzled when she saw a great strong man coming towards her and leading a fair-haired woman like a girl by the hand.

`Can we be admitted for a little, my good woman`? enquired Orrason.

`Hoot aye, I`ll be glad to gie ye a seat – I reckon ye`ll be tired`, and she led the way to her ben room.

`It is not tiredness or weariness`, said Mary, `that tempts us inside your house. We only want to see it, and we will explain the grounds of our wish`.

'Ye're welcome baith o' ye, tae come in an' look roond, and mark whatever strikes your e'e'.

'Thanks for your kindness', and as Orrason spoke he passed into the room and looked out on the restless, glittering sea beneath.

'I know it all – my memory is yielding its secrets – I have lived here before. The fittings are changed, but the walls and ceilings and door and windows are the same. And the sea speaks to me as it must have done in my childhood'. And he gazed with rapture from the little casement.

'Do you say you have lived here before, sir'? queried the woman.

'I feel I must have lived here in my childhood. My memory had lost all trace of it till we were passing just now'.

'In this matter I cannot assist', said Mary, seeing the woman looking enquiringly towards her. 'I have never heard of the place', she explained to the woman. 'We were driving along the roadway when my husband suddenly recognized the house and the scenes around it'.

'It canna hae been in my time; an' then Mrs. Guthrie was only aboot a year i' the hoose before me, an' then Mrs. Carmichael afore her. Aye, it maun hae been back in Mrs. Macintyre's time if ony', and the good woman stopped, satisfied with her tracing of the tenantry.

'At the name of Mrs. Macintyre, Orrason gave a sudden start and turning hastily round said, 'That's the name – the dear name I have been trying to call up. It floated away among my other recollections and you have enabled me to call up and pronounce a name I never framed except with infant lips. But now her image comes to me as the ever blessed of my memory'.

He advanced to the woman, shook her warmly by the hand and pressed his thanks upon her.

'I never heard', Mary whispered to the woman, 'this name before'. Then, turning to Orrason, she asked 'Had you wholly forgotten this dear woman's name'?

'It seems to have been buried in the heart, and I must again thank our friend here for calling it back', said Orrason. Then, turning to the wondering woman before him, he asked, 'And is Mrs. Macintyre still alive, or do you know anything about her'?

'Alive! Aye, indeed she is. Weel in her health and weel aff tae, for onything that I ken. Would you like to see her'?

'I should be glad beyond measure if I could only see and speak with that dear woman once more'. And Orrason seemed carried away with anticipation.

'Weel, she'll no be ill to find', said the woman 'Let me speir, if you please, hoo did ye come alang the road'?

'We came from the west, from the village of Limekilns', said Mary.

'Weel, ye'll easily find Mrs. Macintyre gin ye'll juist drive back the road ye cam' an' tak' the first cottage ye come tae on the south side o' the road. Ye canna' weel pass it, for the rose bushes and creepers are growin' high aboon a little gateway – a bonnie an' enticin' place it is'. The woman came to a sudden stop, for Orrason and Mary were already on their feet.

With a profusion of thanks, Orrason and Mary walked rapidly to the door, called the carriage and, after settling the vigilant tollman's dues, were soon rapidly retracing their former course.

'We are directed', said Orrason, 'to the very cottage we passed on the way. You remember the white-haired woman with the whiter cap, standing under the drooping roses'?

'We are indeed', Mary replied with emotion. 'We are surely, dear John, being taken by the hand, and led into these mysteries, by a Providence that watches over us unseen'.

'Ah! Yes, Mary, there is more in life than we can measure, and more in the guidance of human action than we can know. And now we are drawing near the cottage', and as Orrason spoke, the carriage hurried forward.

CHAPTER XXXIV

The House of Revelation by the sea shore – An auld acquaintance, and an important interview – 'Unkind and cruel' – A 'revealing impulse' – A joyful meeting – 'Orchardhead' to the front – An affectionate parting.

Eagerly did Mary and Orrason look for the figure of the woman leaning over the rose-adorned gateway. No woman was there, however, and a shade of disappointment was seen to flit across their faces. The carriage stopped and the travellers alighted. Bidding the coachman return within the hour, the two entered the garden gate. No one was in view but as they advanced they were met in the shade of bush and tree by the same kindly figure they had formerly beheld.

'Forgive me, but let me ask, 'said Orrason tenderly, as he drew near, 'are you the woman whom I once knew by the name of Mrs. Macintyre'?

'I've been lang kent by that name – langer indeed than I can either count or mind, but whether I'm the same Mrs. Macintyre ye are seekin' for is mair than I can answer for', replied the half-smiling, half-enquiring woman.

'Let us, if it suits you and your household, Mrs.Macintyre, go inside, that we may now explain the reason of our calling', urged Orrason, with a tone of agitation in his voice.

The guidwife led the way and the husband and wife soon found themselves in a small, plain, yet neatly adorned room, the windows of which looked out on a small but tastefully kept garden and, farther away, to the open sea, and were shaded by the boughs and leaves of well-trained bushes.

'You say you have been long known by the name you now bear – will it reach back over twenty-eight years, do you think'? Orrason, in his own agitation, did not wish too harshly or too suddenly to disturb the serenity of the gentle woman he saw before him.

'Yes, it will that, an' twa-three mair – but what for do you pit the nummer twenty aucht'? and Mrs. Macintyre looked enquiringly at her guests.

'Can you not recall any incident of that time in your motherly experience or in the lives of your children'? enquired Orrason, almost trembling, while Mary sat clasping her hands.

The calm countenance of the woman suddenly changed. The light of mingled grief and anger filled her eyes, and a flush of affection spread over her features.

'Do *you* ken oucht o' what happened to me at that fell time? If you really ken – if ye speak frae knowledge gathered frae a better and surer source that the idle gossip o' idle folk – then let me hear. Yes! I can indeed ca' back the griefs o' twenty-aucht years ago – they come oftener than I want'.

Here Mary interposed, 'I should say, Mrs. Macintyre, that the occurrences to which my husband refers are almost wholly unknown to me, and I am only getting to know about them as you and he proceed'.

'If that be sae', Mrs. Macintyre answered, 'you may as weel be tell'd. Twenty-aucht years ago – come the hairst – I lost my ain bairn by an unchancie fate, and Providence, for a time, sent me anither in his place. It was a bonnie bairn, weel faur'd and sonsie an' sae cheery an' guid nature'd, I thocht I had never seen his equal. He grew up wi' me as ane o' my ain, an' my very heartstrings were warpit roond him. My joy in that bairn was owre guid to last. He was ta'en awa' ere he had seen his third year oot, an' I've never seen nor heard aught o' him since', and Mrs. Macintyre drew the corner of her apron over her tear-filled eyes, and looked wistfully out upon the distant sea.

'How was he taken from you', asked Mary, gently taking the weeping woman's hand in her own.

'Oh, my dear', slowly answered the loving heart, 'I can only tell you by letting you know hoo the bairn cam' to be mine. Hoo it was I canna tell noo, but somebody had learned that my ain bairn was deid an', wanting to get a nurse for some lady's love child, they had thocht on me. A' on a sudden, a wee, dark, uncanny-looking man, on a November nicht – when the gloaming` was gane an` the mirk was on – cam` to me an` made a bargain aboot the bairn. At first it was nae more than a bargain – sae muckle siller for sae muckle trouble – an` the thing bargained for was a human bein`. It micht be wrang to bargain for such a precious thing, an` if I was wrang I was sair punished for the sin`. Then, after a long pause:

`The bairn was brocht to me by the same man, an` in the same way. We lived east-bye at the Ferry Toll in thae days, and the bairn grew up there. The saft whinny braes, an` the warm simmer sands doon at the fountain was his playgrund an` mine. Mony a happy oor was spent there. In my partial e`e I saw the laddie grown to be a man – a great, strong, guid-heartit man – but that weary creatur` cam` an` took him awa`. And the old kind heart, still full of love, wept on in silence.

`How could anyone take the child from you`? quietly queried Orrason, scarce able to control his tears.

`Oh, my dear sir! It a` cam` oot o` that unchancie bargain – sae muckle siller for sae muckle trouble, and to gie up the bairn when the mither wantit. I didna think aboot it at the time. I never thocht the bairn wou`d sae twine himself aboot my heart as he did. I was bound to let the winsome bairn gang, but it was a sair, sair hurt to me` – and again the falling tears would come.

`It was unkind and cruel`, said Mary.

`When the bairn was brocht to me at first`, said Mrs. Macintyre, `the dark-faced messenger would ha`e me to believe he had carried the bairn frae Embro` and when he took it awa`, it was only, he said, to let the mither see it, an` it wou`d be brocht to me again. But I`ve never seen either the man or the bonnie bairn since`.

`Had you any name for the child`? It was Mary who put the question.

`Oh! Yes. We had a name, though it was mair by way o` a bye-name than anything else. His ain folks` name neither I nor the bairn ever kent. I would hae a name frae the man, when he cam` wi` the bairn. He said it was an orra bairn – an orra son – an` that I micht as well ca` him Johnnie Orrason as onything else – an` Johnnie Orrason he has ever been to me`. And the kindly, loving soul, staying her tears, again looked out on the restless waters now washing the rocks on the beach beyond.

Then, turning quickly around and seeming to reflect, she said, 'But I've been carried awa' wi' my story, and forgotten to learn and satisfy the object o' your visit'.

'Our reason for calling', broke in the anxious Orrason, 'was simply to learn the story you have just told us and, on my part, to renew the love and re-establish the attachment of bye-gone years'.

'I dinna ken your meanin', nor can I comprehend ye', replied Mrs. Macintyre.

'Would you know, do you think, this same Johnnie Orrason, if you saw him again'? And he turned himself full to the light of the half-opened casement.

The woman and the mother glowed at once in the eyes of Mrs. Macintyre.

'I can fancy he'll be greatly changed – if he be to the fore – but his bonnie hazel e'en cou'd surely never be matched'. And as the speaker looked into the eyes of the man who stood in the glowing light before her, she trembled with expectant agitation.

'But there is a'e infallible print o' the hand o' Providence that should mark him oot for surety to me…', but she could go no further. She sprang towards Orrason and, in the light of a revealing impulse, laid her head upon his shoulder and, with her arms about his neck, wept happy tears.

Orrason pressed her to his breast and, uttering the words, 'my own, my only mother', he stroked the white ringlets escaping from her snowy cap.

Mary covered her face with her hands and wept tears of joy with them.

Then did the quietude of unspeakable unutterable satisfaction fill for the passing moments that little room by the sea shore.

'An' have I found my long-lost son at last? Has my prayer been heard and my joy fulfilled'?

'And has my lost, my vanished mother come up out of the depths to me'?

And then the two were once more silent.

Orrason was leading the joyous woman to a seat, when the door opened and a lovely maiden, the youthful counterpart of Mrs. Macintyre, entered the room.

'My daughter, Christian`, said the still trembling woman, `one that has been to me the bond of the household since her father, John Macintyre, died`. Then, after a moment`s pause, and speaking to her daughter,

'Have the ithers come in, Kirsty? If they have, bring them here. We have no secrets, but rather joyful tidings to tell`.

Two stalwart sons, both of mature age, and three daughters, were quickly within the little parlour.

When all were seated round, Mrs. Macintyre said, `My family, Mr. Orrason – for Johnnie winna dae noo, though I`d rather use the old, familiar name. An` you, my ain bairns, this is the Johnnie Orrason we loved and lost langsyne – and this is his wife, Mary. We often spoke aboot the lost laddie, and noo, after lang waitin`, he`s come back to us, an` the great privilege is given us of lookin` upon ane anither and joyin` in the old love again`.

Introductions over, the table was set, the steaming urn was brought, and the happy company gathered round.

'Can you not guess or tell why it was your foster child was so rudely taken from you`? said Orrason, looking to his hostess.

'I have nothing tae say in the way o` certainty. I only ken this, that a gentleman wha` was stayin` wi` Mr.Mitchell, the innkeeper, for a day or twa at the ferry, had brocht ae day an` Embro` newspaper wi` a short account o` a fierce law plea that had been gaun on i` the Coort o` Session. The Marchbanks up bye in Dumfarlin` there had been tryin`, through some siller transactions, to tak` the estate o` a man named Ralston, wha lived then wast at Cu`ross; and when the tide of fortune was rinnin` sair against Ralston, some ane o` the lawyer bodies put his lordship – the judge – up to the fact that the Marchbanks had tried to force Ralston to marry a sister o` theirs that had ha`en a love child; and syne, because he refused, had in revenge brocht him before the Coort anent this matter o` the siller`.

'My dear Mrs. Macintyre`, said Mary, quickly alive to the importance of this narrative, 'I feel sure, from what I already know, that this law affair will ultimately concern the fate of Mr. Orrason. Can you give the time, or near the time, it happened'?

'It is just twenty-six years past', said the eldest son, helping his mother.

'That is so, James', said Mrs. Macintyre. 'Johnnie Orrason had been wi' me the better pairt o' twa years at the time. An' hearing the story turned o'er again an' again at the toll, I made nae secret o't the neist time I was in Dumfarlin'. Orchardhead, the farmer yont by, happened to be in Dumfarlin' juist a wee time after my visit to the toon, and he gat the whole story alang wi' the rest. He was said to be gey thang wi' the Marchbanks himsel', an' whether he made ony evil use o' the law plea story I canna tell, but it wasna lang after this when the messenger o' evil cam' for the bairn. I aye thocht after that', she added, 'that the law plea an' the bairn were somehow connected'.

With hearts relieved of long-pressing doubts, Mary and Orrason lived, in this humble cottage of Mrs. Macintyre, an hour of unalloyed bliss. To the kindly woman and to her family the hour was an equally happy one. Peasants, farm servants, were they all, and unused to the artificial life of the great towns, and the cruel deeds of commercial heartlessness, but the very simplicity of their lives made them only the warmer participants in a real joy, and the readier sharers of pleasure with others.

But the hour of parting had come and the Jehu outside had long since announced his presence. The younger son of the household had gone out and, relieving him of the reins, had sent him inside to the hospitable table. The horses were not forgotten either, and now when all were ready, when many good wishes were expressed, and many good-byes said, the group of glad-hearted men and women stood under the rose-covered canopy of the little gateway.

'Come to me again an' let me see ye often; ye'll be ever welcome', said Mrs. Macintyre.

'I can never forget you, and whatever my fortune I shall ever have you in mind', he said as he grasped her hand. 'With Mary, I shall follow out this search till I know who and what I am. When these essentials of my existence are revealed, you too shall learn. Trust me, I shall see you as often as I can, but whether my visits shall be frequent, or few and far between, you shall ever dwell in my heart as a joyful remembrance'.

He lifted his hat, bent his head and kissed the cheek that had so often in his childhood pressed his own. As the carriage drove off, he stood up and waved his hat, and the group under the roses signalled their happy adieus.

CHAPTER XXXV

Seeking for printed evidence – `Edinburgh, our next house of call` – A Court of Session case, and its results – A clue at last – An important witness – The landlord of the `Spire Inn`.

Seated in their room in the Spire Inn, Dunfermline, Mary and Orrason earnestly discussed their future proceedings. In the most unexpected way, light had been made to shine upon Orrason's past life and, by reflection, to illumine his future path.

`Edinburgh is our next house of call, Mary, though there our search must be with things rather than persons`.

`Yes, John. Newspapers must there must form the first quarry of our diggings, and there, or by the lead they give, we shall, I hope, find our *lia-fail* or stone of destiny`.

> `The present moment is oor ain,
> The neist we never saw`.

was now at least Orrason's axiom of life and of the use of time.

Next morning saw the industrious pair inside the Edinburgh coach driving to the ferry on their way to the city. Anxious still they were, yet both felt that now their seeking was not directed by mere blind chance, but ruled by a fair degree of directness and intelligence.

In the grand old capital of the Northern Kingdom our travellers, now that their line of duty lay clearly before them, lost no time with other affairs. Opportunities for scanning its history and lingering over its monuments might again present themselves; meantime, the duty that lay nearest to hand must engage them first.

To scan the pages of the *Edinburgh Courant* in the newspaper office, and run over its yellow-brown and ill-printed columns, was a work of weariness to the mind and flesh. Again and again did the seekers believe they had found that for which they sought, and again and again were they deceived.

But the long-sought-for came at last. The case of Marchbank Brothers v. Thomas Ralston of Craigneuk and The Drums was clearly that for which they sought. The paragraph, after a mere rubric of the case, stated that the defender had been assoilzied from the conclusions of the summons, and a short note of news below informed the legal fraternity and general public that the case had, in its latter stages, taken an unexpected turn. A hint dropped by the defending counsel had clearly indicated that the whole case had developed from certain persistent endeavours on the part of the pursuers to cover the weakness of a female relative by a marriage, in which the defendant was to be the 'sacrificial lamb'. His Lordship probed this insinuation and found it verifiable and, after a careful sifting of decisions given on the points raised, found for the defendant.

The dates given in the paper gave them a clue where to search in the tomes in the Library of the Advocates. How valuable this little clue was to Mary and Orrason can only be appreciated by those who have had to wade, helpless and guideless, through the vast labyrinth of law books stored in this warehouse of legal history, quackery and wisdom.

Volume after volume, and work after work, was searched and wistfully examined. In the long run, the help of one of the clerk assistants had to be solicited by Orrason even to put them on the track. He was able, however, from the dates given in the *Courant*, and the rubric printed there, to make a clear statement of what the case was. In a few minutes, a long row of huge, brown-skinned volumes was spread out before Orrason's and Mary's unaccustomed eyes, and the obliging assistant led them in patient search, through indices and contents, till at last 'Marchbank *v.* Ralston' met their gaze.

Here, however, to their disappointment, only the dry decision was given, with the recorded opinions of certain of the Lords upon adverted points of the statutes relied on, or the differences to decided cases.

They found, however, what they omitted to note in the *Courant*, that this decision was an Inner House one, and therefore that the evidence taken would be preserved. Taking such notes as were necessary to guide them elsewhere, they left the great Scottish store-house of legal knowledge and, elated by their progress, they got to a comfortable inn in the Old Town, and set themselves to regale and replenish the inner man – and woman.

Comparing notes and preparing themselves for the coming day, they finished such tasks as they could then accomplish. The hours of the evening were spent among the deep sunk wynds, the queer 'lands' and historical buildings of this most wonderful and attractive of olden cities.

The following forenoon early found them in the vicinity of the Parliament House. Here, by industrious speerin', they found at last the official necessary to help them. The written detailed evidence of the case was easily got at, and with it the address of Ralston, and that part of the cross-examination where he was recalled and questioned as to the motivation of the prosecution.

Here is the part referred to:

HIS LORDSHIP – 'You have been recalled Mr.Ralston, with regard to your relations with the Marchbank family. Were you intimate with that family'?

RALSTON – 'Yes, for several years'.

Lord SISTON – 'Were your financial relations with them of long standing'?

RALSTON – 'From about the first year of my acquaintance'.

Lord SISTON – 'Did these relations form any bar to your friend-ship'?

RALSTON – 'They did not, until recently'.

Lord SISTON – 'What happened then to alter the tone of your intercourse'?

RALSTON – 'If your Lordship would allow me, I would rather refrain from explaining'.

COUNSEL – 'Was there a lady in the question'?

RALSTON – 'I must admit there was'.

COUNSEL – 'Who was the lady here referred to'?

RALSTON – 'As I esteem the lady greatly, I would rather, with your leave, avoid the question'.

Lord SISTON – 'Had you intimate relations with the lady'?

RALSTON – 'I was frequently in her company'.

COUNSEL – 'Was the lady the sister of the pursuers'?

RALSTON – 'I must unwillingly admit the fact'.

Lord SISTON – 'Why unwillingly'?

RALSTON – 'Because I am sorry the name of the lady's relations should be mentioned in any way here'.

Lord SISTON – 'You say you were intimate with the lady; did anything happen with her as between yourself and her'?

RALSTON – 'Nothing – except that we were separated'.

COUNSEL – 'Were you not asked to marry her'?

RALSTON – 'If I must answer – yes'.

Lord SISTON – 'And you refused'?

RALSTON – 'I did'.

Lord SISTON – 'Might the Court be informed why you refused to marry the lady'?

RALSTON – 'Because the marriage would have involved a relation and suggestion I could not accept'.

COUNSEL – 'In other words, while you respected the lady, you must also respect yourself'?

RALSTON – 'Well, you may possibly put it in that way'.

Lord SISTON – 'Did your refusal break off your friendly relations with the pursuers'?

RALSTON – 'We were never friendly afterwards'.

Lord SISTON – 'That will do'[70].

With this scrap of legal illumination – carefully copied out in the now well-nigh forgotten engrossing handwriting – Orrason and Mary were content. They secured their new treasure of scrip, and hied them from this field of legal warfare.

The afternoon saw them once more atop the Defiance creeping down the steep Drumsheughbrae to the village of Water of Leith, up the opposing bank, and bowling along the road to Queensferry.

Arrived at the Spire in grey Dunfermline, Orrason and Mary looked over their results and exchanged congratulations.

In response to a call, the rough, genial landlord again appeared.

`Let me ask you, Mr.Laidlaw, do you know one Thomas Ralston of Craigneuk and The Drums, Culross`?

`Yes, Mr. Orrason, he is here occasionally. He is an excellent good-hearted man, a capital horseman, and as steady in his conduct as he is in the saddle`, said Laidlaw, waiting.

`Is he anything accessible – approachable`? queried Orrason.

`Well, he is a little stiff in his style at first; but if you are fair and sensible with him, he soon opens up – but you must be on your guard with good sense`.

`That is reassuring`, said Mary, `to find a man who insists upon sensible conduct – there are so few who are that way`, and she smiled towards her male auditors.

`An` let me tell you`, replied Laidlaw, `Ralston wasna aye an example o` sensible conduct or speech – but he has lang gotten o`er that, an` noo is ane o` the best an` maist sensible men you cou`d find i` the wast`.

`Well, Mr. Laidlaw`, said Orrason, `will you kindly arrange to drive us west after breakfast tomorrow`.

`West to Mr. Ralston`s house at Craigneuk, I suppose`? questioned mine host.

`Well, if the gentleman`s house is there, that is where we want to go. We want to find Mr. Ralson himself`, said Orrason, laughing.

`Very good, sir, I`ll arrange it`, and the tall man bowed himself out.

CHAPTER XXXVI

A glimpse of Culross and the Sands – With the Ralstons at Craigneuk – A startling revelation – The child of destiny – A timely visit to Dr. Hardie.

The day following that of the visit to Edinburgh with its absorbing revelations found our pilgrims retracing the road they had followed when driving in the mail coach from Stirling. This beautiful and deeply interesting line of travel disclosed new charms at every turn. The entrance to Culross and the drive towards Sands made the travellers almost wish that their final settlement in life might be by this quiet sylvan shore.

Making their way northward from this region, they sought and found the unpretentious, yet finely situated, mansion of Craigneuk. Luckily its owner was at home and he received his strange visitors with a firm, undemonstrative courtesy that promised, at least, attention and consideration, if not effusiveness and display.

Orrason presented his card, and the uncommon device attracted for the moment the scrutiny of Mr. Ralston. `You are certainly welcome, Mr. and Mrs. Orrason. I am pleased to see you, though wholly ignorant of what may have induced you to call at Craigneuk`, and he waited an explanation.

`We have called`, said Orrason, `on a matter which once intimately concerned you, Mr. Ralston, and which now as intimately concerns myself and my wife`.

`Indeed! Please explain, Mr. Orrason`.

`I shall be glad to do so`, replied our hero, `and if I should touch on a delicate subject it is not because I wish to do so, but because it is necessary to our present quest`. Then, after a pause, `You were defendant, Mr. Ralston, some twenty-eight or twenty-nine years ago, in a case in the Court of Session raised against you by Marchbank Brothers of Dunfermline`?

`That is so, Mr. Orrason, pray proceed`. And the Laird of Craigneuk and The Drums became all at once earnest and close in his attention.

`You were recalled towards the close of the case, and questioned as to your relations with a lady who, though not named, was known to be a sister of the Marchbanks`.

`That is also true, though, before we go farther, I think I should know to whom I am making these admissions. Your name, no doubt, is here`, lifting the card, `but who is John Orrason that he should claim a right to rake up matters that had far better be allowed to sink into forgetfulness`?

`John Orrason is deeply interested – intensely concerned – in everything to which reference has been made. He has no idle curiosity to satisfy, no gossiping appetite to appease. He has simply the claims of affection, and the honourable ambitions of life and character to fulfil`. Then, pausing for a moment, he added, `Allow me, Mr. Ralston, before I explain my position, and give my reasons for being here, to have one more answer from you. The question is a delicate one, but it is vital. Did the lady of whom we have spoken become a mother about the time of the trial`? Orrason waited anxiously the answer.

`There was a time, Mr. Orrason`, said Ralston, `when I could not, under any consideration, have replied to your query. Now, however, I am free from the promise I gave so many years ago to be silent on this matter, and I am divulging no imprisoned secret, or breaking honourable engagement, when I answer you truly – Yes`! And Ralston looked earnestly into the faces of Mary and Orrason.

`Then`, said Mary, rising in her seat and addressing Mr. Ralston, `the man you see before you is the child then ushered into the world`.

It were a mere commonplace to say that the Laird of The Drums was startled, that he was excited and confounded by what he had just heard. He literally sprang to his feet, and stared across the table to where Orrason sat.

`You`! he exclaimed. `You the child of Madge Marchbank! You the child of unfeeling wrath! The infant scapegoat of family pride! The castaway of cruel respectability`! He stopped for an instant then, drawing his hand across his brow and looking into vacancy, he exclaimed, 'Oh! My God! But Thy ways are wonderful! A voice comes here to me as if from the very gates of oblivion to re-vindicate my name, and to set my honour clear in the sight of Heaven and men'! Then, calming down, he turned towards his hearers and exclaimed, 'Forgive me! Forgive me! I was carried away and forgot myself. But to think – after all these years – the very child, the unconscious innocent, which pride and folly cast into the vortex of oblivion, should come back as a living protest against a barbarous iniquity; the thought staggers my powers of belief. Yet I feel there is truth in your claim of birth'. He stretched his hand to Orrason, and the two men – the young and the middle-aged – were gripped by a powerful emotion.

For a passing moment both were silent. Then Ralston, seeing his wife pass the window of the room, sprang to the door, and presently returned with the companion of his life.

'Mrs. Ralston, Mr.and Mrs. Orrason'! he exclaimed. Then, turning to his wife – 'My dear, our visitors to-day have brought us, all unsought, a revelation which, I am sure, will give no less satisfaction to you than it has given to me. That it is an amazing surprise you will readily acknowledge'. Then, after a moment's pause, he went on:

'We have sometimes in recent years spoken together of my Court of Session experiences and of the child then brought into the world by Madge Marchbank, and we have often wondered what fate had overtaken it, and asked ourselves whether it might be still alive. We thought over it, and imagined things about it, but we never dreamed, in our wildest moments, that he would walk into our house here at Craigneuk, as he has done to-day, and sweep away in a moment the mystery of his life. Behold'! he exclaimed, addressing his wife, and extending his arm, 'Behold, in our visitor, John Orrason, the child of destiny, the infant of contention of twenty-nine years ago', and the excited man stopped short.

'Madge Marchbank's son'! broke out Mrs. Ralston in astonishment and, stepping suddenly towards Orrason, she took him warmly by the hand. 'You, indeed, the son of poor Madge? The unwelcome! The forgotten to memory! The cast-out of the heart! Welcome you are here today. You came at your birth as Dead Sea fruit and now again as the very Balm of Gilead`. Then, running round to Mary, `And you are Mrs.Orrason! I am happy to see you and to welcome you both to Craigneuk`.

Then, turning to her husband, she cried `Oh! What would Doctor Hardie say were he here today? What raptures he would get into`. `That is well minded`, exclaimed Ralston, with a glad surprise in his eyes. `The day is young yet. We`ll drive north at once to see him`. Then, speaking to the mystified Orrason and Mary, `Your beast will be tired a wee; we`ll get out our own trap and run up on Hardie in no time`.

Hurrying out for a moment, he gave the necessary orders to bring round the `soddy` – as he called his carriage – and to arrange for the Spire Inn coachman to stable up for a few hours. Returning into the room, he addressed his visitors, `Excuse Mrs. Ralston and myself for a minute or two while we make ourselves presentable – we`ll be with you both in a crack`.

Husband and wife retired and rattled off their few orders to members of the family and to the one or two domestics in the house, and bustled rapidly through their personal preparations.

`Are we all right with this business, Thomas`? queried Mrs. Ralston, when the two were alone. `Is there no possibility of our being mistaken? Of Orrason himself and his wife being – well, to put it mildly – mistaken too`? And the lady of Craigneuk looked at her husband.

`Well, your question is justified by the circumstances`, replied Ralston, `but, for myself, I have no doubts whatever. However, our visit to Dr. Hardie will put your difficulty to rest. He has all that is necessary in the way of documentary evidence, and he has, as I know, very clear medical means of testing and proving. Now, I`ll go in and talk to our visitors till you are ready. You won`t be long`?

`Only a minute, Thomas, and I`ll be with you`, Mrs. Ralston answered, as she put some finishing touches to her rough-and-ready toilet.

`But who is this Dr. Hardie`? questioned Orrason, when his host had returned. `And where is he located? Is it far away`?

`He is the medical adviser of the Marchbank family. Of course, he is an old man now, and his advice is sought only in severe emergencies, but he was the medico who attended Miss Marchbank, as we may call her, when you were born, and would doubtless be your very first acquaintance in this world`, said Ralston. `He lives near Dollar in the Ochills`.

`This is more and more wonderful`, said Mary. `We seem to be treading by some unerring impulse – or by the help of a guiding enchanter – the very footprints of your earliest life`.

`Wonderful it is indeed` repeated Orrason. `And now, since I know who this professional gentleman is – this Dr. Hardie – I feel as keen an anxiety to see him as anyone here can. Are we ready to go`? And he looked round enquiringly as Mrs. Ralston entered, accompanied by her eldest daughter, who could no longer repress her curiosity to see the visitors, and fill her eyes with the image of the `long-lost man newly come again`.

`This is my eldest daughter, Mr. and Mrs. Orrason – Miss Jessie Ralston – and she will keep the castle till we return and keep the inmates in order and subjection. And now we are all ready and the carriage waits`, and Mrs. Ralston moved towards the door.

All soon followed her and the spanking greys were soon threading their way by Kincardine, Forrest Mill and the old, rough, flower and bush bespangled road that leads to picturesque Dollar, wending under the sheltering Ochills, crowned with the stronghold of the Campbells.

CHAPTER XXXVII

*With Doctor Hardie – His professional books – A sure mark of identity –
'Is my mother still alive'? – A committee of the whole house.*

Doctor Hardie's modest mansion lay somewhat off the beaten highway that follows the line of the hills, and his library windows looked straight down upon the approach.

The doctor was still, though approaching the limit of three score and ten, a man of sharp wits and wiry activity. He spied the greys of Craigneuk – well known to him – as they drew near the house, and he was already out on the lawn in front of the door when the party drew up.

'What star is in the ascendant to-day, Ralston, that you are out imitating Phaeton, and oppressing me with honour and pleasure at your visit'? queried the lively and cultured veteran as he handed down Mrs. Ralston.

'Allow me', quickly answered Ralston, 'to introduce to you my two visitors – Mr. and Mrs. Orrason. And now, doctor, we want to go inside to talk to you in the library where we will need the help of your wisdom and recollections'.

The doctor led the way without hesitation, knowing from Ralston's manner he had something of importance to disclose. Placing his visitors and arranging for their comfort and ease, he waited announcements.

'Are your professional books in good order, Doctor'? questioned Ralston, with a curious look towards the medico.

'They always are – always have been', said the doctor.

'Well', continued Ralston, 'these books of yours will doubtless bear record that you once attended at Dunraggan House, on a very interesting occasion, somewhere about twenty-nine years ago'?

'Doubtless they will – though I have not *vised* that entry for a long period', and the doctor looked puzzled.

'Well, you can look your jottings over again – but, meantime, you know what happened on that occasion'?

'Yes, Ralston, an addition was made to the general population – a son was born. Do you wish me to be more particular'? queried the doctor, looking towards the ladies.

'You will presently', rapidly answered Mr. Ralston, have to be as particular as you can; but just now I must more fully introduce our visitor, Mr. Orrason. I ought perhaps to have allowed him to tell his own story – and he may still favour us with the recital – and if I have said overmuch, I beg his pardon most sincerely; but possibly it is better that I should tell you, Doctor, that Mr. Orrason claims you as his first acquaintance in this world, and that acquaintance was auspiciously begun at Dunraggan House'.

'What'! exclaimed the doctor, twiddling his spectacles and turning towards Orrason, 'you Madgie Marchbank's son. Well, that is a surprise; give me your hand'. Then, after a pause,

'What a goodly and gallant frame to have grown from that puling and quickly hurried-off child. What a history lives behind all this! What complications lie before you! A very network of difficulties already rises before my mind and may cross your path to recognition at every turn'. The doctor stopped short then, twitching his whiskers and recalling his thoughts for a moment, he said to Orrason, leading the way to a small inner room, 'Come with me for a little, and you had better come too, Ralston', and then the door closed on the three men.

'Now', began the Doctor, turning to Orrason, 'if you are the son of Madgie, I shall make the statement sure; if you are not I shall make it equally clear'. Turning to his journals, carefully labelled in volumes on the surrounding shelves, he took down that bearing the year of his enquiry.

Opening at the date, he bade Ralston read, and the Laird of Craigneuk found a carefully written statement of the incidents occurring at Dunraggan House, when, on the –th October 1796,

Doctor James Macintosh Hardie was witness and assistant at the birth of a son there. The mother's name was fully written out and the body of the child described with scientific accuracy.

'That description is of no value without the corresponding proof of identity', observed the Doctor, turning again to Orrason. 'If you are the grown-up child here described, I must see you, and not merely your clothes. You will excuse my plainness since you will see the need'. And the quick business fingers and movements of the little man were rapidly and silently exerted to the accomplishment of his wishes. The special skin mark noted at the Refuge and written down also by Dr. Hardie here with scientific detail, was carefully noted at once by Ralston and the doctor.

'Can there be any doubt, Doctor'? Ralston enquired.

'Not a shadow. So far as a medical man can speak, I have absolute confidence that this man, John Orrason, is the same being born on that October day, nine-and-twenty years ago at Dunraggan. You have read the description and – with the exception of certain professional words and phrases – understood it all. You have seen the proof so far as a non-professional can see it. I claim to see a deal more than you, and I have to tell you, and all whom it may concern, that I have no doubts whatever that John Orrason is the son of Madge Marchbank – the same son who was born in October 1796. Give me your hand once more', he said, wheeling round to Orrason. 'The proof of your identity, so far as I am concerned, is complete – the circumstantial evidence is an affair of your own'.

'Yes, sir', replied Orrason, 'an affair of my own! For your clear and indisputable statements I thank you from the bottom of my heart. Hitherto in my line of search, gentlemen', he said, addressing both his hearers, 'I have sought only for the facts of my life, and for the persons involved. Now that, with your kind help, I have been able to trace my connection to the hour of my birth, my enquiries must take another direction. Is my mother still alive and, if so, where can I find her? And then beyond this, who were the parties responsible for casting me adrift and what were their motives for doing so? These searchings being satisfied, I shall then know how to regulate my future. Are we done here? Should we not now join the ladies`? and Orrason moved slowly towards the door. He was anxious that all should hear the proofs of his identity.

Returning to the Doctor`s library, the three gentlemen found the ladies *tete-a-tete* in the drawing-room with their hostess.

`Ah`! said Dr. Hardie, entering with a smile, `we are bound to, however unwillingly, to break up this little cabal. You, ladies, will undoubtedly have important matters to settle, but we feel you will not be unwilling to leave off, and join with us in discussing the absorbing matters brought before us by Messrs. Ralston and Orrason`? and the active little man bowed to the ladies enquiringly.

`We have no cabal, no conspiracies. How could you think so`? replied Mrs. Hardie.

`So far as being conspirators, you three gentlemen are the only parties who have, by your action, earned that title`, smilingly observed the Lady of Craigneuk.

`That is certainly true`, said Mary. `Yet, I must admit, we three are simply waiting the result of your conspiring – pray tell us your conclusions`.

Marchbank House, Dunfermline

CHAPTER XXXVIII

Dr. Hardie's summing up – The form of Marchbank & Co. – 'A mounted Diana in the chase' – The scapegoat – A wise suggestion – An arranged visit to Ravenshall.

Mary Orrason will doubtless be excused by the indulgent reader for the eagerness she displayed at the end of the last chapter to learn the results of what she believed would be an all-deciding examination of those purely physical claims a medical man would look for in making up his mind on the subject of Orrason's identity with the child of Madge Marchbank. The facts she and her husband had unearthed in their search could all be explained away and possibly turned in favour of some other unknown child, but she knew sufficient of medical science to be aware that a man of such skill and accuracy as Dr. Hardie could make no mistake here, and therefore it was that she so eagerly hurried the deliverance of his testimony.

'Our conclusions', replied Dr. Hardie, 'are, in a word, that John Orrason, the stranger of an hour ago, is none other than the son of Madge Marchbank. There is absolutely no doubt – from a physical, medical point of view – the evidence is without a flaw. And now Mr. Orrason explains that, having satisfied his own first line of search – a search for the facts of his life – he now seeks to know who were responsible for casting him adrift; what were the motives which ruled their conduct, and – above all – where can he find – his mother'. And the doctor stopped for a moment in his discourse.

'You all know', he resumed, 'that my lifelong connection with the Marchbank family gave me, as their medical adviser, almost unlimited opportunity of familiarising myself with the private life of each of its members. The confidences of the entire family were given to me, and I should degrade my class, as well as do violence to my conscience – my sense of honour – were I to disclose, or make use of these facts, except where the interest, honour and character of the family were involved'. The doctor's five listeners now drew themselves into attitudes of eager attention.

'I can see, however, that without some statement on my part, parties who are innocent may be blamed, and suspicions may point in an untrue direction. It is asked who were responsible for the abandonment of the child of poor Madge. I cannot answer this fully, but I believe that the *onus*, if not indeed the detail of the whole scheme rested, and will rest, with Robert Marchbank, the head of the firm. Casual hints and occasional statements by the other two members of the firm left no doubt of this in my mind. But Mr. Orrason will doubtless learn more, and find out definitely – in the next stage of his enquiry – who were most anxious to put him – when a child – out of sight and remembrance. He will note, I hope, what I have said on this point.

As to the motives', continued the Doctor, 'these are always difficult to find out, and are ever liable to misconstruction. There is another – one Mr. Orrason will soon meet – who will speak this secret. When he meets his mother at Ravenhall, many things will be told him. I prefer he should hear these there, and there only.

Let us say, however, that I have indicated that the head of the firm, Robert, was the prime mover in this act of unmerciful banishment, and I must now, as clearly, state that the mother, Madge, had no hand in the matter. I will say no more on this point. You, Mr. Orrason, will know it all in time and better elsewhere`. Then the Doctor stopped and looked at his hearers.

Each of the little company joined in a chorus of congratulations and, as Orrason rose to reach the hand of the aged Mrs. Hardie across the table, all the others sprang up and, after shaking his great rough seaman`s hand, made the little drawing-room ring with their cheers.

`The doctor has spoken of Ravenhall`, said Mr. Ralson, looking towards Orrason, `but he forgets that this reference is without meaning to you – and equally so to Mrs. Orrason. The doctor will perhaps allow me to explain`?

The little man nodded assent and Ralston continued.

`Your mother married – perhaps a year after your birth – the young laird, James Graham, of Ravenhall in Strathearn, and has lived there ever since. She seldom comes south, and has kept up only a formal friendliness with the other members of the Marchbank family. She is the mother of some two sons and two daughters and is now, of course, greatly changed from her young days. Oh! Mr. Orrason, allow me to say it, who knew her better than anybody else – she was a splendid, a wholly unmatchable woman for dash and spirit, and even for beauty in her young days. I can recall her image yet – a very mounted Diana of the chase, managing her mare with the ease and grace of an athlete, following the hounds over every hazard and giving the lead to every horseman on the field. She was lively, generous, piquant and full to overflowing with the spirit of youth and daring. She and I were intimate as brother and sister. Our friends would have it that a feeling of even greater tenderness bound us together, and her brothers – possibly, after all, with the best intentions – insisted I should become the scapegoat of Madge`s mistake. You know how I refused, and you also know the consequences but – mark this – Madge, I know, had no part in this action`.

'Capital, Drynaps [71], capital, all through', said Dr. Hardie, enthusiastically.

'Thanks, thanks', said Orrason, with deep feeling in his voice.

'Thanks, too from me', said Mary, 'for this generous defence of a woman'.

'And not a whit overdrawn', observed the doctor's wife, 'for I kent her well, and often wondered she didna get her neck broken'.

'Simply because', broke in Ralston, 'she had strength and skill and nerve to keep herself safe'.

'Let me add a bit to Thomas' record', observed Mrs. Ralston, glancing towards Orrason and Mary. 'He has told you that Mrs. Graham, for we must now know her by her marriage title, has but a formal intercourse with the Marchbanks. There is to a large extent an immediate reason for this:- Robert, the eldest of the three brothers, died a good many years ago; one brother still lives with his family in Dunfermline, and the other, who did not marry, lives also in that town – his household being ruled and guided by a distant female relative. The name of the firm is still retained, but the family is now separated from all its business responsibilities. Their fortunes have greatly subsided and, although Dunraggan is still nominally held by James, it is known to be really the property of bond-holders – in short', added Mrs. Ralston, with some feeling, 'the fate the brothers destined for Mr. Ralston – in their rapacious Court of Session business – has fallen upon themselves. We have risen from our humiliations; they have steadily sunk in the vortex of business, misfortune and mistakes'.

'Well, now, what shall we do'? queried the host. 'I have been thinking while some of you have been talking, and my idea is that I shall write to Mrs. Graham, explain roundly what has happened, and who has come again into the land of the living, and send it north to her tomorrow. I believe Mr. Graham is not at home just now – has been away for a time, I believe – but that is anything but a misfortune as matters now stand. The letter will so far prepare her to meet you, Mr. Orrason, and if you follow the letter – you and Mrs. Orrason – the remaining mysteries of your infantile life will be cleared up and – and

– well, we can only imagine what train of events will follow your visit. Does this please you, Mr. Orrason`?

`It meets my full approval, and I thank you for the suggestion of the letter; but possibly, doctor, while you should certainly send the letter, I would like you to form one of the company with myself and Mrs. Orrason to this place, this Ravenhall. How far is it from here? I know something by hearsay and otherwise of the Ochil region and know we must get through the hills to reach Strathearn`, and Orrason waited.

`A matter of eight or ten miles from here, right away through Gleneagles`, said Ralston.

`Can we not arrange then, Dr. and Mrs. Hardie – though it must be tiring for you both – to go together to Ravenhall? I shall also feel proud and greatly obliged if Mr. Ralston will go and his lady with him. With your company, your presence and your assistance, we might be able to meet all the delicate difficulties that could possibly turn up and which, as we sit here, we cannot even guess. I am loath to press this matter, dear friends, but it will be a case of once-for-all. I shall esteem it a privilege, and none of you may ever have cause to regret that you assisted the `castaway``!

The earnest manner of Orrason and the appealing looks of Mary, at length prevailed. The arrangement was completed. The letter from Dr. Hardie would be written that night, and sent by mounted messenger in the early morning. Mr. and Mrs. Orrason should drive from Dunfermline, and take up the Ralstons on the way, and be joined at Dollar by the worthy Dr. and Mrs. Hardie.

Things thus settled to the satisfaction of everyone, dinner – for which all were well-nigh ready – was served. The guests drew to each other over the viands and the vivers, and talked and joked with each other as if a life-long acquaintance had found them under the roof of the `doctor of Dollar`.

The return to Craigneuk in the falling grey of the evening was succeeded by the return of the Orrasons to the Auld Grey Toon, and the hospitable roof of the Spire Inn.

CHAPTER XXXIX

An important interview with two 'samples' in the Spire Inn – Important revelations – Preparing for a journey – A budget of news to the 'old folks at home' – Arrival at Dollar and Ravenhall.

The reception which our hero met at the Spire Inn was beyond his expectations. In the feverish excitement of the past few days, Orrason and Mary had forgotten their former visits to the master of the song, and its possible consequences. Our two travellers had, however, scarcely gained the interior of their own rooms when they were waited on by Boniface himself.

'Pray excuse my seeming hurry, Mr. Orrason – and you, too, my good lady – but I have had a visit from the parish precentor – Mr. Rankine, master of song – with reference to the little puzzle you put before me, sir, the first night you came here – that was to find out who were the parties 'C.G. and his wife C'. Well, Rankine, as I say, has been here, and has brought a couple of male samples with him that he thinks may answer the conditions you laid before him'.

'Are the 'samples', as you call them, here now, Mr. Laidlaw'? enquired Orrason.

'Yes', replied mine host. 'Rankine was here just a little before you returned but as he has some exercise meetin' doon bye i' the Abbey, he coudna wait, but would have his specimens bide till you came in'. Then, collecting himself a bit, he added, 'They are both here and you may see them at once if you wish'.

'By all means, Mr. Laidlaw', answered Orrason, 'bring them here just now. My wife will be as pleased to see the samples as I can be – bring them in'.

Within the space of a few seconds, the exhibits of the registrar's selection had transferred themselves from the bar of the Spire, and the gratis gill stoup of the landlord, to the private sitting-room of Mr. and Mrs. Orrason.

It was some time before Orrason and Mary could put together to their own minds the various items that made up the important personality of 'C.G.'. At length, recalling the writing in the books of the Refuge at Glasgow, the descriptions given there by Emily, and afterwards by Mrs. Macintyre at Rosythe – not omitting the transcripts in Mary's letters – Orrason and his wife had a better conception of what to look for in the two unknown men sitting opposite them.

The two callers were as dissimilar as two men well could be. They were both of the working class – evidently weavers – and familiar with the disasters and depressions too common in that business then. One was a big hulking man, with large heavy features; the other an elderly, small, dark, sharp-featured creature who, by the cosy way in which he handled his snuff-box and looked round him, was evidently one often engaged in, and fond of, a twa-handed crack.

When Orrason had made up his mental image of C.G. and surveyed the two figures before him, he had little difficulty in fixing on the more probable man of the two.

'Would you kindly give me your names, gentlemen', said Orrason. 'Of course, you know to some extent why you are here. I may explain further to one of you as we go on. Your names, please'.

One gave the name of Campbell Gillespie, the other that of Charles Graham, and both announced that other cabalistic item – that the wife's name was Catherine.

'Now', said Orrason, addressing his visitors, 'though you are both here on the same message, the business can only ultimately concern one of you; it will therefore be more convenient that one should retire for a little. Possibly, Mr. Gillespie will wait downstairs for a few minutes'? Gillespie at once rose, and Graham was left alone with our travellers.

'We need not waste time, Mr. Graham', broke in Orrason, when the door had closed. 'Let me ask you at once whether you can recall anything in you own life that happened, say, twenty-nine years ago. Had you at that time anything to do with carrying off a child from a mansion, possibly in the south of Perthshire? If you had, tell your own story – tell it in your own way – but do not, in any instance, vary from the truth, as far as your mind will carry you. Pray proceed`.

`Weel, sir`, slowly answered Graham,` I dinna ken wha you are, an` I canna, therefore, tell what may be the consequences o` my communication, but I can see plain eneuch that you`ve got haud o` the bairn story some way, an` as the chief man i` the plot has noo gane to his account, I see naething to hinder me – for a fair consideration – frae tellin` you and the lady here present the hail affair`.

Graham stopped to take a snuff and then proceeded, while our travellers smiled to each other.

`There`s no mony kens aboot the affair, for as lang as Bob Marchbank was to the fore, I dursna, for the life o` me, say a word aboot it to a livin` soul; but noo he`s dead an` awa``. Then, after a pause: `There`s nae doot aboot it, I was hired to gang up to the mansion o` Dunraggan – in a gey hurry tae – to tak` charge o` a bairn an` carry it doon, inside the family coach, to a Mrs. Macintyre at the Ferry Toll (I had arranged wi` her aforehand), and persuade her that I carried the unchancy thing frae Edinburgh. She was to speir nae questions; ca` the bairn what she liked, an` be sure to say naething aboot it to onybody. An` that`s true, an` a` that happened twenty-nine year syne come October next`. And here Graham halted to take another pinch. He then went on:

`It would be the better pairt o` three years after this when I was again sent for, an` was told by the man, noo dead an` gone, to gang doon again to the Ferry Toll – i` the same way wi` the coach – an` persuade Mrs. Macintyre, wi` a fine story, to gie up the bairn; an` then I was to carry it by Torryburn an` get by the canal to Glasgow, an` to leave it there for guid an` a` at a place named the Refuge. This I carried through to the very letter o` my orders, an` this same bairn was there for the better pairt o` ten year. That would be, say, sixteen year syne. At that time something had come o`er Bob Marchbank`s hardened disposition, for he then sent me doon to the Links o` Kirkcaldy to ane o` his weavers – a Peter Saunders – there to arrange wi` him to tak` o`er the laddie frae the Refuge, an` learn him the weavin` business. This pairt o` the business I also carried through, an` no a livin` cratur was a hair the wiser for anything I ever said. But hech how! , the last thing I heard o` this castawa` bairn was that he was carried aff wi` the pressgang. Since that time I`ve never heard oucht aboot him, an` never likely will`. And Graham finished his story with a pinch of snuff.

`As I happen to know a good part of this story already`, intimated Orrason to his invited visitor, `I believe you have missed no essential part of it, and you will kindly accept my thanks for your careful narration. You may also rest assured that your hint about a consideration will not be forgotten; but I am not quite finished with you yet, Mr. Graham. Can you, hold yourself in readiness for to-morrow morning? I desire to have your company – in this matter of the child – for the greater part of the day. Please try and refresh your memory as to details, prepare yourself, and be here by eight tomorrow. Can you promise`?

`I can baith promise and perform`, answered Graham, `an` you may depend on my bein` here in time. I suppose I`ll better keep the story o` this interview to myself``?

`Well, at least for a day or two, and say nothing to Gillespie as you go out`. So saying, Orrason rose and bowed Mr. Graham to the door.

He had scarcely disappeared when the landlord was rung in. `I wanted to see you, Mr. Laidlaw, to arrange some things. Can you have a carriage – hackney or otherwise – capable of carrying eight comfortably, ready to-morrow by eight , and horsed for a journey of twenty-five miles out by Dollar and Gleneagles, and possibly back again`?

`Certainly, sir! I shall have everything ready`. The landlord was about to retire when Orrason recalled him.

`You can arrange with that man Gillespie downstairs. The other man, Graham, will be here in the morning. And now, I want you to send the coachman who drove me by Rosythe the other day to intimate (from me) to Mrs. Macintyre that I will feel greatly obliged if she will kindly accompany me tomorrow. Your man can warn her to-night and run down for her early to-morrow morning, and be up here again in good time for the carriage starting here at eight`.

`I quite understand you, sir – you desire this man Graham and Mrs. Macintyre to accompany yourself and Mrs. Orrason at eight to-morrow.

`Precisely so, Mr. Laidlaw, and you will see that things are in order`.

The landlord bowed himself out, and Orrason turned to his wife, who was now busy writing.

`Just what I wanted you to be about`, said Orrason. `I imagine you are writing to your father and mother. You can give them the good news, as far as we have gone, and say that better is yet to come. These have been wonderful days to us, Mary; and now when we are nearing the climax of our search, I feel as if urged by a new impulse to greater cheerfulness, hope and energy`. He stopped, for he saw that Mary's nimble pen had also stopped.

`I want you to add a bit in your own hand, John, for I know both father and mother will be pleased to see a proof you are not forgetting them`, and Mary rose as she spoke. Orrason pressed her to his breast and, taking the pen, wrote a page or two, for letters were longer in those days, and then closed this budget of news to the old folks at home.

They had only just sat down to supper when the master of the song was announced. He was at once invited to take a plate and be one of the party. Nothing loathe, Mr. Rankine sat down and soon, by his wit, his geniality, his power of expression and his love for the poets and poetry of our country, made his presence a very joy at the table. Orrason used, in after years, to speak of the intense happiness of that night with Rankine. The songs of Scotland – those especially requiring emphasis and expression – were never rendered in such perfection in his hearing ever again.

The night, however, sped on. Sleep refreshed the weary, soothed the excited, and then passed away like a life-giving influence as the light of the morning dawned.

The next morning witnessed a fierce hurry and bustle of preparation at the Spire. The two expected ones had come, and the full-bodied, beautiful, sedate Mrs. Macintyre seemed a very contrast and counterfoil to the dark, thin, rather ominous-looking man – Charley Graham – that sat opposite. Orrason and Mary were full of the spirit of enterprise, tempered at once by anxiety and hope. Somewhat within the hour the house at Craigneuk was reached, and Mr. and Mrs. Ralston taken in.

Graham was at once introduced. `He has kindly consented to be of our party and enterprise today`, explained Orrason. `He has acted a part in the little life drama over whose field we have for a time been hunting, and he will be able to put some few things in the clear light of fact`.

Mary introduced her particular charge, Mrs. Macintyre, and Orrason supplemented:

`This is the good woman to whom I owe my life – such as it is. Such strength as I have, and much of the spirit that has borne me over years of loveless trials and unsympathetic difficulties, must be traced to Mrs. Macintyre. But it is too soon to explain all. Everything shall be known in time`.

Ralston and his wife looked in wonder at each other and seemed to feel themselves as pawns in the plot of some deft novel-writer. The scattered cottages of Kincardine and Kilbagie and the woods – the sylvan glories – of Forrest Mill, were soon left behind, and the strong, steady-pulling horses were quickly threading the old rough road to Dollar. Dr. and Mrs. Hardie had seen the vehicle from afar, and were waiting at the gate. They were lifted in by the strong arms of Orrason and Ralston, and the carriage again sped on.

The Yetts of Muckhart were turned, and Glendevon Church already passed. The stream of Devon itself had given way to that of Ruthven, and a sharp turn in the road had drawn the travellers westward to near the spot where the tiny head waters of the Allan freshen the fields around Blackford village.

They were now nearing the end of their long drive, and all were looking with expectation – some with anxiety and uncertainty – for that `approach`, that avenue with bush-fringed edges and soft yielding surfaces, which would indicate the nearness of their haven of rest. That point came too at last, and the gates being open, the carriage drove on towards Ravenhall.

CHAPTER XL

A startling interview – Mother and son – The Lady of Ravenhall wants to know all about it – Orrason meets his mother – His life story – Charley Graham relegated to the kitchen below – Long separated, joined at last!

Ravenhall was partly ancient, partly modern in design. Roughly, its form was that of the letter L – the older portion forming the lower part of the letter. The small windows and narrow gables, and many curious carved devices in shields, bas-reliefs, and gargoyles, told at once the olden part of the structure. The more modern erection, receding from the gabled front of its ancient neighbour, made no pretensions either to ornate or classical features of any kind. The floors were loftier, there was greater abundance of light, and space in every quarter was given with a more generous hand. The angle between the two differing structures was filled in with a kind of staircase tower rising in height to the level of the ridges, and crowned with certain ill-proportioned open letterings. The newer part was of two, and the older part of three stories, with the addition of a basement storey throughout. A low screening wall maintained the height of the ancient gable and, running parallel with the 'new house', provided the means of a flat battlemented arrangement, and gave also an opening to a covered way leading to the staircase already mentioned [72].

The arrival of the carriage was evidently expected, and the occupants were at once attended to by a knee-breeched male servitor and ushered to their respective quarters. A short respite for rest and refreshment was succeeded by a gathering of all to the dining-room. Here a son and daughter of the house did the honours of the table and received the guests, being introduced in turn by the doctor and Ralston to all who were strange to Ravenhall. Their performance of the duties and conduct of the little feast was not without spirit or gaiety yet, although they tried their best and both Ralston and the doctor told some of their best anecdotes, it was evident that thought weighed on the spirits of everyone present.

The mistress of Ravenhall was not present – and her absence seemed to be expected and understood, for only slight friendly enquiries were made concerning her, even by Ralston and the doctor. That she was in the mansion everyone seemed equally to know, and nobody felt surprise when, at the close of the dinner, a message was received at once by Dr. Hardie and Orrason to attend elsewhere.

Leaving the company to finish their repast as best they may, we must now follow the specially-called ones, hear the averments of the one, and watch the fate of the other, in the presence of the woman whose fate was also being measured out to her that day.

When the doctor and Orrason were ushered into the private chamber of Mrs.Graham, they found her seated in a small, beautifully adorned and brilliantly lighted apartment. She rose as they entered and, without touching hands, begged to be excused, and asked both in a trembling voice to be seated. This conduct troubled and surprised alike the doctor and Orrason.

`I have read your letter, doctor`, she began, speaking to Dr. Hardie, `and I need not attempt to conceal from you, my lifelong friend, how much anguish of heart and distraction of thought it has already cost me. That letter, as you must be aware, Mr. Orrason`, turning to our hero, `relates to you and your relation to me. I know what *you* are and have been, doctor, and your letter instructs me as to Mr. Orrason. You are both men of the world and can feel the almost insurmountable difficulties of my position`. She then added, after a pause, `I had thought at first, doctor, to have you with me by yourself – but second and better thoughts made me decide to see you both – to see you together`. As she paused the doctor said:

`It is better for my sake you did so, and better for all concerned`.

`Forgive my silence,` said Orrason, looking towards Mrs. Graham, `for as yet I know not how to speak`.

`I feel – deeply feel – for you, Mr. Orrason`, observed the lady of the house, `and, equally for you and me, it is necessary we should clear the path to some form of understanding – some goal of settlement'.

'I am glad to hear you say so, my dear Mrs. Graham', ejaculated the doctor, 'for now it is impossible to escape the conclusion you have already reached'.

'I am equally glad, and rejoice to hear your words', said Orrason, 'for the oppressiveness of uncertainty borne through so many years has now become more than I can bear'.

'Well, now,' ejaculated Mrs. Graham, rising to her feet, her whole manner and expression changed, 'this will do no longer. We may talk sentiment and lamentation without moving a single step towards doing justice towards ourselves or to others. If a wrong has been done – if others have been made to suffer by my act – my first duty is to undo the wrong, and to heal the wound. I am bound now, and am anxious', she continued, 'to recognize you, Mr. Orrason; to receive you as my son, and to sweep away even the breath of suspicion, or lingering cloud of blame, from everyone connected by act or implication with this incident in my life'. Then turning to Dr. Hardie, she resumed:

'You say there is no doubt – there can be no doubt – that the John Orrason here is the very son born long ago in Dunraggan House'?

'So far as human skill – exercised then and now – can go', said the doctor, leaning forward with an earnest look towards the lady of Ravenhall, 'this is your son – the son born at Dunraggan twenty-nine years ago'.

There was a long and awkward silence – a silence broken at length by Mrs. Graham.

'I accept your statement with the most implicit faith', she returned, 'but there are others besides us to satisfy. And now that I think of it, it would be better that you both return to the table – and you, doctor, will kindly send my son and daughter down to the lodge for old Mr. Moodie, that he may come here and form one of the company – things will then arrange themselves. This man', the lady continued, 'was an early actor in this drama of child abduction – he it was who, all unknowingly, as coachman in the family, carried an unwelcome infant, my now restored son, from the mansion house of Dunraggan.

His presence at Dunraggan was rendered useless after the death of my brother, Robert, and with Margaret, the old housekeeper, he is now a pensioner at Ravenhall. He still has a fair recollection of what happened then – to me and to my bidding he has oft rehearsed the tale. Let him tell it in the hearing of our guests to-night, so that the chain of evidence may be full – wanting not a single link`. She spoke in firm tones, though her agitation could not be concealed as she pressed Orrason's hand, parting with him at the chamber door.

This commission was executed and the old man – sharp, clean, and tidy, with hair of whitening grey – entered the room. And now the lady of Ravenhall came in to where her guests were seated. The company rose as she came forward and crowded round her with excess of good wishes as she took her seat among them. Glancing round the little company, she seemed to balance in her mind the position and character of each, and an anxious, yet pleased, expression kept possession of her face till her eye rested on the form of Charley Graham. The glance of dislike, the look of aversion, was at once perceived, and Orrason rose, advanced, and whispered to Dr. Hardie, while he, in turn, explained matters briefly to the lady of the house.

`I am told your name is Graham, Charles Graham`? she queried, looking towards that worthy and playing with a pencil she held in her hand.

`That is, indeed, my name`, was the ready, if trembling, answer.

`You have made some communication, I understand, to Mr. Orrason as to your being engaged for a strange purpose by Mr. Robert Marchbank some twenty-nine years ago`? And the lady waited his reply.

Graham pulled a rather loosely-written paper from the recesses of an apparently omnivorous pocket and Orrason, reaching across the table, begged the document from him. Glancing rapidly over its contents he passed it to Dr. Hardie, with the rapidly written remark:

`Everything we want from Graham is here set down. Keep the paper and assign the writer to the care of others and elsewhere for a time. He`ll be happier and better there`.

The nimble little man, understanding in a moment the drift of the mission, and being previously assured of Graham's reticence, had no hesitation in consigning Charley to the happier quarters of the kitchen below.

'Now, my dear friends', began the mistress of Ravenhall, 'we are as one in sentiment and perception; I feel sure of this when I look around me. You know, each of you, what purpose has brought us together – yours, to connect my life with that of Orrason; yours, to testify that he is my son; mine, to gladly acknowledge him as such. My life-long friend, Dr. Hardie – a man who never deceived either myself or anyone I loved – tells me from his intimate knowledge there is no possible doubt of Mr. Orrason's identity. I accept his statement with implicit trust; but the story of how the lost life came back into the world of recognition is as little known to me as it can be to anyone here. It will prove to me, as it will to you, a revelation of providential guidance and care such as seldom comes to any of us. If the story is to be told, let John Orrason tell it'. And, despite her somewhat reserved bearing, her whole woman's soul looked from her eyes as she bent them on her son.

The hero of our story, thus appealed to, rose, bowed low towards his long-sought mother, and with tear-blent eyes and voice, began:

'My earliest realisation of life came to me while an inmate of an institution erected for the reception of the unfortunate in Glasgow and while a schoolboy at the Wilson Charity School there. Where I had come from I did not know, or had utterly forgotten. I dreamed and mused of what and who I was with weary repetition of sameness and want of satisfactory answer till my thirteenth year. I was then wheeled by coach to Edinburgh and by boat to Kirkcaldy, and there spent four or five of the happiest years of my life. All of a sudden, I was seized by that institution of oppression, the pressgang, and carried off to sea; and I thought then, and for a time, that the sunshine of my life had become eclipsed in storm and disaster'. He stopped for a moment, overcome with emotion, while his mother, listened in earnest yet tearless anxiety, to this revelation of life.

Orrason resumed:

'In my joyous life in the Links of Kirkcaldy I had for frequent companion and dear friend the woman who is now my wife. During my life in the Navy – at the siege of Algiers, for years on the African slave coast, and among the far west Leeward Islands, we kept alive the flame of life and love by writing such rare letters as opportunities permitted. I left the Navy and, attaching myself to the mercantile marine, remained in the Gulf till I had earned sufficient to start me in life with Mary Seaton. I came home and found her in the City of Glasgow and we were married. I told her and her family such part of my life as she, or they, did not know, and then we set ourselves the seemingly hopeless task of finding my place and connection in the world`. Pausing for a moment to find the train of thought, he continued:

`Seizing on my recollections of the school, we made that our first call. We found my name, and dates of entry and leaving. The Refuge books – for such the place was named – gave me the date for my infant entry there. The letters C.G. were set against that entry and the date was, and is, 25th October 1799, and remembrance told the aged and dying governor and the chief female assistant that I had been brought from the town of Dunfermline. We visited that ancient place and, by a wonderful and fortuitous succession of experiences, we found this kind-hearted woman, Mrs. Macintyre, and found, too, that she it was who had nursed me and been a mother to me in my infant years. Proof of this is now in the hands of our tried and prized friend, Dr. Hardie.

This good and noble woman`, he continued, `furnished a clue to the Court of Session case of twenty-seven or so years ago. Searching through newspaper files and multitudinous volumes and manuscripts in the Advocates` Library gave us the very details of the case. This brought us to the house of Mr. Ralston and to hearing the disclosures he was able to make. From the kindly roof of Mr. and Mrs. Ralston, we were guided again, by Providence and fact, to the no-less kindly home of Dr. Hardie. On all the points I have touched, there exists either a living witness to bear out my statements, or the unswerving testimony of the dumb, yet speaking, sheet or book, written or printed by those who knew nothing, and cared nothing, for John Orrason, or the claim he now pleads for parental acceptance, and brotherly, sisterly, recognition`.

The recital of this short life-story filled the eyes of the listeners with tears – tears of joy as real and intense as ever smile betrayed.

His story finished, Orrason approached the seat where his mother, her face buried in her hands, sat weeping. She sprang up as he drew near, flung her arms around his neck and laid her head upon his breast. In silence and rapture, the two long separated ones clung with unutterable joy to each other.

CHAPTER XLI

Dr. Hardie on the situation – 'Speak kindly of the dead' – Entangled thread of life.

The silence which succeeded the scene which I have described in the last chapter continued for a time after Orrason had returned to his seat – and his mother to her natural firmness and decision of conduct. Dr. Hardie's voice was the first to break the almost hallowed stillness.

'You have heard', he quietly observed, 'the simple yet wonderful story of John Orrason's life. It is brimful of lessons to us all, and pregnant with subjects of thought for every one of us. A great injustice has evidently been done to one who, I feel sure, never deserved to be so treated; but who has magnanimity enough to forget the past and forgive everyone concerned in meting out the evils and hardships of his life'.

He stopped and looked towards Mrs. Graham and, finding a look of approval on her face, he continued:

'But this I would, and must, say. The one most closely connected with the child born at Dunraggan – for John Orrason was born there – had no hand in that child's banishment. The entire scheme was conceived and carried out by one who is now in his grave. We are told to speak kindly of the dead, and I shall say no more of Robert Marchbank than necessity compels – yet we must mind the living even more than the dead. The mother was too ill to know aught of what took place and this illness continued for weeks, and grew upon her till her life was despaired of, and she seemed as one going down into the shadow of death. But she recovered – her splendid constitution carried her through, though several months elapsed ere she was able to leave her sick room.

All this I know even to details', said the doctor, 'for I was then of necessity her most trusted attendant. I had therefore the privilege also of knowing that she had no sooner recovered her powers of reflection, than she enquired for, and pled for, the restoration of her child. Yet she pled in vain. One scene I can never forget – one in which the mother's affection and the mother's right was urged without effect against Robert Marchbank's idea of the family position – in society and the church – and his high reckoning of what constituted respectability'.

The doctor once more paused, and once more looked in the face of Mrs. Graham. In response to a sign he saw there, he resumed his seat and the mistress of Ravenhall continued the recital. 'I should just like to say', she began, 'that when James Graham – the father of my child – returned home, having been detained in the West Indies for long months beyond his calculated sojourn there, we were married and unitedly we pled for the return of our child. Our united pleadings proved, however, useless against the iron will and stony heart of my elder brother. I must also say – for justice must be done in this matter to everyone – that my other two brothers, James and John, knew nothing of what was done with the child, and could not help in securing its restoration. The man Graham, whom ye saw but an hour ago, was a servant of Robert's and obedient to his every wish. I knew the man when I saw him to-day, but did not know till now that he had been an active agent in the plot against my peace'.

She stopped as if overcome with her own thoughts, paused for a moment, and then resumed:

'Certain members of my family, as well as my husband, know as much of this story that I could tell them; they must now, each one of them, learn it from me in its entirety. If I did not, the world would brew it in the vats of scandal, and poison the public ears with it. The law makes my restored son the possible recipient of every privilege his brothers enjoy. The law is more merciful than the world of human-kind, who would tie his good name for ever to the crushing wheels of malice and obloquy because the manner of his birth displeased them. But mere law – human law – I hope, shall never alone rule my house. Rather let it be the rule of justice and right, and generous forgiveness, and all-abiding love that shall dominate my floor and roof-tree. And now that we have all heard this tale, let us lay it to heart and muse over it. Come with me, ladies, and you gentlemen retire for a time; we shall meet again within the hour`.

So saying, the lady of Ravenhall rose, and the company followed her example.

She took with gentle and kindly force the hand of Mrs. Macintyre, and led her away; while Mary, Mrs. Ralston, Mrs. Hardie and Dora, the daughter of the house, brought up the rear.

`While we are together`, observed Mr. Ralston, soon as the trio were alone, `we must not miss the opportunity – which we may never have again – to set down the facts of this strange yet verifiable story and, as Dr. Hardie is the only really neutral person amongst us, I should beg of him to have such measures taken, even to-night, as will prove the foundations of a clear statement of facts – a statement which, I hope, he will undertake to write without delay`.

`If the doctor`, said Orrason, `will undertake this important task, I will gladly furnish him with all the statements I have in my possession, and with the names of persons, places, books, and documents where such may be found. He already has the paper of the man Graham, and the good Mrs. Macintyre, with others present, will not fail to fill in each their necessary parts`.

`As this duty`, replied the doctor, `is one which must be under-taken; and as I am – I must also admit – the only one who could rightly discharge it, I shall, with Mrs. Graham`s leave, proceed with it at once`.

`That shall not be difficult to gain`, asserted Ralston, and as he spoke the doctor rose and hied him to the mistress of Ravenhall. Returning almost on the instant, the enthusiastic little man exclaimed, `With all her heart, and all her help! And further assist-ance may be obtained from old Moodie and Margaret. They were both concerned – though unwittingly – at the birth and the taking away of the hero of to-night, and will be able to give the links in the chain of this history.` And the ardent medico looked the picture of satisfaction.

'But let me understand`, enquired Orrason, `though it looks like going to the beginning when the end is near, where is now the master of the house? Where is Mr. Graham, whom I must now call father? Where *is* he, and what is the reason of his absence? Can any of you gentlemen explain`? and Orrason looked from one to the other of his auditors.

'That is a matter`, said Ralston, `I should have made clear to you before now. But other matters supervened, and besides, as we can easily see, it was useless, not to say indelicate or absurd, to explain these circumstances to you, Mr. Orrason, till it was clear you were the actual son of Mr. and Mrs. Graham. That has now been proved and the way is clear`.

The family of Ravenhall`, continued the Laird of Craigneuk and The Drums, `have long been connected with land and mercantile interests in the West Indies – in the Island of Antigua. It was during one of his earlier absences in connection with this business years ago that you, Mr. Orrason, were born at Dunraggan. Ten years ago, one of the sons – Robert – was sent out there to push his fortune – and he has already pushed it to some purpose. He was recommended to a rich, long-established planter – a Mr. Syme – at the little town of Falmouth, and he is now married to a daughter of old Syme, has a plantation of his own, and is evidently pulling up a fabulous fortune. So well has he succeeded that he is contemplating taking over the entire family business there, and it is with the view of fixing the arrangements in legal form that Mr. Graham has found it necessary to go out to Antigua. You look surprised, Mr. Orrason – is there any coincidence`? queried Ralston, stopping short and looking towards our hero.

'If I do look surprised`, said Orrason, `I certainly have good reasons for doing so. I will tell you why. When I left Antigua I arranged a settlement with a Robert Graham of Falmouth, who was married to a daughter of Mr. Syme, to take over my belongings, so as to permit me to return home. When I did so, I had not the most distant notion that he was my brother, nor did I know that my father had any property there. Mr. Graham must, therefore, have gone out to arrange matters with the very man with whom I had most intimate and important business connections'.

If Orrason was surprised at first, it was now the turn of both Ralston and the doctor to look in wonder at each other, to ask explanations, to lay the threads of connection together, and to be astonished at the little web of life these threads had formed.

While they are doing so, the ladies are enjoying each other's company in their own rooms and in their own way. Mrs. Graham, Mrs. Ralston and Mrs. Hardie were old friends – they loved and respected each other, and rejoiced with each other over the light that had so unexpectedly come out of darkness. Mary's quiet, yet decisive, ways made her at once an object of interest and regard to them, but the unobtrusive sedateness and calm demeanour of Mrs. Macintyre made her the central figure. Mrs. Graham petted her, while Mary and the others knew not how to show their respect and gratitude to the motherly woman.

The evening was now advancing, the family was gathering, and the social tea table brought the members together once more. The night sped on and, as darkness came, lights gleamed on the windows and figures moved too and fro in shadows on the blinds.

It was Saturday evening, and the guests were constrained to wait over the succeeding day, and see at least one Sabbath at Ravenhall, ere the parting came.

CHAPTER XLII

A family gathering in the parish church — The 'old spirit of adventure' — On for Glasgow, and ship for Antigua in search of his father — The elder brother.

The calmness of the Scotch Sabbath morning broke over Ravenhall. The noisy rooks, however, cawed and gurgled and screamed among the tall trees, now bursting into leaf, and all around the quietly ascending smoke from cottage fires told of the peace and holy purpose of the day.

Orrason was early abroad and with Ralston consumed the morning hours in quiet converse amid the surroundings of the olden place. The breakfast bell summoned all to the dining-hall, and the good and still noble-looking lady, in the absence of the master, performed alike the social and sacred duties of the hour. All were happy, for all now understood each other and, to some sufficient extent, knew each other's place and influence in the family circle.

The family coach carried all to the parish church, where they found seats within the family pew. The strange faces among the family of Ravenhall drew many a curious look, and doubtless elicited many a searching question. The precentor, assigned his task, read his lines and sung out in thin, tremulous tones:

> `Love no unseemly carriage shows,
> Nor selfishly confined;
> She glows with social tenderness,
> And feel for all mankind.
> Love beareth much, much she believes,
> And still she hopes the best;
> Love meekly suffers many a wrong,
> Though sore with hardships pressed`.

And so on to the end of the paraphrase – the voices of the congregation rolling roughly over the sacred poet's sweet refrains. The long prayer followed and the people gladly seated themselves at its wished-for close. Then the preacher arose, and in sad and solemn tones gave out his text:

'For this my son was dead, and is alive again, was lost and is found'.

It was no sermon premeditated and made to suit the occasion. Like everything else in Orrason's carefully warded life, it fell into its place as the dewdrop falls, and gave wonder, mystery and beauty to the hour.

In the fashion of the time, the preacher split and divided, and cut and carved his theme, till every possible phase of fatherhood and sonship, of faith, hope and trust, and of life and death and the resurrection were spread out before the patient listeners.

The service over, the kirk soon emptied itself, and groups of village gossips stood on each side of the exit path to mark the visage and the dresses of the strangers.

As they went forth, kindly greetings assailed the eye and ear of Mrs. Graham and, less so, that of the Ralstons, yet all looked with pleased and happy expression on the white-haired comely dame that leaned on the arm of John Orrason.

The day sped on in mingled converse, in mutual intercourse, and in growing respect and love for each other. Between Mrs. Macintyre and Orrason the lady of Ravenhall seemed lost in her preference, but with her son she had much to say and many things to settle. Claims to rights in property and place, it was agreed, should neither be entertained nor spoken of till Mr. Graham returned. Orrason assured his mother that the recognition of his place and connection had bred no fresh ambitions within his mind, nor had he any wish to disturb the possessions of any member of the family.

In the evening the minister called at Ravenhall – curious as any other to verify rumours that had reached the manse, and troubled its usually placid waters. He and Dr. Hardie had it all their own way for a time. Then they were joined by Mrs. Graham, the other ladies, and

Orrason and Ralston. Soon the whole family circle had contributed to the story the minister came to hear, and had put him in a fair position to guide and correct the floating gossip of the parish.

When Orrason came to know that several months must elapse before the master of Ravenhall could return, he formed a project in his own mind, and let that project grow into resolution. He talked about it to Mary, who raised no insuperable barrier against it. The old spirit of adventure rose within our hero's breast, and business considerations and family connections spurred him on, and gave it shape and form. He would go out to Antigua and find his father and brother there.

When the idea was mentioned to Mrs. Graham, she felt at first surprise and then also possibly a shade of alarm. But carefully thinking over its possible details, she found that many useful, many essential purposes could be served by Orrason's going 'out into the west'.

On the following day it was talked over with the help of Dr. Hardie, Ralston and the ladies, and finally made part of the programme of the future.

And here, had I, the privileged narrator of these chapters, been wise, and were I simply telling a tale of entertaining romance, I should here have closed my story of John Orrason's life, and made the long ostracised castaway come back into society, with a grandly affectionate scene in the drawing-room of Ravenhall. But as I must lead where Providence, in this weird and wondrous history, has led before me, I must also trace my hero to the far west, and wait anon the further guidance of His will.

Mary, it was arranged, should leave Strathearn with the others, and after her husband had sailed, return from Glasgow to Ravenhall. Her father, she knew, had more than one good ship in which her husband could find either command or passage to his old haunts in the Leeward Isles. The voyage would result in bringing home the father and master of Ravenhall, and put all other matters in final train for the settlement of Orrason's troubled life, his position and place.

Another day had passed the meridian ere the well-rested horses from the Spire Inn were brought out, and the great lumbering machine wheeled into the courtyard. Many a fond good-bye was said ere the cortege drew away. Mrs. Graham and her family of sons and daughters stood at the entrance to the covered way and waved off with tearful eyes the visitors from afar.

The long drive through Gleneagles to the Yetts of Muckhart and thence to Dollar had been successfully accomplished and Dr. and Mrs. Hardie found themselves once more in their own house. `Good-bye` once more and the spanking horses, knowing they are going home, are soon at Craigneuk, and the Ralstons bid all `good speed` as the travellers strike eastward to Dunfermline. At the Spire that worthy, Charley Graham, had his `consideration` fully paid, and Mrs. Macintyre rested for a while from the fatigues of the journey and then, after many affectionate assurances, was carried down to Rosythe.

Orrason, ere he left Dunfermline, visited Marchbank House and made himself known to the surprised brothers there – his uncles. Here he had no herald to announce his approach, yet he was received with the warmest demonstration of respect and family regard.

A few days more saw our hero and his loved and faithful Mary on their way to Edinburgh, and thence, in due time, by coach to Glasgow. As they went, he pointed out to her the flower-covered braes and woods that had attracted his young eye in the now far off days of his youth. Arrived at the western city, they were met at the Trongate by the anxious and joyous Captain and Mrs. Seaton and, at home in Tradeston, they had a grand night of telling of stories and listening to wonders that had never had their parallel before! They retired to rest ere the tales were half told – indeed, with the Seatons, the stories lasted for weeks and cropped up for months after.

An arrangement was soon made by which Orrason was enabled to traverse the Atlantic and after some weeks to find himself at last in St. John's, Antigua. From here he quickly found his way to Falmouth, and early one morning wakened the son-in-law of the Symes – Robert Graham.

`In the words of the old song, Orrason, let me ask `hoo cam` ye here``? said young Graham, laughingly.

`Your question is a double one`, replied Orrason, `and seeks to know at once the means and reason of my coming, is it not so`?

'Yes, it is so`, and Robert Graham still smiled enquiringly.

'Is your father within earshot`? queried Orrason, making his first effort at announcement.

'My father`! ejaculated Graham, in astonishment. 'The question is a kindly one but, coming from you, a strange one. Do you know ought of my father`?

'More than you might possibly suspect`, and Orrason smiled in turn.

'If that be so, then I must try to find him. He`ll be over at Mr. Symes` place. Will you wait a minute, Mr. Orrason, till I despatch a messenger in search`.

'Well, no`, said Orrason, 'I`d rather go over myself – though possibly, if you had time, you might bear me company`.

'With all my heart`, replied the cheerful Graham. 'It is not every day we have you here. Besides, I hear by script and letter you`re not the same man now. Got married like other folks and given yourself away. Still, it`s the way of the world`, and he strode rapidly towards the office of Mr. Symes.

Arrived there, the old-new friend was received with all the glowing heat of the tropics.

'I am glad beyond measure to see you, Mr. Orrason and I hope no frown of fortune has hailed you hither or bleak disaster`s blast blown you over here`?

'No, nothing of the kind – quite the reverse`, said Orrason. 'Never was one so blest or had better prospects for the future. But where is Mr. Graham, senior? Excuse me, Mr. Syme, if I express a desire to speak to him first as to my business here`.

'Surely, surely, Mr. Orrason, come this way,` and Orrason was led to an airy, wind-blown chamber of flowers in the garden behind the office, and here he and Robert Graham found the senior resting and chatting to one of the estate managers.

This functionary dismissed, our hero approached and drew from his pocket a long and clearly-written letter from 'Dr. James Macintosh Hardie to James Haldane Graham` and handed it to the gentleman before him.

As Graham read the letter, he changed colour – flushed and paled, and flushed and paled again; then, raising his eyes to his new visitor and letting them wander to the features of his son, Robert, his countenance seemed as if suffused with a new light. He rose up, suddenly seized Orrason and Robert each by the hand and, looking from one to the other, he whispered in hoarse, passion-fraught tones, `Robert, this is your elder brother`!

CHAPTER XLIII

The heir of Ravenhall – Life in St. John's, Antigua – The slavery question.

It would be bootless work to describe the sequel of the scene introduced in the last chapter. The little conservatory did indeed witness a passionate outburst of affection between grown men, such as is rarely witnessed anywhere. The vision of his lost son had often floated through the mind of James Graham, but he had never once pictured him as the strongly-built, broad shouldered, yet mild-eyed man, clad in seaman's garb, and bronzed by the weather and storms of varied climes, he now saw before him.

The story of his life was told by Orrason himself to the father and son – his father and brother. The manifold searches by himself and Mary to find out his connections were soon described, and the culminating visit to Ravenhall set before them in all its details. No doubt was left, no lingering suspicion lagged behind in their minds. The man before them was fully accepted as the son of James Graham and the heir of Ravenhall.

The head of the house and, in a less degree, the son, too, felt that the newcomer had changed the world for them both. They felt neither regret nor grudge at this change, but possibly sensed that they were dealing with a man whose magnanimous nature would scorn to give occasion for any merely worldly apprehension of loss or gain. If good fortune came to him, he would not forbid it, but the channel must be pure and the fountain one of sympathy and affection.

The visit, however, so far as the Symes and Grahams were concerned, had made business considerations a matter of hurry and despatch. Old Mr. Graham, now that he knew how he stood, and having learned that Orrason could, if wanted, return to the homeland in a few weeks at most, determined to arrange his affairs in such a way that he could go home with the same ship. All this was agreed to, and the details fixed with the cosy, nonchalant celerity of the western planter.

After this and until the eve of departure from St. John`s, the days were spent in close application to business in warehouses, shipping port, office and field and the evenings in tea parties, balls and junkettings, such as only the easy-going dwellers in those western isles could imagine or struggle through. Orrason made himself as free to these, and as happily abandoned in them, as his nature would permit.

He was more inclined to enjoy this new social life as he learned more and more of the true Negro character. The old and almost forgotten debate with Lieutenant Schellsey came again to his mind, as he viewed the slaves at labour and at play – the body and mind bent in the one case to the performance of enforced tasks, and in the other flowing out in song and grace of movement and innocence of intercourse. He could not help concluding that the dark-skinned race was as capable of enjoying and guiding themselves in freedom as the white man was. At a gathering – assembly, soiree, and concert rolled into one – at the house of young Mr. Graham, he could not help admiring the grace and dignity and natural courtesy with which the young and old among the Negroes tripped through the mazy dance, interpreted their songs, and joked and laughed with each other.

Orrason contrasted this happy meeting with another of a higher and grander kind at St. John`s. Here he was the invited guest of the chief men of the country, the local Parliament and Council, and the rich grandees with their ladies and their daughters from the six parishes and rich districts of Antigua.

All these were fully aware of the superior caste, manners, and nature of their dark-skinned labourers and, though both harsh and cruel to them at times, they boasted of them and pointed them out and seemed to feel a pride in their doings. Orrason did not fail to note the inconsistency of the planters in retaining as slaves those whom – they willingly admitted – would, in any land, adorn the status of freedom.

During the weeks he spent in the island – visiting in every quarter and being welcomed by every planter, as one newly come from the homeland, and who could tell of all things new and wonderful going on there – he never missed an opportunity of reiterating the arguments of Buxton, Brougham and Canning, and showing that the system of slavery was doomed in the Windward and Leeward Islands, and that great honour ought to attach to that colony which would first sweep it out of existence.

These arguments and statements of Orrason gave occasion to a series of district meetings at which the whole subject – by help of the multitudinous newspapers and publications our hero had brought with him – was fully discussed. A general meeting of the whites was held at St. John's, at which John Orrason was invited to speak. This was a new experience in his career but, as his heart and mind were fully thrown into the arguments for freedom, he made a deep and, as it proved, a lasting impression in favour of his dark brothers and sisters. For it is but the ABC of facts in the history of slave emancipation to know that the island of Antigua – thanks to the advocacy of John Orrason – was even in advance of the home country in granting full freedom to her slaves.

Mr. Graham, senior, though busied largely in business affairs, could not help feeling proud of the son who could thus move a whole community to such a noble purpose. He aided Orrason's arguments by every means in his power, and urged his son, Robert, to set an example which would resound to his credit for ever after, and which would be sure to be followed whenever it was begun. At Falmouth, in Antigua, we know the movement for emancipation began [73], and here was first lifted the voice of praise and thankfulness to one whom, coming from afar across the trackless sea, had raised the flag and fought the fight of liberty.

Business matters had gone well with Robert Graham during the years he had been in the colony, and he was able to make such a settlement with his elder brother as to send that favoured one homeward, not only a happier, but a wiser and richer, man.

But time passes eternally onwards and the hour for the homeward voyage was now at hand. The ship – after many a warm God-send and wet-eyed parting – sailed from English Harbour and, bending her spars gracefully to the breeze, was soon, to the aching eyes that followed her, hull down on the horizon. The voyage, with the usual luck of trips by sea in the tropics, was one of varied experience and fortune, but at length the ship entered the Clyde and was soon berthed at the Broomielaw.

A few happy days and nights under the hospitable roof of Captain Seaton proved a cheerful set off to the house in Strathearn. Going by the very paths over which Mary and himself were guided in the first dark days of their search, Orrason took a pride in showing his father where he first found traces of his parents. He saw evidence of the hand of Providence as he followed up these traces in his ardent seeking for the infancy of his life.

I have but little now to add. My tale of the castaway is drawing to an end, though my interest in his career must dwell with me while life shall last. The lady of Ravenhall and Mary – there were two ladies of the keep now – received with joy the wanderers of the deep. The whole family, apart from Robert on the Western Isle, gathered round the cheerful festive board, and rejoiced that they had found their son and brother again.

Many a family council was held, and many a consultation with Dr. Hardie, and the legal guides in matters patrimonial. Since love and goodwill ruled every question, the difficulties of settlement were never seen. Our hero was lifted into his proper place in the family. He was known no longer as John Orrason, but as Charles Graham – curiously, the very 'C. G.' after which he had so long been seeking [74]. He added the middle name of Orrason, to keep his life of banishment ever before his eyes and ears. He never forgot the guides and nurses of his infancy and, as he came in good time to rule in Ravenshall, many a poor, neglected soul looked up as he passed and blessed Charles Orrason Graham.

CHAPTER XLIV

A parting word in explanation – The young Laird of Craigneuk and Madge Marchbank – A `sudden eclipse` – A Court of Session case.

The narrative of facts – the footnote to history – which Dr. Hardie undertook to write, came in due time into existence. He had determined that it should not be a mere *précis* of dry, hard statements; these, doubtless, must be prominent by their presence, but the whole story had proved so full of romance that he found it impossible to exclude the form, if not indeed the essence, of romantic composition. He traced the tale of love and hate from its very beginnings, and, while he drew warm and lively pictures of the actors in his little drama, he no less delighted to expand in descriptive essays the scenes in which they were engaged.

He described the nature of the business in which the house of Marchbank had been engaged; he portrayed the different characters of the three brothers, their country and town residences, their friends and customers. Among the latter he placed the name of Thomas Ralston and, picturing this genial west of Fife laird at the time of his first connection with the brothers and with Madge Marchbank, he thus presented him:

`Thomas Ralston had come into the possession of the paternal acres when still a young man, and he showed his peculiar appreciation of his position by pushing his claims to notice and assuming the lead of the more dashing spirits among the landed gentry of the district. He rode his own hunter when the pack was out, and in the whole field there was no finer mount than his and no more daring follower of the hounds than the young Laird of Craigneuk and The Drums. When any wild work was on hand, any heavy field to cross or ditch and fence to leap, the lead was sure to be given by young Ralston.

At any rout and ball in the wast owre he was in urgent request and constant with his presence. If he was the envy of the young swells of his neighbourhood, he was no less the favourite of the younger and aspiring ladies of his acquaintance. His person was formed in a mould of fair, manly proportions, and his manners were as frank as his countenance was open and free.

His 'animal spirits' – to quote an almost scientific term – were ever overflowing and effervescent, and no one could ever feel sad in the presence of Thomas Ralston. Yet, with all his love of fun and merriment he never allowed himself to forget his own self-respect. Indulgence was the common social vice of the time, and the swiller of unnumbered glasses and bottles was the accepted hero of the after-dinner debauch. But neither here nor at the chance foregatherings at the Dunderawe Arms, could it ever be said that Craigneuk was beyond his own control [75].

Yet his expenses were heavy, and his outlays beyond his legitimate means. He had in the earliest of his transactions already impaired the extent of his patrimony, and burdened the remainder with IOUs which, if they did not greatly damp his spirits, were destined, at no distant date, to put an imperative stop to his present career.

The Marchbanks were known to be wealthy. Their mortgages were planted on properties big and small around their ancient town of Dunfermline and were – as might have been expected – well-secured. The holders of these were fairly numerous and, unfortunately, included our dashing young landlord, Thomas Ralston.

And now, having described *sans courtesie* the leading man in this interlude of youth, let me introduce the lady – Madge Marchbank – of our story. The death of her mother at an early period of her life and the more recent demise of her father had left Madge Marchbank to the care and keeping of her wealthy brothers. These regarded her with an extravagance of affection that displayed itself on every public and private occasion, and in a thousand different ways.

Her life, spent sometimes in Dunfermline, sometimes at Dunraggan, was one long round of pleasure or, at least, of time spent wholly in the satisfaction of 'her own sweet will'. Her health was robust to an abnormal degree – her strength and agility were the source of endless comment. She had been well trained and educated in all that category of curious things which go to make up the accomplishments of a lady.

She was fond of riding and, if any obstreperous colt wanted a little breaking in, there were few better fitted for the task than Madge Marchbank. In the north, when living at Dunraggan, she was more familiar with the saddle than with the sofa and the young bloods of the district had a hard task to keep themselves in countenance when Madge was allowed to lead the cry.

Her most constant companion in private or general turn-outs was the irrepressible Craigneuk as our friend Thomas Ralston was always named. In every way he seemed to suit her, in every way he appreciated and esteemed her. If he was reckless, she was no less fearless, and both seemed to understand each other so entirely that everyone believed that not only attraction but confidences of a much more tender kind had passed between them. They were allowed to lead the field, the ball, the rout, the play, not only because they desired to be matched together, but also, as it was believed, they were pledged and bound to each other.

All this came suddenly, and without apparent reason, to an end. Madge paid one of her usual visits – it turned out a long one – to Dunraggan, and if the young country gents of West Fife heard of it with regret, they had no reason to wonder. But when the visit extended to many weeks, and was gradually counted by months, the feeling of surprise grew in intensity till it reached its height. And then, as Madge came no more back into the sunny slopes of West Fife, it died down, till the name of Madge Marchbank became only a glory they could refer to with expressions of bygone exultation and present regret.

The real cause of her sudden eclipse was known only to Madge's family and to Ralston and, when the parties concerned were made aware that the irrepressible Madge, the heroine of the hunting field, the toast and boast of every hopeful swell in West Fife, was about to fall from her pedestal of high respect, the consternation of the one could only be matched by the astonishment of the other.

The brothers thought first and only how to save their own and the family honour. Their line of enquiry was as obvious to them as it is to the reader hereof – though it must be admitted that here every move and effort utterly broke down. Speculation and suggestions as to the paternity were as endless as they were useless. In this matter Madge was as self-willed as in every other. She would make no statement, give no hint, or relieve anxiety by giving an explanation of any kind. At all times, strange, wilful and positive, she proved in this crisis of her life and fate more strange, wilful and positive than in any other event in her dashing career.

In these circumstances, the brothers could only fall back on what they knew – Ralston and Madge had been inseparable companions whenever possible chance or occasion gave an excuse for their meeting, and they had both been openly spoken of as entertaining for each other the warmest attachment and fondest affection.

Craigneuk was therefore taken into the confidence of the brothers Marchbank – and that filled him at once with the deepest regret and most intense surprise. It was now that he had his first intimation of Madge's condition, and the first indication of the imputation which the Marchbank family had attached to his character. Constrained by his liking for Madge and respect for her family, he voluntarily and at once promised that what he had learned should be communicated to no one.

But the further insinuation that he was bound to marry the lady – and that at the earliest possible moment – he would not on any condition entertain. He had respected, he had liked Madge Marchbank and all her ways. He had enjoyed and exulted in her company, and it had ever been a pleasure to him to meet her, but his intimacy and intercourse had presumed no further.

This refusal of the delicate impeachment on the part of Thomas Ralston, the Marchbank brothers could not accept. They knew there were good points in his character, but they believed also there were strong inducements to a young man and member of respectable society, to refuse acknowledgment in a case like this, even against fact. The obdurate silence of Madge herself might be construed as being part of an understanding with Ralston, as well as being a possible exoneration of his character. To the first of these hypotheses the brothers committed themselves.

Partly through their displeasure, partly through policy, the brothers kept Madge in entire ignorance of their dealings with Ralston, and when these utterly broke down, any reason for intimating or explaining to her the course taken with that gentleman had equally vanished.

Ralston had the very strongest reasons a man can have for rejecting the insistent demand of the Marchbank brothers. They, however, did not, and could not, see his inner soul, and the feeling left with them at the close of all their interviews was one of anger and displeasure, rather than that of satisfaction.

The brothers, having utterly failed with their weapons of appeal – mistaken as these were – sought, if not to secure their original purpose, at least to satisfy their desire for revenge and here, as already hinted, poor Ralston's financial condition, and his commercial relations with the Marchbanks, offered not one, but several openings for attack.

The mortgages had been neglected, interest payments had been forgotten, and the securities were now endangered. To seize these last, to alienate The Drums and Craigneuk, and strip the dashing Ralston of his all, was now the settled purpose of the Marchbanks. The intimation of a process in the Court of Session proved a terrible awakening to the gay and hitherto unthinking young laird. The stern realities of his condition burst at once upon him with a grim force he could no longer withstand; and he vowed, like the `Heir of Lynn`, that he would fight the battle of his patrimony and, if he won, he should be at once a new and better man [76].

The Court of Session is a field where everybody loses – it is only a question sometimes of who loses most. The legal campaign in which the firm of manufacturers and the young laird-farmer now engaged was fought for weeks and months of dire and fitful waiting, and though Thomas Ralston came out of it a poorer man than he ever believed he would become, he had saved his acres and his position, and he was proud and exultant in the midst of his losses.

As the case progressed it became known in the Court that causes other than those on the surface had led to the introduction of the litigation. Law Court judges like nothing worse than to be made fools of by pretending litigants, and when a hint was dropped by the defending counsel that Thomas Ralston had been dragged into the legal vortex in connection with a wholly different and exceedingly delicate matter connected with a female – a sister of the pursuers – the defender was recalled and questioned from the bench, and, though he held honourably to his compact with the Marchbanks, he was compelled to admit a knowledge of facts which gave colour and venue to the whole case. He was, as the lawyers have it, assoilzied from the conclusion of the summons.

The reader of this little personal history knows all the rest. The doctor's introduction has served well as our valedictory, and as we extend our thanks and bid him good-bye, we think of him with nothing but happy thoughts and pleasant recollections as the central figure of that now shadowy group of friends, called together by fate and fortune round the person and being of John Orrason.

❦

THE END

NOTES

1. The Court of Session paternity case is probably that of Kerr versus Syme. In 'Anent Dunfermline', Vol. II, item 53, January 23rd 1893, 'A child mystery', Thomson writes the following. 'To-day running over old stories of older times with my friend at Castle Blair, Geo. C. we fell upon the Kerr family. He told me that, early in the century, his grandfather (of the same name) and his grandmother, with his uncle, travelled on one occasion to Glasgow. His uncle carried a 'cut' or roll of cloth all the way to Torryburn and on the other side after they had crossed the Forth. His grandfather carried something else and his grandmother carried – a child. The child was handed over by the brothers Kerr for delivery to a party in Glasgow. The child was so delivered but what became of it no record sayeth. This child would probably be one borne by a relative of the Kerrs to one Syme, farmer, Primrose, who refused to acknowledge paternity even in the Court of Session. The brothers Kerr were somewhat scandalised and got the evidence of their relative's weakness, in this quiet way, out of sight'. There are several points of comparison between the Kerr family and the Marchbanks of the story – not only were both families were caught up in a paternity case but they shared a Dunfermline manufacturing background and the same names for the three brothers – Robert, James and John. For further details of the Kerr family see 'Anent Dunfermline', Vol. II, item 256-7.

2. The Ferry Toll was one of many toll-bars set up to collect dues from road users. It was situated at a crossroads south west of Inverkeithing between North Ferry and Rosyth Castle. In 1895 the toll-house was refurbished and opened for Glasgow policemen as 'The Police Convalescent Home at the Ferry Toll'.

3. There no longer seems to be an Inn of this name in North Queensferry, though there is one at nearby Limekilns.

4. Probably near the well or series of wells at the junction of Main Street and Old Kirk Road where the Waterloo Memorial now stands.

5. Ba`hill Road, probably Ballingall Road to the west of Milnathort.

6. Kilbagie near Kincardine was the site of a well-known distillery.

7. There is no trace of this now but the Bridgend Hotel stood here for many years. The Salutation Hotel still stands in the High Street.

8. Queich Bridge spans the burn to the south of Kinross. Another of the same name lies to the north.

9. Inhabitants of Inverkeithing named for the ancient Hat and Ribbon Race that takes place in August.

10. Kirkcaldy is known as the Lang Toon for its long High Street running parallel to the sea.

11. See note 2.

12. The North Kirk of Dunfermline lies at the eastern end of Golfdrum Street. `Mount Allan` is a mystery but may refer to one of the hills to the north or north-west, e.g. Craigluscar, Knock or Saline.

13. The Path is probably `the Fit-paith` or Chalmers Street/Woodhead Street, which were roughly paved on the eastern side.

14. The `check` road (or Lundin Road) ran to Crossford from what was known as Mount Hooly check toll just beyond Milesmark. Check tolls were set up to catch anyone who might try to cheat the Revenue by taking to the hills.

15. The 35-mile long Forth-Clyde Canal was opened in 1790. A `swift boat` was smaller and lighter than the `big` boats and carried 60 passengers, 36 in steerage and 24 in cabins. `Anent Dunfermline` II, 1023

16. There were several refuges for children and young people and the one Thomson has in mind may be the Children`s Night Refuge on the south side of Rotten Row near the High Street.

17. Wilson Charity School for boys was opened in 1780 to the north of the Trongate, after a native of Glasgow, George Wilson, who became a wealthy London merchant, bequeathed £3000 in 1778 to clothe and educate 48 poor boys. A new school was built

in nearby Montrose Street in 1823 at a cost of £2000. By the 1880s, there were a master and two mistresses and 86 boys who were accepted at 8 years of age and stayed for four years. The school seems to have provided a good basic education. Details from `Report by the Town Clerk as to the Several Educational Endowments in the Administration of which the Magistrates and/or the Town Council of the City of Glasgow are interested, 1881`.

18. For a description of a mill-owner – Alexander Struthers of East Mill – travelling from Dunfermline to Kirkcaldy to buy his flax see `Anent Dunfermline`, II, 247.

19. The baron bailie was a baron's deputy with both civil and criminal jurisdiction in the Baron Court of the barony. A baron might be a member of the lowest rank of the nobility or could be anyone holding land directly of the Crown.

20. Vous Rocks, south of Kirkcaldy, appear on O. S. maps as East and West Vows, and Dawtle Mill, near Raith Lake, appears as Datie Mill.

21. Fréjus is a Riviera town in south east France.

22. This mutiny about poor food and low pay took place at Sheerness in May – June 1797.

23. In a fable, the baby Orson was snatched and suckled by a she-bear and grew up to be `the wild man of the forest` and the terror of France.

24. HMS Impregnable was launched in 1802, a second rate, wooden-walled vessel of 2406 tons. It was a training ship in Devonport from 1862-88 and in 1891 it became HMS Caledonia Boys` Training Ship, anchored to the west of the Forth Bridge. It accommodated 1000 boys and crew mainly from Scotland and northern England. It was withdrawn from active service in 1906. HMS Impregnable was second in order at the bombardment of Algiers where 50 of her seamen were killed and 170 injured.

25. The Dey was the pasha or governor of Algiers.

26. This should probably be Bone (now Annaba), a Mediterranean port of north-east Algeria.

27. Gibraltar.
28. As a rule, the title 'commander' was used for the chief officer of a smaller ship; 'captain' for the officer on a larger or 'rated' ship. Thomson sometimes uses them interchangeably.
29. The voyage across the Atlantic from Africa to the West Indies on board a slaveship.
30. Boglily is south east of Kirkcaldy near Raith Lake.
31. Banana Island and Yawry Bay are in Sierra Leone.
32. L.E.L was Letitia Elizabeth Landon, a well-known poet of the early 19th century. Married to George Maclean, Governor of Cape Coast (now part of Ghana), she died in mysterious circumstances in 1838 aged 36.
33. Suicide.
34. Thomas Clarkson (1760-1846) was largely responsible for the abolition of slavery in the British colonies, 1833. Sir Thomas Fowell Buxton MP (1786-1845) was Wilberforce's successor in the anti-slavery battle in Parliament. Baron Henry Brougham (1778-1868), was a Whig politician involved with reform of all kinds, including slavery reform.
35. Guadaloupe and Grande Terre.
36. Maria Galante, an island south east of Guadaloupe.
37. The Gulf of Mexico.
38. The Golden Horn was a fabled harbour of the Byzantine Empire in Constantinople, now Istanbul.
39. As Christopher North, John Wilson (1785-1854) published *City of the Plague and Other Poems* in 1816.
40. The firm of Sproul and Laurie is probably an imaginary one.
41. St. Mungo is the patron saint of Glasgow.
42. Clough should probably be Cloch, which lies on a bend of the Firth of Clyde near Gourock and has a famous lighthouse.
43. A 15th century anonymous verse.
44. The new suburb of Tradeston was established just south of the Clyde opposite the Broomielaw and its first house was built in 1790.
45. Now the Glasgow Bridge.

46. James Law, Minister of Bethelfield United Presbyterian Church (U.P.), Links, Kirkcaldy, 1799-1859.

47. William Kidston, Minister of East Campbell Street U. P. Church, Glasgow for over 50 years. First Moderator of the U. P. Church in 1847.

48. The First Secession of the Kirk took place in 1733 on the question of patronage.

49. Rev. Robert Shirra was a popular minister in Linktown, Kirkcaldy from 1797-1840.

50. Stories about Ralph Erskine were part of the folklore of Dunfermline. For a recent account see `Erskine, Ralph (1686-1752)` by D. C. Lachman, in the *Oxford Dictionary of National Biography*, (New DNB), 200

51. Toussaint L`Ouverteur led a slave revolt against the French in Haiti (1791-3). He capitulated in 1802 but died in a French dungeon in 1803.

52. In the Peninsular Wars against the French, Torres Vedras were lines of defence built around Lisbon in 1809-10. The Battle of Busaco was won by the Portuguese and British led by Wellington.

53. In his testament, George Wilson stipulated that beneficiaries of his charity should hear a special sermon at St. Andrew`s Church on each anniversary of his death (April 26th).

54. Anonymous, ancient ballad.

55. John Mayne (1759-1836), poet and newpaper editor was born in Dumfries and lived in Glasgow 1782-7.

56. The Brown Bear Inn may have been based on the ancient Golden Lion in King Street, Stirling, whose frontage featured the figure of a lion.

57. A broadsheet of the time shows that a riot against two resurrectionists occurred in Stirling on the night of April 19th 1823. Thomson used alternative names for Mitchell and Mcnab, the actual `disturbers of the dead`, and for Forrest the medical student, but kept the real names of Sheriff Macdonald, Provost Thomson and Captain Jeffrey. An account of the trial that gave rise to the riots can be found in the Stirling Journal and

Advertiser, April 24th 1823. The broadsheet 'Riot in Stirling' begins: An account of a serious riot which took place in Stirling on Saturday the 19th of April 1823, when two disturbers of the Dead were almost torn to pieces by the populace, and a party of soldiers being brought from the Castle to quell the riot, fired on the mob, when several persons were wounded'.

58. St. Ringan – an alternative name for St. Ninian.

59. A famous old whisky.

60. The Battle of Bannockburn between the English under Edward II and Scotland led by Robert the Bruce took place on June 24th 1314 and resulted in a resounding victory for the Scots.

61. Source of this verse is unknown at present.

62. Kate Simpson's Brae lies at the east end of the village of Crossford.

63. The Spire Inn and Hotel was established in 1817 in the Guildhall (or Cross or County Buildings) of 1807-8. It was let as an inn to Mr. R. Laidlaw for 19 years and remained an inn until it was sold in 1845. *Anent Dunfermline*, Vol. II, item 174

64. Sang schools existed before the Reformation but records for Dunfermline exist only from 1640 in the Kirk Session minutes. The words precentor, music master, reader and clerk changed over time and sometimes one person would combine two of more of the positions. The precentor was responsible for the singing in the kirk and was generally a teacher of music.

65. James Rankine came to Dunfermline from Glasgow to be master of the song school, precentor and registrar in 1819. He died aged 52 in 1849. He would have been a little younger than John Orrason. E. Henderson, *Annals of Dunfermline*, 1879, p. 659.

66. Then a wild area, now site of the extensive Mossmorran petrochemical complex.

67. Carnock had a history of argument and debate being the site of covenanter unrest in the 1640s and, under the minister Thomas Gillespie, playing a leading part in the first secession debate.

68. Abercrombie is the older name for Crombie; its meaning – the mouth of the Cromb or Crombie – may refer to the Torry Burn.

S. Taylor, *The Place Names of Fife*, Vol. 1, section on Torryburn Parish.

69. Rosyth Naval Dockyard was built on the site of Orchardhead Farm.

70. This Court of Session case has already been mentioned. `Lord Siston` appears to be an invented name.

71. Name probably derived from one of Ralston`s farms.

72. Thomson probably had a house in mind for the mansion of Ravenhall in Strathearn and for Marchbank House in Dunfermline and Dunraggan near Dollar, though none has been identified to date.

73. There was a slave revolt in Antigua in 1736. Emancipation (in name at least) eventually came in 1834.

74. It seems curious that Thomson has two Charles Grahams in his story, especially as one is a far from likeable character. He may have been influenced in his choice of name for Charley Graham by stories from the 1770s of `a gypsie` Charles Graham who was a `crafty pickpocket and thief`. `Anent Dunfermline`, Vol. IV, item 49.

75. This may be based on the Dundonald Arms, Culross.

76. In an old ballad the reckless Heir of Lynn sold his land and title but managed by a stroke of fortune to buy them back, becoming a sadder but wiser man.

GLOSSARY OF SCOTTISH WORDS
AND OTHER REFERENCES

Angle-berried: lumpy and bumpy
Arcana: mysteries
Arles: earnest money
Assoilzie: decide in favour of; absolve
Athort: all over, about, across

Baron bell: official bell of a barony
Bathochtit: thoughtful, pensive
Bawbee caun`le: halfpenny candle
Beaver: fur hat
Bedrall: beadle
Beit: relieve, ameliorate
Ben: inner, inner or best room
Bien: comfortable, cosy
Birkies: smart fellows
Black-a-vised: dark-faced, swarthy
Blue Town: the sea
Boniface: innkeeper – several sources
including a hospitable pope.
Bottom: a weaver, after character in A
Midsummer Night`s Dream
Bound thirl: bound with sense of duty,
obligation or affection
Braid: broad
But the house: through the house

Cabal: scheming group of politicians
Can: chimney pot
Carse: low land along a river
Caunle: candle
Cautioner: guarantor
Chiel: fellow
Chuckie: pebble or marble
Clashin`: noisy, bustling
Cockery: shaky
Collyshangie: uproar, skirmish
Cosy: intimate
Couthie: cosy, sociable, agreeable
Cracky: chatty
Cranage: fees for use of crane

Craw-fit: crow-like, crafty

Dark-vised: dark-faced, swarthy
Dead Sea fruit: traditionally said to be
fair to the eye but bitter to the taste.
Dook: prob. duck, coarse linen or cotton
Dottal: daft
Dowlas: coarse linen cloth

Embro: Edinburgh
Ettle: purpose, intention

Fia fail: stone of destiny
Fell: stern, energetic
Flou o` saut: pinch of salt
Flee: fly
Furthie: bold, go-ahead

Gar`d: made or done
Gey: very
Gilpie: lively
Gin: if
Gleg-eyed: sharp-eyed
Gudesake: heavens sake
Guerdon: reward, recompense
Gustful: hearty

Hairst: harvest
Haughs: river-lands, bank
Hauvre-meal bannock: oatmeal
bannock, oatcake
Heart: hurt
Hech how!: heigh-ho! dear me!
Heddles: vertical cords of hand-loom
Hempie: a rogue deserving to be hung
Hiddling: secret, hidden, mysterious

Ilka: every, such
Iron-tongued: forced, reluctant

Jaupit: splattered (usually with ink)

Jehu: coachman – after biblical Jehu, 2 Kings ix, 20.

Kail: cabbage or other greens
Kitchen: extras in food
Kittle: tricky, difficult
Kythed: turned out or proved to be

Laft: church loft
Linties: linnets
Loupers: travellers

Marrow: companion, mate
Mavis: song-thrush
Merle: blackbird
Mool howkers: earth diggers
Mother Carey's chicken: a seabird

Naig, naigie: small horse or pony
Near-hand: almost

Orra: extra, odd, unwanted

Partan: crab
Pawky: shrewd, astute
Phaeton: driver of the chariot of the sun
Pock: sack
Pree the parritch: taste the porridge

Ranz des vaches: an alpine horn tune

Sanctuar: sanctuary
Sans courtesie: without flattery
Seat tree: weaver's seat in hand-loom
Shools: shovels
Smerten them up: enliven them
Sonsie: fine
Soople: supple
Speeled: speeded
Speiring or sperring: enquiring
Spiel: climb

Steer about: bustling, busy
Stoor: commotion
Strath: river valley
Surtout: greatcoat
Swarfed: fainted

Tacksman: tenant or lease-holder
Tak tent: take care
Tape it out: measure it
Tapitless: daft
Tappit-hen: decanter with top like fowl's crest
Tear-blent: tear-filled
Thang: close
Thegither: together
Thieveless: useless
Thirled: obliged, traded with, bound
Thowless: lacklustre
Tongue-tackit: tongue-tied
Toom: empty
To the fore: alive, still in existence
Treddle: foot lever on loom
Trysted: arranged to meet
Twa-handed crack: discreet talk between two people

Unchancie: unlucky

Vised: looked over

Wa' gaun: departure, going away
Waled: chosen
Wame: belly
Wark: building(s)
Warpit: wrapped around
Wast owre: over the west; westwide
Weel-faured and sonsie: fine and sturdy
Whilom: former, formerly, once
Whitrick: weasel
Wist: know
Wirakow: demon

Yont: along

DUNFERMLINE HERITAGE COMMUNITY PROJECTS

The volunteer organisation publishing this book evolved during 2005-2007 with the publication of *Historic Dunfermline*, in the Historic Scotland Series of Burgh Surveys. There are now eight project groups:

Publications Group: researches, creates and publishes heritage titles. *Your Guide to Dunfermline*, a 40-page pocket guide in full colour. *John Orrason (or the Adventures of a Social Castaway)* by Daniel Thomson, edited by Dr Jean Barclay. *Jhone Angus and Scottish Reformation Music* by Dr Jamie Reid-Baxter, Dr Pat Dennison and Prof Michael Lynch (coming soon).

Website Group: created to make information about DHCP and Dunfermline's heritage available through its website: www.dunfermlineheritage.org

Abbey Graveyard Survey: initiated to record and chart more than 800 gravestones and monuments.

Dunfermline City Archive, Walmer Drive, off East Port (Open 10-12 am, Wednesdays & Fridays).

West Fife Family History Group: provides help and resources for local residents to trace their family roots.

Hinterland Group: set up in connection with RCAHMS initiative 'Scotland's Rural Past' to trace abandoned agricultural sites.

Burgh Survey Follow-up Group: monitors sensitive and 'at risk' sites in the City Conservation Area.

Liaison: maintains links with Fife Council, heritage and other organisations.

DHCP welcomes new members. Please contact:
Secretary: Sue Mowat, 49 Grieve St, KY12 8DN,
Tel: 01383 724 960 Email: suemowat@dsl.pipex.

COMING SOON

"Jhone Angus
&
Scottish Reformation Music"

To celebrate the 450th Anniversary of the Reformation in Scotland, an illustrated book will be published by DHCP featuring the music of the Dunfermline monk and composer Jhone Angus. The 16th century was a time of turbulent religious and political movements which changed lives throughout Europe, and especially in Scotland. The replacement of Roman Catholicism by Protestantism brought fundamental changes to ecclesiastical music. Angus wrote simple but beautiful music for the new religion of the Reformed Kirk which has been preserved in the 16th century Part Books of the 'Wode Psalter', which will be featured in this publication.

The story of Reformation music is told by Dr Jamie Reid Baxter, Fellow of Glasgow University. He traces the transformation from the elaborate, polyphonic music of the Roman Catholic Church, to the simpler form required by the Reformed Kirk which, would be sung by the congregation.

To set the scene, Professor Michael Lynch, outlines the origins and spread of Protestantism and its effects throughout Europe. Dr Patricia Dennison, focuses on the Reformation in Scotland, and especially Dunfermline in the time of Jhone Angus.

DoubleBridge Press
Named after the ancient bridge in the Glen,
Pittencrief Park, Dunfermline
**DUNFERMLINE HERITAGE
COMMUNITY PROJECTS**